LOST BONES

BOOK 1 OF THE BONE READER

Mab Morris

———————————— ⫷◆⫸ ————————————

For Claire
Without you, the series would never have happened.

Contents

Chapter One   5

Chapter Two   27

Chapter Three   51

Chapter Four   66

Chapter Five   73

Chapter Six   90

Chapter Seven   119

Chapter Eight   126

Chapter Nine   136

Chapter Ten   149

Chapter Eleven   172

Chapter Twelve   197

Chapter Thirteen   207

Chapter Fourteen   216

Chapter Fifteen   231

Chapter Sixteen   245

Chapter Seventeen   298

About the Author   306

Other Books by Mab Morris   307

CHAPTER ONE

⟪◆⟫

Cemirowl Dusane almost missed the bits of skeleton, nearly stepped over the rib hidden in the leaf litter and spring forest growth.

She knelt, and put her red-stained fingers to the yellowed bones. Crouching, she rummaged through leaves, and found more than a lone rib carried there by a carnivore. She picked up what might be a femur or a tibia picked almost clean by crows, ants, and yellow ground bees, then she touched the bone with her mind. Some of the animal's spirit still lingered within. A faint echo, nearly gone.

"Wait, wait, wait!" she cried.

The spirit froze, caught, crouching and waiting for danger, but no longer running away. No longer fading any more.

Relief nearly loosened Cemirowl's control over her grief. She crumpled onto the ground, catching herself with her free hand. *Oh! You I will not have to send away*, she thought to the young animal, as her trembling subsided. "But where is the skull?"

Animals had scattered the bones from the kill, taken some away. Cemirowl rarely found a complete set. She used fresh animal carcasses to practice wrapping, and did not disturb their rest when she was done. These bones she'd add to her basket for readings. She moved carefully as she gathered up leg bones, brittle ribs, and the fragile vertebrae, putting them in her carry bag. She finally found the skull under a young shoot of fern where a fresh yellow asfodel bowed over the left eye like a pale star, the color of hope. She sat back for a moment and then dug up the bulb. The root was poisonous, but the flowers were pretty.

After nipping the flower off, she pulled her carry bag off her shoulder and put the dirty bulb inside with the rest of the bones and the other herbs she'd gathered. She wove the soft stem of the flower through worn holes of her bodice. Then, she picked up the skull and lifted it to face her.

She thought of Meelac. She rubbed fresh tears from her eyes with hands stained with red dye and reeking of funereal herbs steeped in, unfortunately, rancid oil. She missed her mentor, already, though she'd just buried him. It hurt more than she could bear, but she put the thought aside again. This time it was easier. She stared into the eye holes of the skull.

"Come to me. Stay with me," Cemirowl said. She sensed the spirit of the little grey fox pup on the other side of the veil. It was still caught by its fear—disconcerted, surprised, lost. She sensed it heard her.

The fox pup emerged from the otherworld, cringing, slinking as it saw the other ghost pets. At first afraid, it joined the entourage of animal spirits swirling around her skirts. They welcomed him cautiously, but as part of their odd pack.

"Come, let's go home," she told them.

She carried the skull in her hands, and caressed it lightly in her fingers. After a moment, she paused. She realized she could breathe again—more deeply than she had in the past three days.

The sharp pressure of Meelac's death eased into a bearable grief. Also, she now had new bones to help her reading.

Her mentor's passing—was that the change her other Bone Readings had told her would come? She'd do another reading soon with these new bones to see if the signs and signals were different now that her mentor was gone.

It was a better change than finally going as mad as her mother, which she still dreaded and half expected.

"I wish my vision was as clear as the villagers seem to think it is," she murmured to her animal entourage. "Either for seeing the dead, or with the few readings I've done for them!"

She was able to think about Meelac, and his last words—both alive and dead—more calmly. Would he now see how her sight kept barriers between herself and any other person she knew—even him, her beloved teacher?

Dead, would Meelac finally understand that she heard and saw less than he had believed? And far less than the villagers believed, using her mother as their guide? If he came back to discuss these matters, he'd find the conversations far more slow-going than all his teaching before. Ironic that even death wouldn't help. Only in the first moments of death, before the journey to the underworld, were the departed able to converse with her, if they ever did, as clearly as they did before they died.

In his long career Meelac hadn't seen any ghosts or spirits, but he'd wrapped many bodies and walked behind the burial cart in mourning many times. At first alone, then with his pupils, with Cemirowl apprenticed early, at the age of eight; Alcon had come later. She had tried to tell Meelac that second sight didn't help her bury the dead any better than Alcon or himself. Alcon came to Meelac as a student, funded by his gentleman father. Neither

Meelac nor Alcon had ever needed second sight to do the work, and Cemirowl knew that they had done it well. Second sight did not help her as a priest. It only allowed her to see more than others.

Cemirowl was alone in the woods by choice that morning. If she were anyone else, the village would have found this unacceptable. Primary grievers were *never* left alone. But she was. The memory of her mother, and even her strange father, made it easier for the villagers to shy away from her except in need. Overhead, the wind made branches creak against each other. It reminded Cemirowl of the funereal cart. Meelac had been fond of saying that the cart reminded him of death. The left wheel creaked, "harsh and inevitable." They never could fix it.

She'd spent the night before binding Meelac's body in cloth dyed red, so his soul and body would be protected from evil as he traveled the underworld. After she'd wrapped him, Alcon and she had put him on the cart. They'd pushed it through the village of Soft Water, and beyond, so all could see him pass. After he was buried, she'd let Alcon deal with the gathering, while she faded back into the woods to look for bones, as she did each time she'd cut the souls away from the bodies of villagers she'd cared for, and then wrapped them in protective red.

Rising from wariness, the villagers didn't mind her being by herself. She'd heard a rumor once, that they could trust that she wasn't alone. Surely she was surrounded by ghosts. It was one among many whispered rumors, such as her mother's family's past sins, never elaborating what they were. Cemirowl only knew that they were an aristocratic family descended into comparative poverty. Strangely, the local land owner, Sir Thade, considered Ferioul's marriage to Dusane a step up for Ferioul—with or without her madness. Dusane had been whispered about as well, but he was kindly thought of, as he acted as an apothecary. Worse were the whispers about her mother, or rather the fear that Cemirowl would end up like her mother. She didn't see ghosts of the dead the way her mother had toward the end of her life. Everyone expected that she would. It was the change she dreaded the most. She readings for herself hoping never to find it looming beyond rumor and thought.

While Cemirowl had helped celebrate births, weaving a new soul to the community, or a marriage when families were bound together, there were times—inevitably—where her past, or rather the memories of her mother's past behavior interfered. Regardless of what Meelac had said, that past history did mar her role in the village.

It was pure petulance to ask now: but how many priests did a small village need? Three had been ridiculous. Alcon could do the job just as well as Meelac had. If she were gone, who would notice? Or care? Alcon and the villagers could not see what she did any more than Meelac had, and he had been a true scholar from the king's city Elbyrge, by the Pyrandor River. Alcon was a younger son. A local boy. A son of a gentleman, and more admired than she ever had been; there was neither secret taint nor madness in his family's background.

Cemirowl crashed through the woods. Then stopped and shook her head. To calm herself, she took a deep breath, sensed the ghosts around her, those of animals, not of those she had pushed away as was her duty. She looked again at the eye holes of the fox skull. Calmer, she looked about, and saw another good healing herb peeping from the fallen leaves. She stopped, dug it up, put it in her pouch on top of the new bones.

Beyond easing her sorrow, the new bones would hopefully clarify her readings. And this was the fraud: no matter how accurate others believed her fortune telling to be, she could never call them 'clear'.

Bones from her basket had said, 'Change was coming', and coming directly to Cemirowl. But from where? And what kind?

For a month, the lay of the bones she had thrown had been strangely similar. Constancy had not helped her understand the readings any better. It might be amazing to some, spooky to others, but it was frustrating to her. Change. Change would come. Was this change the loss of her mentor, a madness like her mother's, or something else? If she had done these readings for someone else, an event would transpire to prove her skill, and inspire awe and amazement.

Cemirowl snarled out a tuneless, "Euegh!"

She wiped her face again with stained hands, and looked around to see where she was. By the look of the trees and a stream, she had gotten a little off track. After going east a little longer she finally came to her garden, and sat down on her bench beside her largest Compass plant. She breathed in the fresh, sharp scent of the funerary herb while running a spray of its needles through her fingers. She rubbed the tacky oil into her skin. The scent could open the mind and clear away evil.

With sticky fingers she examined her new bones, settling her mind into them and getting a feel for the fox puppy's spirit.

The sharp pain of death, fear and confusion came first, then memories of 'mama.' A longing for comfort—possibly why it had responded to her? There was a sense of curiosity and play, but with an echo that exploring could lead to getting lost, and being the prey of a predator—and the type of predator it somehow knew it would never become.

She called the puppy closer and let it sit upon her lap, something it would never have done in life. She said a few words appropriate to human burial, sending away its pain and fear. She looked into its eyes.

"Now, Little Grey, let me tell you of Meelac. He was hale during the hard winter, but as the tree frogs, the peepers, began to sing their songs again, he caught a spring cough. I tried everything to cure him, but he died." She felt her eyes burn again. She rubbed them.

Running her fingers through the fur she could not quite smell or feel, she held onto the sense of this small, now trusting animal, and let sorrow wash away from her.

A sound startled her and she looked up. Someone was walking up the path to her house. He was shadowed by the trees, but a patch of sunlight lit the man's face and clothes for a moment.

She remembered him: the strange nobleman who had watched the funeral procession from atop his horse the day before, talking to Soft Water's factor. Under the glinting spike and turban, the arrogance of his face matched the bold, purple stripe crossing his surcoat declaring he was a nobleman in King Larthor's employ. Cemirowl was surprised he had not left the village yesterday. Soft Water was too poor a place to offer any comfort to a gentleman of his standing and wealth. Sir Thade's town was not so far off he couldn't have travelled there before full nightfall. Apparently he hadn't. He'd preferred rushes on the floor and poor stews to the greater comfort of Caballier Thade's household, and all his renowned wines.

He stepped out of the trees into the garden in front of her

house. Her chickens scattered with much squawking. Cemirowl watched him in silence. His walk was confident with a hint of easy grace. He was handsome.

She bit her lip. Resolutely she examined his clothes. What gleamed from the white turban of his helmet was etched with arabesques that seemed to rise up the lower portion of the spike. If she remembered her father's stories, the turban around the helmet implied he had been trained to fight against enemies across the strait to the south—primarily Hergila, which was now an ally. The tawny right side of his surcoat implied a worthy ambition. The white field was either empty or indicated silver, which meant he was either a caballier or a baron. With the relaxed cant of his shoulders, Cemirowl decided white was blank. The sickle dividing the purple line declared an expectation of a fruitful harvest. The choice of a young caballier with new property?

He was proud. He was wealthy. The cloth was the finest weave she'd ever seen. Even the field of white was lush with a texture as ornate as the filigree pattern on his silvery helmet. The cloth of his turban was also subtly detailed. The embroidery of his crest and badge were magnificent, shot with color, even while his clothes could have seemed quite plain at a distance. The colors alone, in their vibrancy, spoke of riches. Not even Caballier Thade's wife and daughter wore such wealth.

Cemirowl thought, *Father would have called it 'Arrogant Humility'.*

Her chickens were already coming back.

He seemed to sneer at the surroundings. "Dusane?" he called.

She gathered the bones back into her pouch, then stood and asked, "Good day, Sir. How may I help you?"

"I am looking for Dusane."

"I am Cemirowl Dusane."

He was examining her now, from the worn brown and green dress to the wilting asfodel. He disregarded her. "Hmm. I believe I need your father."

"I am sorry, sir, but he is not here."

He smirked. "He is travelling? Perhaps overseas with Sir Thade's wine merchants?"

"No, sir. He never traveled. He died five years back."

This seemed to surprise the gentleman. "Oh! He never traveled? Or worked for Thade?"

"He did, sir."

"His profession... These are the caballier's hunting grounds? They were friendly?"

"I believe so, sir."

"What was his profession, then? Huntsman?"

"No. He served Caballier Thade as an apothecary."

This surprised the caballier even more. "Interesting. A trifle odd. Hunting grounds and no travel, and served only as an apothecary."

"Yes, sir."

"And you are his daughter. Does he have a son who works for Thade?"

"No, only I."

"You are one of the priests, I believe, that I saw yesterday?"

"Yes. Is there anything I can help you with, as my father is not available?" she asked.

"You are the one who tells fortunes? The... the Bone Reader?"

"Indeed," she said, thinking that it did not take a

fortuneteller to know that he was perturbed about something.

"Dusane is an odd name this far south," he said.

"Is it? I would not know. I grew up with it."

"It is evocative of a northern duchy near where I grew up," he said. "I am surprised to hear the name in a small village this far south. And there are few southerners with hair the same as yours. Auburn, is it? It is why I would have been interested to meet your father. I like curiosities. They make for good stories at court." He paused and then looked at her. Cemirowl could see his mind churning. The apparent oddity that was her father wasn't present, but a fortuneteller was.

He finally asked. "May I have a reading?"

She pushed the door open and turned. "Come in, if you wish a reading."

His hand touched the hilt of his curved sword lightly as he bowed, almost as if mocking her. Skepticism rode his eyebrows. This will be an easy job, she thought. No matter what the bones might offer him, it was clear that the experience of his visit was showmanship enough for any fee. And showmanship was all he expected from her. He did not appear to want answers from bones. As soon as he entered, he seemed to disregard her presence and make himself at home, examining the objects of her house.

She went straight to the table and cleared off the few books Meelac had given her, putting them on the shelf beside her bone basket. The caballier moved to the fireplace. He examined the objects on the mantelpiece while she readied the table. Set among some of the smaller skulls of the creatures she'd found in the woods were a wooden squirrel and raven. The caballier's eyes lingered on them.

"My father carved those," she said.

He picked up her father's pewter plate. It had an intricate pattern nearly lost to tarnish. The caballier bent it toward the light coming from the open door. He grunted in surprise, looked up at her, and then back at the plate.

"It belonged to my father," she said.

"Truly?"

"Of course."

"Did he tell you of the crest? The family that it represents? I can't quite make out whose it is."

"No, sir, my father never said anything about it."

"Interesting."

She wondered if the caballier recognized what he could see of the pattern. Wherever it had come from, it didn't matter: if her father had retreated to the country, as the heraldic squirrel might indicate, the raven meant she had to make her own life. She did know that he'd been well educated.

While he was alive, she'd witnessed her father aiding Sir Thade with various matters on occasion, and with Thade deferring to his tenant as if Dusane was greater than the caballier. Her father's manners were far above that of a peasant, something he'd attempted to teach his wife to no avail. While her mother was somehow connected to the caballier, and their social consequence was supposedly high, their manners were rustic. As far as her father's possible consequence or wealth—if he'd had any—his coffers had run out long ago. Impoverished, living as an apothecary, and more like a peasant except in manners, he'd also refused to let Cemirowl slide into low habits. It was another characteristic that set her apart from the villagers as much as her mother's madness. He'd refused to sell the plate, as did she. She also had a store of wine that Sir Thade had given her father before he had died. It was, possibly, the only wealth she had besides her chickens and books.

The caballier put the plate back and looked at her curiously, but said nothing further. He seemed content, now, as if he needed nothing more from her.

"Please take a seat." She gestured to one of the stools.

"Oh. Yes. The reading." He paused again. In great good humor he asked, "Do you not have a cat?"

"Excuse me, sir?"

"Aren't you supposed to have a black cat? At least a cat, I would have thought. The stories say fortunetellers have cats."

Her fingers were at her mouth as she bit back amusement. Some stories also said she ought to also be a hag, old and bent. It was a rare opportunity to be mischievous without further damning her reputation.

"Oh! I do not need one. There is an herb I use in my thatching. Mice and squirrels cannot abide it. Pests leave in a day or two. Do you need some? Half an ounce is four crowns."

None of it was true. Most vermin avoided her ghosts. She could probably throw something together which might work, if he asked. If he believed her.

"I'd rather have a cat," he said.

Cemirowl smiled watching his shoulders relax as he laughed. He'd been more uncomfortable than he'd believed himself to be. She wondered why. After adjusting his sword, he rested his elbows on the table. "How do you read bones?" he asked.

Cemirowl wondered if he were asking, *What sort of magic do you use?* or *How does this work?* It was impossible to answer the former. There was no magic. Only an inherited curse that had driven her mother mad. She answered his question with, "Your part is very simple; I will lead you through it." She placed the basket on the table, unfolding the square of cloth that covered it.

"Do you need to know the question?" he asked with one eyebrow raised, his face tilted in challenge.

"No, sir. You need not tell me. Just think on your question before you take a handful of bones then toss them onto this cloth. First I must ask your name, for payment and exoneration." She sat down, her hands smoothing the square of red wool flat onto the table.

"Exoneration? I don't understand," he said.

"I am only a translator of any message the bones may give you. I merely relate what I see in the lay of bones you'll have thrown. There are some who believe I cause the readings to come to pass; that is not true. I only interpret." *And that badly, more often than not,* she thought. "So I ask you to exonerate me of causing any future event I might read to you from these bones."

His eyes narrowed, his brows drew in, the corners of his lips pulled together as he examined her. Then his face lightened.

"What would you do if I was not honorable?"

She smiled. "Lie and predict only good things."

He laughed. "Well, then, I am Caballier Mercor. I exonerate you." He pulled out some coins from the decorated, leather pouch hanging from his belt. "Is this enough?" He put the coins on the table.

"Yes. Thank you, Sir," she said, pleased that she had guessed he was no baron.

She slid the money into her hands without looking at it for more than a few seconds before putting it in a small bowl behind her. A glint of silver told her she would be able to buy staples she could not grow or forage. She might even be able to buy more cloth to replace her dress and her worn vestments. More wealth than wine or a pewter plate!

As she turned back, she caught his eyes staring at her red hands.

"Why are your hands red?" he asked.

"My hands? You do know that I am also a priest of the village? You mentioned that."

"Yes. I noticed you and your brother priest yesterday behind that cart of... if I guess right by the objects on the cart... your mentor? I wondered why such a small village had two priests— once three. That's how I learned of your other abilities."

"Priest Meelac taught both Alcon and me in the mysteries of priesthood. Alcon performs most of the other duties. The villagers prefer him. By Meelac's choice and my natural... inclination, I tend to the burials more often than births, or celebrations. I wrap the bodies and perform the other rites for the dead." She looked at her hands. "Do they not wrap in the cities?"

"Of course, but the wrappers do not go about with red stained hands."

Her hands were over the bones in the basket. "Really?" She looked at her hands. "Maybe it's the oil that soaks the fabric or the vegetable dyes we use. We have to dye our burial cloth with what the forest gives us. The stain usually fades before the next burial, unless there has been illness in the village." It had happened once.

He shrugged, looking at the basket under her hands, no longer interested in dyes or burials.

"I do not think you're the sort to be dismayed by the touch of bones," she said.

She stirred the basket, calling her animals closer, calling

them to examine the questioner. They came, swirling around her, some leapt onto the table. Mercor did not notice them, but Cemirowl noticed that the hairs on his arm lifted lightly with the change in the air.

She hid her smile and said, "Try to think of a question that doesn't have a yes or no answer. When you have it, stir the bones, take a handful and toss them gently onto this cloth."

She stopped stirring them and put her hands into her lap while he pondered the question to ask. *It is most likely a love question,* Cemirowl thought. *It usually is.*

As he focused on his question, Cemirowl began to shift her perspective. She breathed in and out slowly till the echoes of smells, sights and sounds of her ghosts were nearly as clear as the young man sitting before her.

She watched her animals investigate him. They batted at his hands, moved silently around and through him, crouching on his shoulders, sniffing his ears and breath. The ghost of her cat sniffed his hands tentatively, then turned and began washing herself.

Time and practice had minimized the two-realm vertigo that had probably contributed to her mother's madness. Even while the room shifted and wanted to spin, Cemirowl found her center between the two realms.

By the shift of his shoulders, Cemirowl knew he was coming close to asking the bones his question. She took the remaining seconds to contemplate him and his movements. There was an edge of pain around his soft mouth. His shoulders were still somewhat tight. Handsome as he was, many women would want to smooth the hurt away.

He shifted on the stool and his chainmail made soft music

as he moved to gather bones. The movement brought an echo of scent. He smelled of horse, and the padding needed cleaning, but his sweat, though a little sour from travel, was not unpleasant.

The bones echoed the music of his mail as they fell onto the cloth. She bent her head to examine what he had thrown.

"Some of these do not look like bones," he said, interrupting her thoughts. He pointed to one or two of the objects. His eyes were bright and curious as he examined the bones and her face.

"Most of the basket is filled with bones of different animals: fox, bird, squirrel and dog among others." She gestured to the different bones. "Some of these are stone or other objects that represent different ideas or talents, such as this tuning pin for a vihuela." She pointed to the worn brass pin she'd gotten from a wandering minstrel. "They aren't really necessary. I only added them recently to add some... immediacy to what I could interpret."

She did not mention the one object that had caught her attention with some surprise. The small black stone roughly shaped like a bird. It represented herself. It had come into other readings without having any significant echoes. This time it was fixed within a reading for a complete stranger.

She bent back down to look at the bones, hoping that her own troubles were not interfering with his reading.

First Cemirowl looked at the different positions of the bones and their relationship with one another, as well as their relationship to their former selves. She contemplated their symbolism in heraldry or popular tales. This was only to help her hear what she called echoes. It was the one part of her talent that felt touched by magic. Even for her the process was mystical.

She was confused. There seemed a great deal of

information in the lay of bones divided between his immediate question and one that had come through despite any relation to his inquiry. The answer to his immediate question was clear.

"You are traveling to the king's city," she murmured.

"Does it tell you that?"

She looked up into his surprised face. "Even if they did not, it was quite obvious. You came from the east yesterday. The king's city lies in the opposite direction." She gestured at the glittering purple line of his surcoat. "You are clearly the king's man."

His eyebrows lifted. He'd not expected her to explain herself, but rather expected she'd claim higher knowledge. It would come, though. Sideways and strange as always... and useless.

She bent her head again.

"You are a younger son, but have already surpassed your inheritance. You are leaving someone of importance, but going back to someone you believe to be of greater importance. The first is a man and related to the young woman to whom you are returning. She is a pretty creature, but sly. I believe she sings quite well. She places you high in her plans, without true affection, merely for the promise of your position."

"She does not!"

Cemirowl glanced up at him, eyebrows raised. *Do you wish to be entertained or not?* she wondered silently and waited for him to subside back into his chair.

"Do you have proof?"

She laughed gently. "From these bones?"

"How can I trust them? You?"

She did not know how to answer him. How could he want proof that this reading was true? What could she give him? She'd enough experience to know that the information was real, but it wasn't exactly practical or necessarily helpful. She was surprised when she saw her cat butt up to Mercor's chin affectionately, giving him a ghostly cat kiss. Then, as only a cat can do, live or dead, it disdainfully turned away and sauntered to the dog, butting its head in a gesture of affection. Cemirowl could almost hear it purr.

Her animals were not usually this blunt if they aided a reading. Most of the information came from the echoes of imagery, sound, or even feeling. Things half seen or felt. She looked away, slightly embarrassed, even if she could not explain why.

"I believe her actions toward another might give you the proof you seek." Another echo, another flash. "Possibly later this spring, or early summer?"

She glanced back at Sir Mercor, who looked every inch of a caballier capable of using the scimitar or knife hanging from his belt. The movement of his head in the fire light flashed on what she'd thought were decorations circling his turban. The spike of the helmet underneath the cloth, alone, could kill her. Surely there were more weapons on his person. She swallowed and bent back to the bones, forcing her breath to steady.

"To continue, the nobleman you left probably has some connection to a wolf, perhaps in his heraldic device? He will travel to the city in some weeks to come, giving you a positive answer to your request—an engagement? By then it will be too late. You will have decided to reject a course involving either of them."

"Is that all?" Mercor's voice was dry and colorless.

Cemirowl was examining the other part of the lay and said, distracted, "About that question, yes."

She closed her eyes and dropped her head further. She had not meant to say anything. This part of the reading would not be as entertaining as the answer to the love question—which he already disregarded as pure fiction and would probably turn into a source of derisive amusement later.

"There is more?" he asked.

She looked up at him. He was leaning forward. His eyes and shoulders were strangely intent. His hands far from his weapons. The sickle on his tawny field seemed to loom over the small pile of bones. *Fruitful harvest?* she thought.

Cemirowl did not know what to do. She turned back to the bones. Normally the immediate question did not play such a minor part in the reading. With her little raven stone so clearly within the swirl of these bones, she had great doubts on the truth of her perceptions or this reading.

Yet there is the fox tooth and the bear knuckle and the way this lays over that, she thought. *It does have something to do with this young caballier sitting across from me. Maybe the raven just means I'm influencing events by giving him this reading. But I don't like how those eagle claws are clenched around me. No, it can't be. I'm never going to see this man again. I don't have to tell his fortune to know that. I can see that just from the look on his face.*

It was strange because the echoes of this reading were similar to those she'd thrown for herself. It made her feel small and helpless and strange, as if the changes predicted for her life came from farther away than she could ever have imagined. Not Meelac's death, nor Sir Thade's men finally catching up to her for non-payment of rent or taxes her father had never paid, or that somehow playing with the Realm of the Dead for so long she too would go mad like her mother. It was something else. And more frightening for being something completely unlooked for. If the caballier's reading had anything to do with her.

The fox pup, whose bones she had not yet added to her basket came and sat on her lap. It laid its head against the arm she'd rested on the table. It pressed its nose between her elbow and chest as it whimpered. She looked down at it, wanted to comfort it, but could not move.

Careful Cemi, she told herself. *Focus. Concentrate.*

She hoped Mercor expected something eerie for his entertainment. She'd give him his money's worth. She felt an eerie chill glide up her spine as she spoke.

"Sir Mercor, from what I read here, there will be a time of difficulty coming for you. Sometime within this year someone very important to you will die." Saying it, Cemirowl winced softly. She could hear the classic story-tale charlatan's line.

She swallowed back a nervous laugh. "Because of the tasks you will be called on to perform, either by association, duty to the king or other influences—I cannot see that clearly—you will be hard pressed to act with probity. Oddly enough, I believe that you'll have all the tools or abilities to see many things clearly, during these events, but will be either incapable or unwilling to act. It is as if you will not be able to bridge some gap between what you know and the confusion caused by this person's death, or even some other loyalties."

She shifted on her stool and looked up at him. She wasn't sure how to convey what she could see in the lay. It reminded her of the cart wheels, but three of them spinning independently. "The whole lay is interesting. Circles within circles. It is as if your hope for your young woman is one wheel or circle, bright and clear.

Unhidden. This upcoming death is another wheel, but more hidden by yet another larger, more obscure wheel. This last is associated with only you, not these people who participate in either of these other events. One girl is easily forgotten... another is... treacherous, and the last one hinting at information held by one small thread. One wrong move and these wheels will clash into each other and wreak havoc. Speak with caution and care. One wrong word will bring about more added difficulty."

And that added difficulty might mean difficulty to me, Cemirowl thought.

Cemirowl did her best to present a calm front. That her raven was part of the reading was information she did not want to give. None of it made sense to her. She reminded herself, *Assumptions defeat intuition!*

Yet there was no future she could imagine that would involve her with this man again. They were nominally equal in rank, but their differences of wealth, upbringing and location were far too disparate to include her entrance to the level of courtly affairs he moved in. More, except for this reading, he and his world were wholly unconnected to her.

She finally focused on his face. Her heart sank, but she said, "I think you must school yourself against corrupt thoughts."

He did not believe her, though he was now very much entertained. All he said was, "The priest says this." She gathered, by his wry condescension, that he was not overly fond of priests.

Cemirowl did not know if she should feel relief, or dread because he did not believe her, and thought she was trying to preach to him. A wave of tiredness settled into her shoulders, down her spine. She wished he would go.

She had seen that look on many faces. Usually from people

who had lived in the village for a long while. Her mother had died mad, her father eccentric, her mentor merely kind by giving her a job. In their eyes, as she saw now in that of Caballier Mercor of King Larthor's employ: she was the future village crazy, and his morning's entertainment. Not priest. Not healer. She had no ability to see a truthful future.

It hurt, even though she agreed with him.

He stood, for he'd had enough of the village's sideshow. He tossed her another coin. "Thank you for the diversion."

When he'd left the house she put away the bones, knowing she didn't want to read for herself any time soon. She wondered, *What did I see?* That somehow she would be in his life again? That someone would die and cause him confusion? How rare would that be in the court of a king, where intrigue, tournaments, and action were part of daily life? Her days were only eventful if someone became ill, died, or wanted a reading just as pointless as the one she'd just given.

CHAPTER TWO

————————— «•» —————————

Sir Mercor rejected the dread in the Bone Reader's voice as it echoed in his mind. Speculating on who might die would drive him mad. Most of his acquaintances were noble, which could be defined as important. He thought about the woman he hoped to marry, Llora. She did sing well. Even if Cemirowl had spoken of the wolf in Llora's father's coat of arms, he trusted too much in the foundation of his prospects to believe that Llora would be untrue.

The rest? *Circles within circles?* and *Corrupt thought? ... Treason?*

He gripped his reins tighter, his hand fingering the pommel of his scimitar. He secretly wrote to a woman in Hergila—but that was for love, not treason! What did a peasant priest a two day ride from the king's city know? The plate...? Perhaps she was not what she seemed to be? No. Even with a father of probable northern origins—a man out of place, a duke's son if he remembered the crest on the tarnished silver plate—the priest had lived in that cottage all her life. He would have to check his theory at some point. Still, it was clear to him that Cemirowl Dusane had never ventured beyond the village. The farthest she had gone was to Thadetown, nearly a day's walk from her tiny village. The villagers he'd spoken to had no reason to lie. There was nothing she could really know about him, though he had been surprised she'd said something close to the truth. Her position was not enviable, living in a villrage from which she was clearly somewhat alienated by family history and awe.

He admired that in her own strange way she'd made the best of her circumstances and skill, finding a mentor, a priest. But what could anyone truly gain from a fortuneteller? She had given him few details. He was free to think what he wished.

Mercor laughed, realizing her true art.

He'd received the entertainment he'd wanted, and avoided staying with Sir Thade, whom he knew and despised as being weak. Thade even ran his estate in a way that bordered on trade. Yet here he had been attempting to convince himself of the fallacy of a charlatan's predictions. He was glad to gather up his squire and quit the village.

Relaxing in his saddle, he turned his thoughts on how he would tell the story of Cemirowl's prediction concerning Llora for future diversion. When he might use the tale was also a good question. Augmenting the rumors of Cemirowl's gift, he would have to word his story carefully to not offend his lady—though worded well, even she might be amused.

"The Bone Woman magically appeared out of the trees. Her cottage lined with skulls, but she was no hag! Unless... disguised by a spell? She kept her secrets well!"

He laughed to himself, shaking off the rest of the cobwebby gloom he'd carried from Cemirowl's cottage.

It was late afternoon two days later when Mercor arrived on the outskirts of Elbyrge. He could see the palace Ilturir rising above the city... as one poet stated, "a pearl set in emeralds." The afternoon light lit the pale stone, and gave freshness to the spring greenery that filled the palace walls with lush gardens among the various buildings.

It was a crisp, clear day. In the far distance, across the strait, Mercor could make out the thin shadow of Hergila, just beyond the south-eastern edge of the palace. He stood in his stirrups for a better view.

"Across these drowning miles
Enemy of mine, come reach for me
Be my friend
Too much lost in such strife
Come to me, clasp my hand
Embrace me as my friend
Let us love the life and liberty
Now shared across waters
That yet divides us..."

He spoke the words he'd penned for Narsina of Hergila. He knew most people in court assumed the song was based on the peace King Larthor had made, even upon the edge of his sure victory. Larthor had not wanted a weak colony, but a strong ally. The king had married Tidyri of Hergila for peace.

Mercor stood in his stirrups staring at the shadow of the queen's former land. Tidyri had come to Pyrann, but the woman Mercor still secretly loved had not. Could not. Her father had refused—despising Mercor's country and resenting the treaty. And since he could not marry her, it had been futile to stay in Hergila, even in service to his king. He found it much better to return to the land of his birth.

Narsina's brother, once a companion at tournaments all

over the region, and now one of the Hergilan ambassador's knights, had been cool to him since that rejection. Amec's loyalties were firmly in Hergila, and was doubtful of any good Pyrann might offer his country. He had admitted to Mercor that Ambassador Itrizeu had brought him to Pyrann because he voiced such opinions, and wanted to be reminded of that opinion when working for their own king. Amec had warmed when Mercor had openly declared his intention to ask Lady Llora's father for her hand.

Mercor sat back down and looked to see his lone squire Rimmel slowly riding up the lane. His squire stopped him from moving on, dusted off the travel dust, and made his knight as presentable as possible. After a quick polish of spike and scimitar, Rimmel brought out and unfurled Mercor's standard. Though Caballier Mercor eschewed the regular and, to his mind, bloated mass of traveling households, he was still a caballier of some note. Before his appointment into the ambassadorial liaison office of his king, Mercor had gained much wealth and standing in tournament. He could not enter the city without some pomp and circumstance. They went through the city to the palace gates, recognized and cheered along the way. The delight of his return did not diminish when riding past two levels of gates and into the huge rotunda where he dismounted and let a page take his horse. He was greeted with great cheer. He walked underneath the wide balcony, and then through the large entryway, and finally down the long courtyard with flowering shrubs that lined the reflecting pool guiding all eyes to the entrance of the king's audience chamber, as well as his and his queen's private chambers.

Having already ascertained he was not yet needed by his king, with letters from merchants to the east already sent to the king's offices, Mercor went straight to the queen's solar, where he knew Llora would be. Upon entering the brightly lit room overlooking the sea, he bowed to Queen Tidyri, who was composing letters to her friends and family overseas. There would be no politics in those letters. She and Larthor had agreed she would not leverage her heritage for either country's gain. There was still too much fear of betrayal from camps on both sides. Her most political position was to act for the continued goodwill and peace.

"Your Majesty, I have come to see Lady Llora," Mercor said in the queen's native tongue, nodding toward Llora, who was sitting by the windows, alone, embroidering something. He gave a quick glance to the other women scattered around the room in various labors.

"Ah, I see you have a gift for her," she replied in Pyrannian with a wry smile for the language game they both played.

"I went to Turksan expressly for this gift, but I have not forgotten my liege's love. This is for you," he continued in Hergilan.

Her face softened as he handed her the gift. She unwrapped the silk cloth and ribbon from the box. "Mercor! Why, this is beautiful!" She turned the box in her hands and looked up at him with a smile. "Thank you."

Mercor inclined his head again. "You're welcome. I thought you might wish to have a special place for your letters from Hergila."

"Oh Mercor, it is lovely! My thanks to you. Is this... this cannot be wood..." she paused and looked up at him. *"Inlegsel?"*

He smiled and gave her the word in Pyrannian, "Inlay."

She repeated the word carefully. "But not wood. What was

used?" She examined the decorations on the box.

He watched Llora carefully lay down her embroidery and glide over to them. "It is lovely, Sir," she said, giving him a graceful curtsey, but there was an edge of disappointment in her voice.

He grinned. "I have one for you as well. The inlay is stone," he said to the queen, bringing Llora's gift from behind his back.

The queen's box was elegant and large enough for letters. Llora's box was a little smaller, but the inlay more elaborate. Forgetting the queen for a moment, he watched Llora's small fingers caress the box. His lady was absorbed in her gift, and the one that the queen held in her hands. To his surprise, and he was not sure why, perhaps because the pressure around her mouth, or the way her hands held the box, he found himself thinking he ought to have bought a more expensive present. He bit back his self-reproach. Llora's box, though smaller, had cost him more than the queen's. *She should be happy!* he thought.

As he waited for a thank you, or some word of appreciation, Mercor recalled the reading from Cemirowl. Surely the predicted betrayal was just a charlatan's tale. Paid entertainment. He was too canny to miss many rumors about the · ladies in the palace, including Llora. However he'd been gone a while. Something may have changed.

He turned to look out the windows, feeling a bit forgotten over the charms of elaborate inlay. As he crossed his arms, he reflected sourly that Llora's affections did not matter as long as she was loyal, pretty, and entertaining. Her connections were valuable. He wanted sons. He was annoyed to feel a fear of rejection.

But he noted that she'd seen his gesture, that he'd turned

away. With a quick intake of breath she looked up at him. "Oh my dear Mercor, here I am in awe of this beautiful gift and I have not greeted you!" She reached out to take his hand and held it tightly. "I have missed you so sadly!"

Before turning back, he caught the wry expression on Lady Harlyn's face. He grinned back at her. He smiled down at Llora, aware that she had not yet given him a thank you. "Surely you have employed yourself with other activities than sorrow!"

Tidyri laughed lightly. "Indeed, Caballier, she has, yet not the whole time. She has learned a duet."

"Indeed? With whom?" He could not keep the hard edge from his voice.

Llora laughed and leaned toward him. "Our queen is teasing you. I have learned a duet with Lady Harlyn."

"Ah, that is interesting," Mercor said.

Tidyri said, with a bell-like laugh, "Harlyn has gained a new love for courtly verse as sweet and sad as anything you've written."

He looked at Harlyn as Llora and Tidyri exchanged speculative looks. It explained the weariness in Harlyn's eyes, despite the mockery in her smile. He had suspicions about whose love Harlyn wished to have. He was unwilling to gossip, or build upon the vague rumors he'd heard. The stories he told in court came from his own carefully chosen misadventures or experiences. His apparent willingness to laugh at himself made him many friends. And gave him many opportunities to listen.

"Your Majesty, with your permission, I ask that my Lady Llora accompany me. Would you allow her to visit my room, or is her duty required further? I have something from her father, which my squire has surely unpacked by now, as well as news."

Tidyri nodded. "As it pleases you. My other ladies still attend me."

Mercor's room was nearby, down the stairs, near the king's sitting room and audience chamber. During the day it was his sitting room, but at night his bed chamber. He left the door open, as was proper. His bed and changing area were discretely behind a screen. As soon as a page sent away for wine, Llora threw her arms around him and said, "Oh Mercor! Tell me all. Is my father well? Has he given us permission to wed?"

He laughed, pulled her arms from his neck. He thought to himself, *She is so young thinking that marriage in court always includes love.* He stepped away and sat down in his favorite chair, carved in Hergila and upholstered in cloth embroidered by his lost love. Before he was fully settled, Llora was there, sitting on his lap, unconcerned by who might pass by.

The carved Hergilan wood under the velvet bit into his hands as his fingers tightened. For a few seconds Mercor could only think of the golden sunlight of Hergila. Mercor took a deep breath of Llora's scent and sachets, and the wood burning in the fireplace against the chill of the early spring evening. He moved his hands around the slim waist of the girl on his lap.

"Well, what did he say?" Llora asked.

He stopped his hands from moving further, and took his eyes off the pale flesh above the bodice, grateful for both padding and mail, and all the layers under her thick brocade skirts. Mercor looked into her eyes and forced himself to smile.

"He said he would think on it, and let me know soon. I have reason to hope he will agree."

She squealed and threw her arms around him again.

Rimmel followed the valet who carried the wine.

"My Lady," Rimmel said with a bow, and handed Mercor a packet of letters. "Diplomatic letters, for your attention, Sir. These are from your home," he said, as he handed Llora the letters and gifts from her family. Mercor lifted Llora from his lap.

She seemed a bit surprised by his abrupt removal of her from his lap, so he asked, "Will you pour us some wine? Excuse me; I need to look these over to know if there is anything urgent."

"Certainly," she said, but there was wine on the stem when she handed it to him. Her hand trembled as she poured some for herself, spilling more on the table.

While he looked over the letters written in Hergilan, Llora sipped her wine and picked up his vihuela and strummed it quietly. She ignored the letters and gifts from her family. He paid only enough attention to what she played to think, *Yes, Llora and Harlyn have certainly been playing some rather maudlin music.*

Quarter of an hour later he'd finished.

"Forgive me," he said.

"I hope my playing eased the return to your duties?" she asked.

"Indeed, thank you. One letter was important, but not urgent," he said.

"I will be happy to continue playing, if you so desire, while you compose a reply," Llora said.

"No, it will wait. Surely you would like to read your own letters?" he asked.

She shrugged.

"Be that as it may, I must get out of this chain mail." He stretched, standing. "I am glad that I have no need to wear it for another two weeks."

He began pulling off the throwing stars from his turban,

35

and then unwound the cloth from his helmet.

"Mail must get hot in spring. I don't understand why you wear it."

He chuckled and kissed her forehead. "I've been on our sovereign's business and... Llora, you've been here for a year!" he said with a laugh. "This is a royal palace with the king currently in residence. Peace with our new friends to the south is not yet so old that we must let go of caution. While there's peace in the north, there's always rumors we must lend mor than half an ear to. We must always have a certain number of men prepared to defend both queen and king at a moment's notice." He scratched and ran his fingers through his hair, and walked behind the screen.

"But we are not at war with anyone, are we?"

Mercor shook his head, laughing to himself. He took his sword off. "Of course not, my dear romantic girl. You might want all the caballiers to wear court dress all the time and read you poetry, but there are such things as treason, stealth, and intrigue. I'll admit that in spring and in summer, I look forward to my time out of mail! Tournament is sufficient time for full armor." Rimmel helped him remove the chainmail, and brought him his court clothes. Llora played more on his vihuela as he washed himself. He would be glad to spend more time in the bathhouse later, but this would have to do. She broke off her playing to make a comment.

"You did well in the war, correct?"

For a split second he stiffened, and thought *I did well in the War! To see men and friends die or maimed?* He shrugged. She had only seen the survivors, cleaned up—a dim memory from when she was eight. He shifted the thought. He knew she was thinking of the bounty from successful campaigns. "I did better in

Tourney." This was also true. He came out clean and dressed well enough for her company.

She laughed. "It made you rich!" Her eyes glittered as she picked up her packet. "You are dressed to see the king. You must go to your duty. Will I see you at the queen's dainty, after dinner? You must hear me perform with Harlyn."

"Indeed, I look forward to it," he said and pecked her cheek. Rimmel finished dressing him, and she left with a swirl of her brocade dress.

During the queen's dainty, the king's brother, Lord Arthan, took the time to examine the faces in the room while he listened to Llora and Harlyn play music and sing. The queen's cousin, Ambassador Itrizeu, and two of his knights were present, along with other nobles.

The Hergilan ambassador, Itrizeu, was present with his caballiers Amec and Quormen. The envoy from Gastren echoed Amec's usual glowering, whenever his gaze ventured towards another corner of the room. The current representative king from Pruan was there, with his exotic niece, instead of the queen. She stood out among the darker people present, even the queen's gold haired glory. Her skin was pale, and he knew, up close, that she did have eyebrows and lashes, but they were as pale as her white blond hair. The northern traders, once raiding along the coastline, was surely in her genealogy, no matter her birth in the southwestern mountains of Pruan. Larthor's invitation to bring her was as pointed as her presence.

Arthan noted when Mercor entered the room, moving to the table where many of the small pastries and savories were laid out. He and Amec stood together for a while, which surprised him. Amec was formal to everyone in the court—with the rigid skill Hergilan men could adopt, and so very different from the more open passions of Pyrann. Arthan knew that he hated the treaty, wished to be home in Hergila, and had at one point disliked Mercor for his interest in his sister. That dislike had cooled since Mercor's open declaration that he'd requested the Lady Llora's hand. After their brief conversation, Mercor went to sit near his lady.

Arthan noted the Lady Harlyn gazing at him as she sang. There was no place in the room where he could hide. The music was not inducing him to more romance, it grated against the edges of his thoughts. But Harlyn was not a lady to notice his stiff jaw, and the way he avoided her gaze. She was a true romantic.

The two ladies finished their song, and Mercor stood to declaim some of his poetry, as if to Llora—though Arthan was one of the few who had heard the same ballad before, and knew it was written for another woman from Hergila.

Avoiding Harlyn's stare, Arthan looked at tapestries vibrant with color against the pale walls of the queen's solar. Two were made by his lost wife.

The trebuchet impact of her loss still bruised, as if his ribs were still cracked from the blow, making it hard to breathe. Looking at those complex weavings, he remembered a heavily pregnant Boduscia had attempted to befriend a young queen, new to the country.

Almost like a tapestry was the memory of Boduscia embroidering a baby's shirt as she attempted to teach Tidyri Pyrannian. Days later, her labor pains began. She bled to death, holding their baby boy— born blue, and dead.

To this day he suffered to be in this room filled with such musical cheer. There could be no poetry in that, except something tragic, and it was not suitable for the queen's dainty. And now it had the extra irritation of Harlyn's intent gaze upon him.

Mercor launched into one of the poems that spoke of the peace between two countries. Arthan waved away a servant bringing around trays of the food and wine. His stomach roiled. Still, his humor so black, he thought, *My tenebrosity is as dark as the White Princess' silvery gleam. That alone makes it a bad match.* He forced himself to smile and participate.

He watched Larthor smiling down at Tidyri, both of their eyes filled with joy. While she would not touch him in public, like any well-bred Hergilan lady, her eyes were eloquent. He knew that as soon as may be, Tidyri would retire to her private chamber, and her husband would come to her there, from his own apartments— to respect the privacy of his foreign wife.

Arthan had come to this meal because he had to speak to his brother, and soon! He looked at Harlyn who would have, in a moment, sat at his feet on the queen's Hergilan carpets as rich in color as Boduscia's tapestries. He knew that Harlyn would make him miserable. Knew it better now after she'd forced a greater intimacy upon him.

The walls of the palace grounds were well guarded day and night, but people inside could roam the various palace buildings freely. His palace was down one long balcony from the apartments held by the queen and her ladies.

Arthan could not help but cross his legs as Harlyn tried to catch his eyes—so clear and obvious, as if she owned him. To some extent, she did. Weeks ago, dreaming of Boduscia, he'd woken to Harlyn when she'd snuck to his apartments. His dreaming body already responding, Harlyn was most willing to take what she wanted.

He turned to look at Mercor as he finished his poem. Arthan noticed, instead, the grim look on his brother's face as he watched Harlyn. He knew he would have to find another, more appropriate time to discuss matters with him. He was glad that this poem was the end of the night. The room slowly emptied, but as he went to the garden side doorway, his brother caught his arm.

"I've seen the Lady Harlyn looking at you," Larthor said low and added firmly, "End it."

Arthan took a breath. The conversation would have to happen now, then. "Brother, I must marry her."

"I'll pretend I never heard that. I have other plans for you."

"She is hard to miss, but brother..."

Larthor raised his hand. "She has already been offered a more appropriate marriage arranged by her overlord, Baron Ross. I have approved it."

"Larthor..." Arthan wanted to tell him why it was necessary, that he needed to make atonement for his mistake with Harlyn. That he'd already risked a great deal to confirm how grave a mistake he'd made, while protecting her reputation. But the king stopped him with a hand. Arthan noticed that the door to the ladies' chamber was ajar.

"She is not a good choice. I don't care how far you've gone if you've ventured. Even forgetting her property—which is insufficient for a prince of state—she is *not* a good choice for you. Do not ask again. I will not give you permission to wed. She hasn't even helped you forget your wife." His last words were dry and bitter, from a brother who understood him well.

"I'm sending you off to look to my other estates," the king continued. "You'll leave in the morning. The time will allow you to reconcile yourself to a more suitable match by the time you return."

With that, Larthor turned to stalk off to the passageway that led to his own offices and apartments. Arthan leaned back in the doorway, looking at Harlyn's face as she slowly opened the door to the ladies' chamber.

He wondered how much she'd heard. Perhaps only that he was leaving? From the look on her face she'd heard at least that much. He dreaded the thought she heard more. He hoped she had not heard more.

She stepped forward, but he turned away, and stalked down the balcony to his own apartments. He heard her follow him at least to the balcony doorway. He would have to set a guard by his doors to dissuade her if she chose to sneak into his rooms again. Larthor was right. It had to end. The best he could do was write her a letter and let her know he could do nothing against his brother's demand. He would be leaving, but he would help how he could from afar—till his brother was done with sending him across the countryside. He could afford to send her to the countryside if necessary, to prevent further scandal than what was already whispered.

The following days, Mercor focused upon his work for the king, finding little time to gather more evidence for his idle curiosities. He wasn't a gossip, but he filed a lot of information in his mind for future use. With his squire's help, he found an engraving of the plate in Cemirowl's house. It belonged to a large estate in the Dusavan Duchy well to the north, that of the duke's eldest son, whose steward tended the land and wealth even though his lord had not been in residence for over twenty years. It was presumed he was travelling the world. A curiosity, but Mercor could not see how it would serve him.

Landlocked, Dusavan's main focus was the border to the north and the relations with countries of Gastren, Pruan, and Denlan. Dusavan was one of the more powerful dukes. Mercor's duties focused on the south. There seemed to be no connection to his affairs, other than the strange and mystical, though it was near his own family's property.

He filed away the idle information for future reference, and applied himself to his work translating documents for the king.

Weeks after the Bone Reading, none of Cemirowl's predictions had transpired. Mercor threw the last of his doubts into the fire, along with the unusable drafts of the trade letter he was attempting to compose. It was only a memory of an odd amusement.

His work was interesting enough to keep his mind applied to his duties. The trade letter he struggled with was one that demanded subtle semantic precision. Hergilan was not his native language, though he was fluent. He had to find a balance in what he needed to convey without giving away more than his liege and sovereign was willing to part with. Though not something to wreck or rock the peace treaty, the letter was delicate enough where he could ask neither queen nor the ambassador's office to help him with the language. He had rarely struggled with his letters to Narsina; they carried no weight, but those were of love and his courtly life—and he'd not written her after he'd declared his intention to marry Llora.

Mercor had already composed more than eight drafts of a letter now smoldering on the fire. In frustration, Mercor took a Hergilan grammar into the gardens. He hoped to find his favorite bench free.

Referring to the volume from time to time, he walked up the terraces, below the queen's balcony, toward the chapel as he contemplated different verbs and conjugations that he could possibly use. *Nedjer, Nedjerat, Pomor, Pomoreyt, Danten, Denatenat...*

The herb gardens and orchards were farther from the main palace, and at this time of day there were fewer people around as many of the servants were retiring for their evening meals. Throughout these grounds, were small private gardens where people could sit and read with some privacy. Mercor needed that silence. He slowly turned a corner in the path, and heard a hushed laugh, and noticed two shadows in a bower of herbs and oranges. He was about to turn when skirts moved and the hem fell into a patch of sunlight. He froze, staring at the familiar gleaming cloth. Then the woman laughed again, and his senses thrilled inside his head. She laughed again, with a sound that teased in protest to the other shadow.

The figures moved. Clouds moved. Hidden as they were, sunlight displayed Llora's profile so that there was no longer any doubt. She laughed and dropped back into the arms of the other man.

Mercor could not move from the shadows that hid him. He stood under the overhanging archway of espaliered fruit trees and the shadows of the palace complex's southern wall. Blood roared in his ears and he trembled. However long they had been in their quiet corner, shifting sunlight would soon expose them. The last patch of sunlight before the sun ran toward dusk.

They did not see him.

Llora was sitting on the man's lap, her skirts much higher than they should be. His rival's hand ran through her dark hair, the other on her thigh. When they broke from their kiss, their eyes were fixed on each other.

Mercor heard Llora say in soft, teasing tones, "What will you do after I wed Caballier Mercor..."

He dropped the book. "Beyond the gates to hell, you will!"

Stepping forward, he grabbed Llora's arm and pulled her off the man's lap. She fell into a heap of glittering brocade, thrown out of his way. Mercor could see the man now, an archer, who stood ready to defend her.

Mercor almost laughed, and felt his fist break the man's face. His left hand pulled his knife, and used the pivot as he drew back from the first blow to cut across the man's chest, then hammered the knife back down. The blade landed into the man's right shoulder, just below the joint. He would be useless as an archer, even if Llora's father left him anything else in punishment.

He drew his knife out as the man crumpled. As the roar faded from his ears, Mercor reflected that it had taken only two twists of his body and half a step to bring the man down. Thinking of a conversation with her, weeks ago, he thought, *Yes Llora, I was successful in war*. He began to hear the soft sound of the surf far below and the satisfying sounds of the archer's bloody snuffling. The man's arm and face were bleeding.

Llora was gasping for breath. She must have screamed. He hadn't heard it. Mercor turned to look down at his betrothed. She was looking at her fallen suitor. She was not weeping. Her face was flushed, her brows together, rapt in calculation. Mercor wondered if she was unable to decide to go to the wounded archer or her more promising suitor.

He moved a step toward her. She jerked, trying to stand, and looked up at him. She was in shock, pale, trembling. Even so, her gratitude was feigned.

"Mercor, by the great gates, thank you! He—" she began, but he turned and left without another word. His disgust was complete.

People arrived, mainly from the chapel, with a crunch and flying of gravel. One man, a novice cleric, robes flapping, pushed past at a run. It was possible that he'd cut into an artery. Mercor didn't care. With immediate help the archer could possibly survive.

With such an audience at the end of the fight, it did not take long for Llora's humiliation to come to the general attention of the court. Honorable Priest Ferran was infuriated on the queen's behalf.

Apparently some of the ladies in the castle had merely been waiting for the opportunity. The queen, shy of open displays of affection, admitted she'd wondered about Lady Llora, but the passions of Pyrannian people continued to surprise her after years of exposure. It quickly became clear to Mercor that Llora had not been as well liked as he'd supposed. It was a blow, worse than the betrayal. He was not usually this easily deceived.

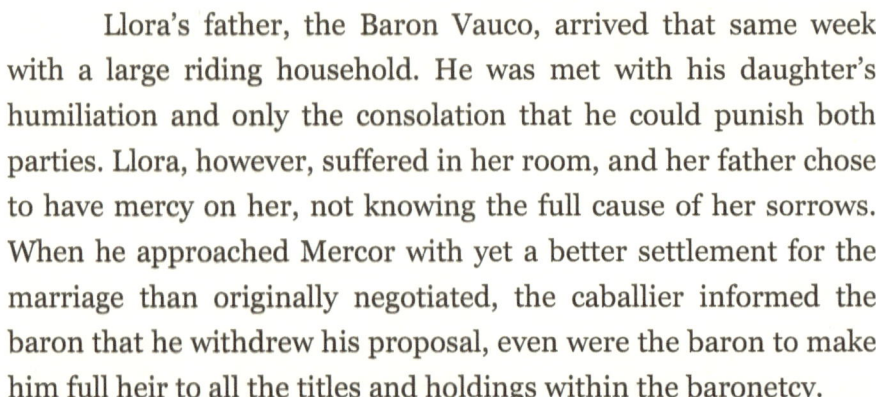

Llora's father, the Baron Vauco, arrived that same week with a large riding household. He was met with his daughter's humiliation and only the consolation that he could punish both parties. Llora, however, suffered in her room, and her father chose to have mercy on her, not knowing the full cause of her sorrows. When he approached Mercor with yet a better settlement for the marriage than originally negotiated, the caballier informed the baron that he withdrew his proposal, even were the baron to make him full heir to all the titles and holdings within the baronetcy.

Mercor knew that Llora was not hiding in mortification—whatever her father thought and tried to convince him of—but was ill with whatever potion the queen's midwife Abenne had secretly given her to kill the archer's bastard. Harlyn had told him, as she was one of the ladies willing to tend the Lady while she remained ill.

"Those potions are terrible when they don't work right away," she'd told Mercor. There was pain in her eyes. "They're terrible even when they do!"

"She is suffering then?"

"Yes. Does it please you?" Harlyn asked.

Mercor shook his head. "I'd rather not have known she was with child!"

"It is news unwelcome for any lady when a match could not come to pass!"

46

"For what care I can barely remember for the Lady, thank you for tending her."

"She's helped me when I was ill. I'm not so petty as to forget her kindness."

After the baron's entourage had left with his dishonored daughter, Mercor remembered the Bone Reader's words. Intentionally arriving late to the queen's solar for the evening's sweet fare and music, he examined the temper of the room.

In the shadows of the balcony above the western garden, he could see the king and queen's favorites all sitting there, listening to the surf and the gentle sounds of a musician playing a vihuela. He felt his brow furrow, but quickly ruled his expression.

King Larthor was there beside Queen Tidyri. Her remaining three ladies were there; Soflia, Terria, and Harlyn mingled with other court ladies. Standing near Terria was the Ambassador Itrizeu's aide Sir Quormen. This was a surprise, as the scandal within the queen's household kept the others away. It was possible, however, that it was a gesture meant to support Queen Tidyri, who would be feeling equal horror, but forced to act like a Lady of Pyrann. Lady Terria's father, Lord Bartemo, stood by the windows speaking to the Pruan representative. There were also a few other men high in the king's favor attending the queen, including the Honorable Priest Ferran. The king's brother was still absent.

What must they think of me? Mercor wondered and shook his head. He readied himself to play the role he intended with a wry smile and a shake of his shoulders. It wasn't enough to be entertained, Mercor must entertain. He could not bear to seem weakened by Llora's betrayal. Especially as she had never been his first choice.

As he entered the room, Mercor nodded to the musician, who was a slight friend. They had worked together on a song or two. Stad nodded back and continued strumming the four rows of double strings of his vihuela. Mercor bowed to the king and queen.

"Are you well?" asked Queen Tidyri and gestured to a stool nearby. Her face was shadowed with concern.

He barked out a wry laugh. "It is truly ironic, Your Highness, but you see I was prepared for it months ago! I merely did not know the truth of my fortune."

Larthor raised his eyebrows. "That sounds like the beginning of a story, Caballier." He settled back into his chair, ready to be entertained.

Mercor laughed, knowing tonight would be the best opportunity of telling the tale of the Bone Reader's prophecy of Llora's betrayal.

Harlyn leaned forward and gave him a wry smile. No cheer filled her eyes. "Perhaps we can arrange a match between both our rejected suitors? Lady Llora might now enjoy the oft lauded Caballier Merald," she said lightly. Mercor sat close enough to see her jaw clenched with tension as she held her goblet for the squire to refill.

He was surprised that Harlyn mentioned the failed match before the king and queen.

"Poor Merald," Tidyri murmured teasingly, winking at Mercor and her king both. It was, again, another effort to damp down scandal in her own rooms. The king clearly appreciated the clumsy effort. Harlyn did not.

"Now for your story," said Tidyri, "If it does not pain you!"

"When my fortune was given me, weeks ago, I'll admit I was at first very angry—such as I was days ago. But then..."

Mercor laughed and told the story about the Bone Reading, telling about all the points that predicted what would happen with Lady Llora and her father—including the details of his crest. He made it as humorous as possible.

Queen Tidyri and two of her ladies laughed gently as he brought wry humor to the tale. He watched their eyes soften in their relief that he was not heartsore. Soflia contemplated him; her expression was clear, though her father had already started negotiating an engagement. Many ladies of the palace would be delighted for him to bestow his attention and favor upon them. He smiled on them all, wondering if any were ready or willing to be wooed for sport or for advantage.

King Larthor gave a robust laugh. "Mercor, how did you come to ask this Bone Reader such a delicate question?" There was a twinkle in his dark eyes. His dark mustache danced as he laughed even as he gestured. A squire jumped up to fetch him more food from the table, but Larthor turned to the caballier.

"I heard tale of her abilities on my return journey from Llora's father," Mercor told him.

"So, of course you went to see her!"

"Of course, my liege. They were burying their priest and this woman was participating in the funeral. In a very common dialect a villager told me that 'she can rayed the bones and be larnin' all sorts of t'ings frome dem!'"

Larthor laughed again and Priest Ferran leaned forward. "No doubt you met a charlatan. There has been little magic in this realm for many years, if there ever was."

"I thought the same, Honorable Ferran! But what she predicted came to pass!" Mercor turned his back to him and looked at the court ladies. "I can tell you that my hands went through bones from her basket!"

The ladies squealed or gasped in horror, then laughed.

The queen shuddered and laughed nervously. "Perhaps we should send for her for our entertainment?" she asked, seeing that her friends were amused.

"She is also a village's priest, your highness," he said, enjoying Ferran's shocked look. "We ought not remove her from her duties."

"But she predicted that Llora would not be true to you?" she asked.

"Yes, without ever having met her," Mercor exclaimed.

The company laughed at his joke.

Mercor was pleased by the court's response, and shrugged off the other predictions that suddenly clouded his mind. Even if the predictions about Llora came true surely the others wouldn't. He felt a shiver of gooseflesh prickle his body. In the glow of the praises that flowed his way Mercor thought, *Surely it was coincidence!* He rubbed his arms and smiled at some barbed joke Harlyn made.

CHAPTER THREE

————— «‹◆›» —————

Dear *Mother,* Tidyri wrote. She wrote in Hergilan, giving her mother her most respectful greeting of "Levestima Anjhem." *I know you would say time... No. I will not complain again. I have said in too many words how different this place is than home; you know it already. I still struggle, but there is joy. As Larthor once pointed out he had married, purposefully, from Hergila just as I have married Pyrann. As often as this land, and sometimes its people frustrate me, I do have the love of my husband.*

There is some pleasant news this early summer amid these petty trials: the cook has been well bribed to stay—despite the thievery by his favorite kitchen clerk; and the hawk master will now take care of Tudjie as she deserves. Once I would have thought Larthor's brother Arthan would have been the dark cloud of my days—for I believed he did not approve of me. I can see, now, why my husband depends on him.

But I am not Pyrannian. I feel different, even though I have learned the language of Pyrann. I still misunderstand so much! I began to think even one of my ladies was jealous of me! I realized I must be wrong, for I have never seen her show any particular feeling for my king but, I thought, for another.

My ladies know of my past disappointments. They have kept me from heartache as best they can, and have kept my heart light despite the slight tension in court because there is no heir. I can only say that duty has been far more of a pleasure, and perhaps soon...

Her letter came to a point where she could not in good conscience go on. She played with the quill feather. Should she write now, or later? What she really wanted to tell her mother she could not—yet—even if the letter took weeks to arrive. She'd waited longer than she had in the past with similar news, to ensure that she was safe. She'd secretly been wearing a Pyrannian braid around her waist that bound a baby to life under her robes. It was such a foolish thing she did that she removed the cord before Larthor ever entered her rooms, and kept it hidden under her shift so that even her ladies would not see it.

Three years of hope and expectation served with pain, weakness, and disappointment. She did not wish to provoke Larthor's sorrow if her body lied to them both again.

With a deep breath, Tidyri put down her pen. She had waited long enough with this news. Even her ladies-in-waiting most likely had sufficient evidence to confirm the speculations generated by the frequent visits of the midwife. Larthor was well aware of the signs as well. It could not have escaped court gossip.

She would finish the letter after she had spoken to her husband.

Tidyri stood and glided down the short hall to the king's chamber where he was already being dressed. "Forgive this crowd, my dear." Larthor dismissed his men, and turned with raised hands to greet her.

She held his hands in her own and kissed him. "You always say that. We could just adjourn to my bedchamber, which is more private."

"Ah, the advantages of a Hergilan wife. I enjoy your privacy," he said with a laugh, while kissing her neck. "Perhaps I ought to recommend it to everyone?"

"Wicked man. I think everyone knows what married partners do. More so in this country."

"True enough. Unfortunately, this morning I have much to do," he said, but guided her to the bed where they sat down.

She knelt behind him, hugging his neck. Her golden hair fell over his shoulder. He brought some of her silken hair to his face.

"I'm glad you didn't cut it," he breathed. "It would have been a tragedy." He turned to gaze upon her while caressing her hair.

"I remember Boduscia's chestnut hair," Tidyri said, "gleaming with that lovely crown of curls around her face. I almost cut mine for our marriage like good Pyrannian women do. She was so lovely with it. Priest Ferran would have been happy that I was a proper Pyrannian wife."

"I did not marry Ferran. Besides, if you had then I would not have been able to run my fingers through your hair," Larthor said, doing so, and using it to hold her head while he embraced her.

It was certainly not a lack of passion or effort that left them childless. When they broke apart, she was breathing heavily. Her hair was mussed, their clothes a bit rumpled.

"Larthor," she began. Just as she took a breath to speak again, there was a knock at the door. They both looked up.

"What is it?" asked Larthor, gruffly, moving his hands from her skirts.

"There is news from Denlan and the envoy from Gastren is waiting," stammered a caballier. The man turned red, looking bleakly at her for one shocked moment, and turned from the door. She could see how well her Hergilan demand of privacy was respected. At least he blushed at his intrusion.

"I'll be there in a moment!" Larthor growled.

He looked expectantly at Tidyri after the knight shut the door. "I gather that you did not come just for a pleasant interlude," he said. "Did you want to tell me anything in particular, my dear?"

"I'll tell you when we can be alone and uninterrupted," she said, moving off of his lap, trying not to be as angry as she felt.

He ran his hands over her back.

"I'm sorry. I do try," she said, relaxing her jaw.

"I know that you do. I apologize as well for letting us be disturbed," he said, and kissed her mouth again, running his thumb against her jaw, caressing her neck and head with his fingers.

She took a deep breath, nodded, but she was still angry. He might apologize, but rarely did the actions of his people change. They would always be disturbed, sometimes even in her bedchamber.

"I understand that you're busy today with the treasurer, stable marshal and a number of vassals. Thank goodness Pruan left with their exotic princess. You only have the Gastren envoy to speak with."

"You're not jealous of this Gezine?" he asked.

"No, of course not. I understand you wish to arrange to

have her wed your brother?"

"Yes, after the other problem we must both deal with."

With a sigh, she let go of her anger. To be angry with him for being a king, or Pyrannian was as futile as being angry at the sun—when her parents agreed to the marriage, she had accepted both king and country with her eyes open.

"Would you like to have dinner alone with me in my chambers tonight?" Tidyri asked.

The words hung between them for a moment. Larthor looked at her, examining her face, contemplating every inch of it, contemplating her.

"I don't speak of the luncheon you must have with members of your court—a good deal of your work happens during that time, as the more private work in your office."

He took her hand again, and stilled their trembling. "You are a good wife. I've made no fixed plans for dinner. Envoys and ambassadors can dine with Arthan now that he's returned, or in their own rooms tonight." Larthor squeezed her hand affectionately. "He has matters of his own household that take him into Elbyrge, but surely this evening he will be free to host."

She relaxed, and then held him tightly. She had not married a stupid man. She was sure he realized the potential importance of her request; she had worked too hard against cultural differences to make such a request lightly.

"Then I will arrange it with the hall marshal and the cook," she said, giving him a kiss on his cheek and sliding off the bed. "I'll see if he'll add an errand for me, as well. There's a book I would like him to find if he's the time."

"Do," he said, then kissed her again on the lips and then yelled for his attendants to help him get ready for his day.

The day was long for Larthor. The envoy from Gastren, Engune, had refused to accept a meeting with either his brother or the Lord Steward Bartemo. The small man was from the country bordering one important duchy and the realm of Denlan to the east, and clearly like many northerners, Engune did not bathe often. Discussing anything with him was unpleasant, more because it also delayed the business with his treasurer, and inquiries about the hunting lands. But wanting to know who Pyrann would side with in a conflict between Gastren and Denlan was a matter this envoy could only ask the king. Larthor was glad that Pruan had left, removing yet more tension from this discussion.

Generally at peace within his own borders, there was still a great deal of internal politics for Larthor to handle among arguing vassals, preventing small but costly civil wars from erupting over the country. War brewing between Gastren and Denlan to the north was not something he looked for—not when he'd done all he could to broker peace across the straits to the south!

It was early summer. *Winter* was the tempestuous season! If there were already hints of trouble now, it would not do to let the arguments turn into war, and certainly needed diplomacy to resolve during the growing or harvest seasons. That was even more costly. Destruction of cropland would only add starvation to everyone on top of the death or disablement of good men.

Larthor guessed at the cause of Gastren's worries and wondered why Denlan even bothered to arouse such worry from such a poor landlocked country. She had a great deal of trade from the east, as well as from across the Einterinne sea. Gastren was good for horses, but little else, but she had her own import, if limited, of the Tashihyellian horses that it did not matter. Pruan, and its hill country had neither offered offence nor even advantage to Denlan's queen.

Irritated, Larthor reflected that Denlan's Queen Rashart always liked to see weaklings dance for her sport. From his brother's accounts, as well as his ambassador, she sported such in her own country as well—making weaker vassals dance for her pleasure. Trying to look diplomatic, he listened to the envoy, working to make sure his shoulders look relaxed and his jaw didn't clench in annoyance. He thought it a poor way for a ruler to prove their power, especially as he believed her more than capable. He knew her to be astute.

Shrewd or not, she enjoyed baiting bears and bulls, and other sports that worried captive creatures. He wished that her entertainments at Gastren's expense would not cause him extra work, even if it came with startling regularity.

He looked casually at his calendar while the envoy repeated himself. Rashart was on schedule, at least. Engune was only a week late. Bartemo had won that bet, but not by much.

He listened to the man because Gastren bordered the duchy of Dusavan. That alone made the envoy's visit important. Though he doubted there was anything but Rashart playing games, he would not discount a man because he looked like an incompetent wot. Larthor was obliged to examine the truth of the rumors. A courier, a letter, and Dusavan would tell him the truth of the matter if the information hadn't already been sent. He wondered if the duke's son could be found. His marquessate touched on all three countries, and had been a brilliant fighter during the Hergilan war. According to his knowledge the man was touring the world, but surely his steward might know where to find him.

Larthor was glad to send Gastren's envoy on his way, letting him know he'd introduce him to Denlan's ambassador at luncheon, and perhaps they could discuss things together.

The morning was full of mental juggling and interruptions; he looked forward to a private dinner with his lovely wife, even while he discussed the price of cattle, the disposition of the salt mines, the haul of the fishermen, and the storage of grain for the winter season if the promise of harvest equaled the hopes of summer. Despite interruptions, the discussion with his steward was more pleasant than the one with the envoy. Bartemo was always organized, and pleased that he'd won the bet.

A page brought in more notes and letters and reports from vassals that would not wait for audience. Bartemo went to the table to draft a letter to the lord who was managing the salt mines. Larthor opened up a letter with the crest of one of his queen's ladies. It was from her steward, and confirmed Larthor's fears. He quickly penned a note for Tidyri, and summoned a waiting page. "Take this to the queen, and send for Lord Arthan."

The page ran off.

"What news, Your Highness?" asked Bartemo. "Your countenance is grave."

"A letter from one of the ladies' stewards. Something I must deal with." He did not often interfere with his wife's household, but circumstances warranted him to finally resolve the problem. His only regret was that his wife had not had better luck with the ladies of this kingdom than she'd had.

"Ah. I see," Bartemo said.

Larthor shook his head. "I see that more than ladies gossip in this court."

"Men speculate. If my... speculations are sound, then you could have resolved the problem by ordering her to marry."

"True enough. By then she'd already paid for her choosing. Why force her to regret the debt?" Larthor said.

"Or burden her with added scandal. You are too kind. She should have been sent away for aiming too high."

Larthor waved the letter. "She will be, but for the sake of her estate, not because of any match she dared imagine I'd condone."

"And save your queen added indignity of her household."

"Exactly. With that inconvenience soon safely out of the way, I can more easily plan for my brother's future. Now! On to other business."

They worked through more of the morning on other important matters that dealt with the internal matters of the palace, the harvest, even while Larthor also read letters and contemplated the political balance of his country. They met with some of his own countrymen in his audience chamber over the petite course, to discuss internal politics.

Later, at the longer luncheon, he dined with them, and various ambassadors and envoys, dining to lighten the import of the business at hand. The Hergilan Ambassador Itrizeu had come with his knights, one who was slowly embracing Pyrann, and the other whose dislike had quickly increased. They were joined by a visiting prince from the Tashihyel, who was still learning the language. There was a pale giant of a sea captain, almost as pale as the White Princess, but sunburnt. He had come from the far north with trade goods gathered along all western coasts. Both Larthor and Itrizeu were quite interested; they worked to prevent other heads of state and their agents from seeing the potential wealth in the strange merchandise.

One of the more important acts of the lunch: Larthor introduced the Gastren envoy to the Denlan ambassador, letting them know quite diplomatically, but theatrically as well—Itrizeu loomed behind him in his stark Hergilan robes and stern Hergilan countenance—that if the squabble was petty on either side, that Larthor had no difficulties calling upon his allies to school both countries. If it was not petty, he would work as a mediator between them to keep the peace he so valued.

The luncheon interlude offered more information to labor over with in his offices. He and Bartemo retired there, and began to read more papers and compose them. A page with his brother's livery came in with a message that Lord Arthan had returned to the castle from his morning venture into the city and whatever private matter pressing to his own household that had sent him there. He'd received Larthor's summons and would join him shortly.

"Let him know there is no rush. It is only information I wish to convey to him."

The page bowed. "Yes, Your Highness."

There was a scream, and then from more than one woman, echoing down the hallway from the queen's solar.

Larthor shot out of his chair. Lord Bartemo followed.

Thinking of the news that he would share with his brother, and how at least one lady would react, it occurred to him that

60

news or gossip must travel fast! But the hopes of the evening's quiet entertainment with his wife would not be laid over coals of the lady's distress.

The hall was filled by people. He pushed past one of the Hergilan knights, who was carrying a letter scroll, with a stamped crest dangling from it. Lady Soflia was wailing by the doorway, held between a page and a caballier, as if caught in a swoon. Larthor pushed past them, and into the room. He saw Lady Harlyn, her hair rumpled as if she'd been woken from a nap, her hand crushing a sheaf of purple wands, leaning against the door frame to the ladies' bedchamber.

Lady Terria knelt over Tidyri. As she fell back, her bottle of smelling salts dropped from her hand, rolling away. Her hands moved to her mouth as she cried out, "My lady!"

Tidyri lay in a heap by her worktable. He took three long strides to her, moving Terria aside, as a caballier helped her rise. She turned to cry into his chest.

Tidyri's eyes were partly closed in a faint. He reached for the bottle of smelling salts, not pausing to wonder why Terria had let it drop from her hand.

As he took her in his arms, Larthor was surprised to see that her hair had been cut. He wondered why she'd done it, wondering if it was the cause of her faint, like some sort of mystical thing from a tale.

He felt disconnected from the room for a moment, wondering if he was in a fairy story. He ran strands through his fingers, and noticed how raggedly it had been done. He grew furious. He vowed he would get some answers when Tidyri awoke from her faint. He waved the salts under her nose. She did not stir, though his own eyes watered from their potent stench. He set it down. Tenderly, he moved to pat her cheeks and wake her.

"Tidyri," he said.

It was then that he realized she was not breathing.

Her cheeks were clammy to the touch and through heavy lidded eyes she stared at him, dark eyed, from an anxious face.

"Tidyri?" he asked.

Gradually, he realized she was dead.

His whole being wanted to deny it, wanted to reject the information plain in her frozen face. He tried waking her again. He'd seen death on the war field, but this threatened to break something inside him he could not control. Dead soldiers on the field of battle were not a wife dead in her own solar.

"Tidyri?" He kissed her lips with desperate force and clutched her body to him.

After a short, stunned moment, Larthor turned to the crowd. "What happened?" he demanded.

His heart thudded slow and harsh in his chest, too loud in his own ears for him to hear anyone else in the room. He felt incredibly numb and removed from all the noise and bustle in the room; it seemed an effort to ask even that question.

He watched Terria sobbing in the caballier's arms, trying to say something.

Finally, he heard Soflia's wail from the doorway. "We just found her, Your Majesty!"

A general commotion of the three ladies wailing and babbling began; he could get no sense from their hysteria. Larthor ordered them away with a gesture, but demanded that the marshal of the guard get some sense out of them. He held his wife to his breast, still feeling numb, struggling to think. His body felt incredibly cold.

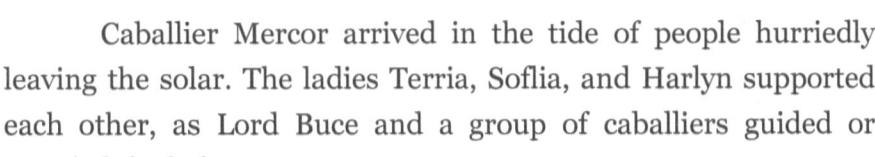

Caballier Mercor arrived in the tide of people hurriedly leaving the solar. The ladies Terria, Soflia, and Harlyn supported each other, as Lord Buce and a group of caballiers guided or guarded the ladies.

Sir Amec stopped him, looking grim. "This is bad! I must give this news to Lord Itrizeu!" he said to Mercor. "What will this do for his treaty now?"

Mercor had known Amec for years, and heard the undertone of satisfaction in his voice. It grated against the horror written on the caballiers' faces, and the desolation on the ladies'.

"What happened?" he asked, surprised that Amec had even bothered to alert him of anything.

"Go see!" Amec said. And for once Mercor cursed his long years in the countries south of Hergila, and in Hergila itself. He could see the pleasure in the man's face, where few others would. "But I must go inform Lord Itrizeu, so he can know what to do with his precious treaty."

Mercor went to the doorway to see the king in a heap on the floor, stony and staring, clutching his queen, one hand in her cut hair. At first he thought it was an awful lot of commotion for a haircut some would have thought long overdue for a Pyrannian wife. In shock as the truth hit him, he breathed the first thought that came to mind.

"Great Gates! She knew!" he said, as he stumbled forward,

in the press of people trying to leave.

The world suddenly slowed as Mercor saw his words pierce the king's perception. The caballier could see the cold and numbness in Larthor's shocked and staring eyes transform. Mercor felt his own stomach turn to ice as Larthor turned to face him. It was the look no man wished to see from a liege lord.

"What did you say?" The king growled, his voice low and dangerous.

Mercor knew the voice. There was a rising anger in his king, but he was too stunned to stop himself. He cleared his throat with an effort and spoke louder. "The Bone Reader, she knew! The reading she gave me. She told me someone would die."

Horror had been rising. Now humiliation grew. He had not, could not have prepared for this situation, but it was horribly strange to realize that he *might* have done so because of the Bone Reader's predictions. Once, during a battle, he'd had to fight up a muddy hill, sliding and slithering, fighting for his footing and his life. This felt agonizingly worse.

With the king's glare upon him, Mercor stumbled backward. He'd never been clumsy in front of his liege and felt his stupidity and desperation keenly. His shock began to die as the cold in his belly grew.

The world stopped. Mercor waited for Larthor's fury to peak. He waited. He listened to the pounding of his own heart, and smelled fear in his sweat. He could hear Cemirowl saying inside his head, *Speak with caution and care. Even one wrong word will bring about more difficulty.*

Like cannon shot out of the clear blue suddenly smashing a wall, it came.

Larthor roared. "Then get her and bring her here. Let her

tell me who killed my Tidyri!"

Even the marshal of the guard and the steward stepped back, pale in the fury of the king's anger.

Sir Mercor paused. "But..."

"Now!" Larthor roared. "And if she doesn't tell me why she did not warn me, you'll both die for the treason!"

Mercor turned and plunged out of the room through the wall of people still crowding the hall.

What a few days ago had been an amusing entertainment was suddenly a source of mortification. If the Bone Reader had predicted Llora's betrayal, how could Mercor not have warned the king of the queen's death? But she had not told him *who* was destined to die, merely that someone would. He felt himself flush and scowled.

He turned, angry, and gathered up two caballiers, Cibran and Tadeo. Running into the stable marshal who was coming up the stairs to find out about all the fuss, Mercor ordered eight of the fastest horses. They would travel light, and switch horses often to make better time.

Mercor, still trembling from shock and his embarrassment, would do his duty to the king. But he was infinitely glad to get away.

CHAPTER FOUR

P rince Arthan arrived in the solar after some of the king's men had taken Larthor to his own chambers and the queen's body had been moved. He stood in the solar, by the windows, with the book he'd bought for Tidyri from a city bookseller in his hands. In a whispered conversation with Lord Marshal Buce, the appalling events of the afternoon were revealed to him from the discovery of Tidyri's body, Mercor's errand, and what had already been done and what investigations they planned. The ladies had not been helpful as yet.

They were not unwilling to rule out murder, most likely by poison. But she had been weakened by miscarriages, and was not strong enough a woman to rule out a sudden fit. The knife that had cut her hair had been found in the room. Strands of her hair were found tangled in her fingers.

Arthan had little to add or to offer Buce. They knew, beyond a doubt, that not all who resided in Itrizeu's household approved the treaty.

"Vipers at our breasts!" Buce had said. "And Sir Amec being right on the spot, supposedly delivering a letter from Hergila to her Majesty!"

"There are people of our country who opposed the match as well," Arthan had replied, ruthlessly.

"True, but where were they?"

Everywhere! Arthan had thought, and the word renewed itself in his mind. He was somewhat uncomfortable. Too many people believed he did not approve of the treaty; and he also knew too well how easily his rooms connected to the queen's, even if along a gallery open to a garden from below.

"That is a question you must ask and find answers to!" he said, almost growling out the words.

Buce left the room to continue his inquiries. Arthan stayed. He looked about the solar where Harlyn, Terria and servants worked on clearing the room. He put the book on Tidyri's desk. He turned to the fireplace. The room was fragrant with the distinct floral sachet Harlyn wore in her clothes. He could not look at her, knowing she was nearby. He stood facing the fire in the solar, though he did not really see it.

Tidyri's harp banged against the floor as a servant moved it. The echo of the strings off the sound box jarred. He shook his head.

"Leave." His mouth was dry. The words croaked out low.

Arthan turned to face the page near him. The boy stiffened and looked up. His face turned red as he began to tremble. From the corner of his eye, Arthan saw the other servants unmoving, staring at them.

"I said leave me."

The words were still low, but clear and full of the authority born to a prince.

He never struck vassals, much less villains. Yet the three servants moved quickly as if he'd strike them once they understood him. He knew that in the past year his temper had gained a reputation for all the brooding calm his body usually displayed. Cruel some called it. He could not help it. As servants scattered, he stared at the two ladies. He took a number of deep breaths while Terria led Harlyn to the balcony and the garden down below.

Terria said, "Come, we will go sit vigil for our queen!"

They would go to the chapel beyond, he knew. And the ladies would have plenty of time to be questioned and to mourn. It would take days before official funerals and burials would take place. Bartemo had already sent the fastest boat they had to inform the queen's parents. He also knew that there were things being done to her body to ensure that the events were not... horrible.

He knew that the emotion carved on his face was ugly, rough, and terrible. He was glad the room was empty. No matter how devastated Harlyn appeared by his coldness.

He breathed deep, strong and steady, as he brought himself under control. Slowly the fireplace came into focus. He felt its heat, but its amber light was drowned by the light coming from the large windows amplified by the whitewashed walls that weren't covered by tapestries.

He noticed burnt paper in the edges of the fire. He bent to pick it up. It had been torn, and much of it burned away. He could see the scrolling letter work that started with Har... and the rest was gone. One piece looked as if it was the embossed letterhead of his brother's office. He looked about for more pieces. There were few enough, with blackened letters, but offering up no more information as they were fragile as ash. Toward the edge of the white ashes, something caught his eye.

He nearly stepped back in surprise. The burnt letter was a curiosity, but this did not belong. He picked it up.

A white spider! It was crushed, but he knew it came from only one place. He stepped back and noticed that the carpets had not been brushed. Near the spider, the carpets had dirt. A slight trail seemed to come from the outside gallery door. He shivered.

Arthan reached out and pinched some of the dirt between two fingers and sniffed in expectation. He drew back almost immediately. His eyes watered, and he felt a cough in the back of his throat. *Ammonia,* he thought. *Bat guano.* It certainly wasn't from either of the gardens. He wished it had come from a barrack garderobe instead of the caverns under his apartments.

It was possible to make a case that it had come from the stables, but Arthan knew it had not. With the evidence of the spider and this bat guano, it would be clear to certain people in the court—Master of the Guard Lord Buce in particular—that someone had gone through the secret caverns. Very few knew of the passage. His heart thudded. He'd used that passage for meetings best left unmentioned. And recently.

Arthan's thoughts moved fast as he bit the inside of his cheek. He considered telling Buce or Larthor, but he had no wish to damn himself.

Larthor himself had placed Arthan's rooms over the entrance to the caverns, trusting his beloved brother to keep them secure. They rebuilt the building to disguise it as much as possible— blocking it off from the soldier and servant tunnels that ran under most of the buildings. The caverns led to a seaside cave accessible at low tide, though hard to get to. If Lord Buce saw the spider here in this room, he might realize that Arthan had, at the very least, compromised the security of the castle.

It would be imprudent to explain why.

Arthan put the spider in his purse; later he'd put it in a glass vial, in case he needed it. Arthan looked around for more incriminating evidence, still thinking fast.

What plausible reasons could anyone have to visit the caves who also had reason to visit the queen? What other rationalizations could be used?

He quickly catalogued the few people who knew the secret of the cave that led down to the sea—and further brave enough to venture deep enough to bring back evidence of the journey. The crushing dark of the caverns was not everyone's cup of tea.

The closest to the dark of the caverns were the palace passageways below ground. But as he'd had an active role in supervising the rebuilding as well as new construction of the palace buildings he'd ensured that where possible those passageways were not dark. As with his own home, there were cunning architectural lanterns that brought light to the passageways. In other places he'd added refracting glass, like those that helped bring light from the main deck to the cavernous dark hulls of boats, wooden structures where torches and fire were not the best choices to bring light.

The coastline of his small duchy, Ardine, had a western coastline. Having sailed, he'd added them where he could during various building projects to make the maze of the guard and servant tunnels brighter. Servants needed to get to storage rooms, for foodstuffs, as well as tables and chairs needed for events, or meals, and so on. Guards needed to be able to move quickly from one side of the palace to another, at need. But the caverns themselves? There were no refracting lights or lanterns. They were dark and eerie.

He knew that the secret passageway had passed into legend, if it was known at all. Once it might not have been a great secret. Even in his grandfather's time, the entrance was boarded up. Larthor and he had started to explore it as boys, but the dark was too crushing. When he'd explored it later, while constructing the palace building for their mother, he'd explored it to ensure that it posed her no threat. He'd discovered that there was a marked passage. He'd informed his brother, and when their mother passed on, Larthor asked him to take over the building and guard a potential threat.

Besides himself, who knew of them and had business in the queen's private solar? It was very possible that any of those few men who knew of the caverns, who might have gone through there, had brought it in during the confusion, except that Arthan knew that Buce had not investigated the caverns recently, nor ordered anyone to do so. They all had to go through his chambers.

Only one lady knew of the caverns, but to his knowledge had never entered them. As far as he knew, he was the only one to traverse them recently, and guide another through.

Arthan knew that the ladies at court were not timid. Though many were silly, most were raised to be strong enough to rule their courts in their future lord and husband's absence. He'd gone through the caverns himself a number of times, and explored others. Their strange beauty intrigued him. He did not know any lady who would brave the tomblike darkness of the caves, much less trail long embroidered skirts through bat guano swarming with insects.

He could not find any more insects or other evidence pointing to the caverns and breathed a sigh of relief. Guano would be swept up as dirt; white spiders and other cave dwellers might be noticed and commented on. And that *must* be prevented!

He looked out through the windows. "Calm yourself. You will find the midwife," he told himself. But now he had two reasons he wished to speak with the woman and ensure her silence.

He'd added two weak links in the security of both this palace and his reputation. His hands trembled as he fought a wave of angry self-reproach. Now it seemed that all his private actions were in jeopardy of being revealed to the court. He had to look for the midwife Abenne, with her herb pouch of helpful herbs and potions mingled in with foul poisons—those that could kill. He was disgusted with himself and what he'd done. He needed to deal with the midwife and finish what he'd started.

Chapter Five

⟪•⟫

Cemirowl loved baking. It was not a skill she'd learned from her mother. The rhythm of rolling and pressing the ball of dough while she kneaded gave her a sense of meditative peace. She became sanguine and centered. The warmth of the day would help the dough rise beautifully. She had opened doors and windows for any breeze. She'd need it when she rebuilt the fire for baking. Dusane came in through the open door and sat in his chair.

"Hello, Father," she said. He seemed to reply. She wondered if he found their apparent one-sided conversations frustrating as she sometimes did. There was peace in his presence, and she was grateful for that much.

The fireplace resembled that of the Thade's manor kitchen. It was extravagant for a house built for a poor man with no property. Her mother, Ferioul, had not coped terribly well with the roasting turnspit, or the baking alcoves, preferring to cook peasant fare in the pot and round peasant loaves in banked coals. Titled though they had been, this was not the life her family had been born to. Sometimes this had been too much to cope with, among many things.

The woodsman Toggas's sister, Gazzie, had worked in Thade's kitchen—a place well-loved in that household. The caballier's inclination was not for war or hunting, but in food and wine. His vineyards were becoming well known for the wine he produced since the peace. Gazzie had been one of his inspired cooks. After she died, Toggas had Cemirowl cut her soul, "Not trustin' the newfangled ways of the manor's priest."

Gazzie had followed her brother to Cemirowl's house after she'd helped him reclaim a family heirloom—her and her mother's favorite cooking pot. Instead of haunting the manor kitchen, Gazzie cooked here while her brother came for pastoral care.

There were worse teachers than ghosts who could not instruct with words. Over time, Toggas's grief faded. When he no longer needed neither the cooking directed by his sister nor Cemirowl's pastoral care, Gazzie's presence had faded. The idea, which Cemirowl did not entertain long, that Toggas had wanted more than pastoral care also gently diminished. Her walls stayed up, while he found a woman in Thadetown.

Now, in the warmth of a summer kitchen, Dusane sat in his chair while Cemirowl baked bread. Even if to most eyes she was alone, bread, or a feast for one when she could afford it, was still shared. She could see the red of her father's hair, and the vague outlines of his body as he sat down. The memory of his strong, though scarred figure added the details his wraith kept from her eyes.

With the long, rolling motion of kneading rocking her whole body, Cemirowl talked comfortably with him about her new books. Though Alcon had inherited the old pony, she had inherited Meelac's four books. Three of the books discussed the four humors, history of the church, birth bindings, wedding celebration, and funerary rites. The prize was Meelac's tiny book of verse. She now had a noble collection. They were good companions to the book of courtly verse she'd inherited from her father, along with his books on herbal lore, and his precious handwritten book on anatomy and his own experience with the herbs available in the forest around them.

The anatomy he had apparently learned during the war—which he had discussed only once, and only as an explanation of why he knew what went where in the body. He had furthered the lesson after a gift of a freshly killed pig from Sir Thade, letting her see what some of his drawings resembled in real life. It had only helped once, when he had her massage a woman's belly in helping turn a baby, when the local midwife was helping another birth elsewhere in the village.

The new book of poetry was a frivolous treat, and when Dusane came to visit, and Cemirowl sensed he wanted to talk medicine, she turned to a new poem to shift the subject. While she was sure the information would be useful and interesting, it was not as if she could hear what he was telling her.

She sang Dusane a verse from the new book the way she imagined it would sound if it were put to music.

> *Your words are woven through me!*
> *My whole body a celebration*
> *My mind has been set free!*
> *There can be no other contemplation,*
> *Sanguine, I celebrate thee!*

She repeated the verse, but ended it with 'me'. She paused, and looked up at him. "Well, that's how I think it could sound. What do you think?"

She sensed a positive response, and said, "I'm not sure that

I could celebrate myself," she admitted. "I like the first refrain better as I'm assuming 'thee' means the Holy One."

Cemirowl could almost hear Dusane's deep, steady voice along with the wave of sympathy. She believed the words suggested something like 'an ideal.' He tried to shift the topic to the herbs she had drying. Cemirowl had the idea he thought her collection of koot mauls insufficient for the coming winter, being a mucilage herb excellent for coughs and more.

"It is early yet, Father. I have linus seeds, in plenty," she said. "I even found some aquill."

Her father seemed surprised.

"I went with Toggas to a sick friend late spring. It was a dry area, and there it was, as you described, with white flowers. I planted some, in some river sand."

She continued to knead and wished that she could really hear his words, because he seemed to praise her memory. A memory of Ferioul came on the heels of that thought. Her mother had sat on the bed at the other end of the room talking, moaning, unclear and upset, hearing the voices of the dead. Cemirowl smiled wanly at her father. She buried memories of Ferioul and felt the wave of sympathy rise again from her father, strong enough that it felt almost as if his hands touched her. She started another verse.

Suddenly, some of her animals leapt up onto the table and began to mill along its scarred length and through the dough between her fingers. Other animals surged by the door. Her head jerked up.

The dog howled, an odd echo that Cemirowl felt more than heard. The bones from her heel to the base of her spine ached, echoing below her lungs. Unable to breathe for a moment, she nearly retched from the vertigo. She gripped the dough and shook her head, coughing.

Dusane stood, moved toward the fireplace and faded deeper into the otherworld.

A crack of a branch muffled by the walls of her cottage snapped her attention outside. Then she heard a sound like thunder and the whinny of a horse. Bumping against the table, Cemirowl hurried to the door, rubbing her hands in her apron. She saw a large horse making a ruin of her garden.

She remembered a horseman coming to Dusane, long ago, once, begging for her father's medical advice, when Thade's son had injured himself while hunting. Cemirowl had gone along as her sewing was finer than her father's.

"What has happened!" she cried to the rider leaping off his horse. His figure and face were obscured by the bulk of the horse.

Herb lore, surgery... Her mind ran through the contents of her still room as she hurried around the horse's head. Then she saw the spike and turban, the tawny field and the white. She stopped cold.

No! She thought. *It can't be!* She almost ran back inside her house, but the cold rising in her belly froze her to the spot.

"You knew!" Mercor barked, "Why didn't you tell me? You're wanted by the king!"

"What? I don't understand you, Caballier," she stammered, shaking her head, stepping back.

"The queen was found dead the day before yesterday."

"The *queen*?" gasped Cemirowl. The cold reached her skin. A wave of gooseflesh ran all over her body.

"Why didn't you tell me it would be her?" He took her by the shoulders and gave her a shake.

"What? How could I know?" she asked him desperately, unable to break away. *The queen?*

"Your reading told me someone would die!"

"True! But the Bones did not tell me *who!* You knew that! You *exonerated* me!" She pulled herself out of his grasp and stepped back.

He glared at her. "Well, the king wants you now. He'll accuse you of treason if you cannot tell him why you did not warn him!" he said savagely. He loomed over her with all the carriage of a knight strong enough to earn a living in tournaments.

She stumbled backward and fell to the ground.

"Get your things," he growled, but a wave of emotion came and fled his face, leaving it hard and frozen.

Before he turned from her, Cemirowl saw a hint of self-reproach. He knew that he'd dominated a frightened young woman who couldn't possibly defend herself against him. He was still a caballier covered in mail with a scimitar hanging by his side and a variety of other weapons about his person, not the least were his fists. She could not forget it. A brief moment of sympathy from him could not make the situation easier to bear.

Trembling, Cemirowl got up from the ground and ran to the house. She stumbled across the threshold and slammed the door. She fell to her knees and began to weep. She swallowed the wail that wanted to rise deep in her throat.

Step by step, don't get lost. Whatever was happening she could not disobey the king. *Deep breath,* she told herself. *Steady yourself.*

Still trembling, Cemirowl picked herself up from the floor and went to put out the fire. Then, calmly thinking of what she might need she realized what her priorities were. Calmly, she gathered up her bone basket. She padded the bones with scraps of cloth and quilting and put them in her herb carry-bag. She collected her newest dress and her vestments, and rolled them into her father's old satchel. Putting both bag and satchel over her shoulder, she gathered up her bread dough. Slowly, she walked out the door.

With a pretense of calm, she walked to the side of the house and tossed the dough into her compost heap and laid the bowl nearby. She took her old chipped spade, shoveled dirt over the mess and turned to the caballier.

"I am ready, Sir." She could not look at his face.

"Why did you do that?" he asked sharply, gesturing toward the compost pile.

"What, the dough? I buried it so animals wouldn't eat it and die of a burst stomach, nor did I want the fermenting dough to cause an infestation of insects in my home. I plan to return here, Sir," Cemirowl ended firmly, finally looking into his blue eyes.

After a brief moment she added, "I would also like, if we have time, to ask my friend Alcon to watch over my chickens."

"Fine," he said, shaking his head.

She watched him lift himself into the saddle, and enjoyed the black irony that her prediction had, at least in some form, come true. *Perverse thought; but at least I know that the predictions were true! Of course readings are never clear. Damned bits and pieces of information! How could I have understood? Besides, the chance of it coming true was not that low. Everyone dies.*

What bothered her was how much the prediction of change for herself and his reading of betrayal and death were tangled with each other. Mercor's involvement seemed obvious now. The chaos of those predictions had obviously begun. Change had not been Meelac's death; it was not inheriting her mother's insanity—though of course this was not ruled out as a future doom. Change was whatever this moment brought her.

As Mercor settled himself into the saddle he reached for her. Mercor took her forearm and pulled her up behind him with sheer proof of his strength. He then maneuvered the horse back down the path, trotting quickly as possible through the trees.

"I have brought two other caballiers for your protection. They, as well as another horse, await us in the village," he said, when they slowed to avoid a low branch. "It will be a rough ride. I take it you've never ridden?" His tone was condescending.

"Meelac had an old pony. I would ride it when I was called to perform my duties as a priest when they were far," she said coldly, hating her rising anger.

Cemirowl ground her teeth. *Most peasants do not ride,* she reminded herself, *and it is very possible that he had not meant to be demeaning, forgetting that in rank we are equal.* She suspected that the caballiers were less there to protect her, than to keep her from fleeing.

"Good then," Mercor said. "It will be a hard ride, nonetheless. We do not have much time."

"Indeed, not," Cemirowl agreed and lost all her anger thinking of the body.

They did not have much time before the funeral process became horrible as the body decomposed. She had read in one of Meelac's books that there were ways to preserve the body for a longer wait before burial. A small village could never afford it. A king certainly could. Still, even for a queen, a hundred-weight of spices, oils, and herbs could only delay decay. But the thought flung her into more gloom. She'd not been called to bury a queen. She'd been called to answer a charge of treason. All the consistent readings in the world *might* have warned her of the danger—had she been able to understand them. They certainly did not give advice on how to get out of this predicament.

By the time they were making a late camp, Mercor's anger had lessened. The tone of his orders, even to the other caballiers, was less biting, and his words to Cemirowl less contemptuous. Tension still crossed his forehead, but now his pensive movements spoke of serious thinking.

Cemirowl took the time to examine her own position. Just because the villagers had a certain cautious respect for her did not mean that the nobility would feel the same, no matter her training or ordination.

She stretched and groaned. Arms, shoulder blades, and legs were sore from the rough ride. She was glad that she did not have to move her bags far. The horse she'd ridden was much larger and wider than Meelac's old plodding pony.

Trying hard not to look as stiff and pained as she felt, Cemirowl watched Caballier Mercor as she put down her bags. The caballier named Cibran ordered her to move them elsewhere.

"Get wood," Mercor ordered.

She nodded again. In the failing light she picked up as

many downed branches and twigs as she could find around the camp they were making. By now she realized Mercor was not just grieving his queen, or following orders of his king. She recalled part of his reading: Circles within circles or wheels within wheels. Whatever that could have been, all she could remember was twisting lanes of logic circling round and round each other, like woven patterns.

Looking at the tightness in his shoulders, and in the corners of his mouth, that idea was too general. Whatever was bothering him was more specific. And probably associated with her. His eyes kept darting over at her. Besides the reading, she could not know what else she might have done to anger him.

She straightened her back with a groan. Her arms were not quite full, but she could no longer bend down to pick up another branch. She took the load to Caballier Tadeo, who was finishing the fire ring. He knelt to blow on the tinder he'd set, and began to pile the tiny fire with the branches she'd brought.

"I'll need more," he said.

Having worked funerals since she was eight, Cemirowl quickly noted that all three knights showed signs of shock and disbelief. Tadeo's eyes were tight, but even so, his eyes gazed off into nothing—nearly forgetting the fire. An oath from Mercor blasting one of the horses, brought his attention up. Tadeo said with a sigh, "Wonder if he'll write a song for her."

"What?" she asked Caballier Tadeo in some surprise.

"Nothing," he barked. "Where's that wood?"

She nodded and turned to fetch more downed branches, and she was glad, for it gave her time to think. All three men were struggling with the knowledge that a loved one had died. That their queen had died.

Whenever the subject of the foreign queen had come up in Soft Water, most villagers—as far as Cemirowl could tell—spoke poorly about the match the king had made. The best they could say was that noblemen could disport themselves as they wished, but distrusted most things foreign. It was clear, however, that Queen Tidyri had become loved by those closest to her.

But Tadeo had given her a glimmer of understanding: Caballier Mercor would sing his grief, not attack the people around him. He was fighting back in anger or defense. As a man who had been humiliated?

She turned her attention to watch Mercor and Cibran hobbling the horses. She could see him limping where one of the horses must have stepped on his foot. She did not know what had sent Mercor struggling to bolster his self-esteem, but his brief display of dominance at her cottage had probably been a salve to a wounded ego.

She stood by the fire with her arms full of branches, thinking about this.

Was it possible that he was humiliated because now Caballier Mercor would be associated, for a time, with a peasant priest? Their rank was nominally equal, but there was no disguising the shabbiness of even her best dress or vestments. A rich, well positioned caballier dragging something he brought up from the ash pits. And with a ludicrous story to boot. Because of the ridiculous story?

"Get out of my way!" Caballier Tadeo barked.

Cemirowl nearly dropped the wood in her arms, but laid it down and stepped out of the way.

Her next efforts to help—trying to set up the tripod for the cooking cauldron, and attempting to bring the food satchel—

brought on the same barked orders.

Cemirowl sat down on a large rock near the fire pit, and held her hands in her lap. She watched the other three set camp and cook. When the stew was ready, she held out the bowl they'd given her. Tadeo filled it, and then ignored her. She ate in silence, and continued watching them.

Caballier Cibran's grief was clear despite his wan smiles. His eyes were rimmed pink, but she knew he would not cry. Cemirowl was not surprised that she became a source of his painful attempts at humor. Caballier Tadeo was rather more morose. He kept his distance, grieved in silence, stared off in the distance—Mercor yelled at him once for nearly letting the fire go out again. Roused out of his grief, he barked out comments or orders. Mercor could hardly sit still. His right foot tapped up and down while he sat, his face intent with troubled thinking.

Cemirowl found herself shrinking into herself. She felt separated from their companionable if grief stricken activity.

Four people and their horses were ringed by darkness and silence. They were in their own little world. Their own tiny village. Breaking the silence was the sound of spoons scraping wooden bowls, slurping, eating, the crackling of fire, and Cibran's very few comments.

Cemirowl had never been in a group of people without having something to do. Having something very important to do. When she was not wanted, Cemirowl lived alone, hiding in her cottage, or wandering in the woods with very few live companions to break the monotony. She stayed out of village life except at their need. She had rarely run to them, or brought herself into their lives. Except for occasional visits from the dead, her ghostly pets were her only regular companions.

She watched Mercor spoon more stew into his trencher. He made some comment to Tadeo, and she could see how—though she understood the meaning of the words—they spoke a different language from hers. She was foreign to them in so many ways. Fleeing back to everything familiar was barred by the threat of all the weapons that glittered in the firelight whenever any of them moved.

As she stared at Sir Mercor, he gulped the rest of his stew and then scraped the remnants into the fire. His face displayed more calm, as if he'd come to some sort of resolution as he'd chewed his food. Her heart pounded when he stood and approached her.

He sat down beside her.

"You truly did not know that it would be her?" he asked softly.

She blinked back tears with a savage thought, *Suddenly he is kind?* She looked up at him and said as clearly as possible, "No, Caballier, I truly did not know it would be her. I do not know of any form of divination that can be so clear. Though I'll admit my experience is limited. Perhaps it is the fault of my ability. There are many things I cannot learn or interpret or even impart."

Mercor was silent for a long while, looking into the fire.

"Will you... can you," he began finally, but could not finish. Cemirowl wondered if he knew what he was attempting to convey.

After another long moment, she asked him gently, "What, Caballier? What is it you are trying to say?"

"Will you be capable of telling him how the queen died by reading your bones?"

"You mean read how she was killed?" she asked.

"Possibly. I don't know. He was rather angry with me at

the time, so I did not stay to find out his exact wishes for you. I do know that he wishes to know why you did not warn him. We may be saved if we can prove you could not be clear. But can you do that? Find out who or what killed her? It might save us."

Cemirowl blinked and stared. Mercor seemed so hopeful. She caught sight of Cibran and Tadeo watching them intently across the fire. She could see that the two caballiers were also very interested in what she had to say. She realized that Sir Mercor was somehow also bound within the accusation of her treason.

"Sir, I do not know what to tell you."

The look on Cibran and Tadeo's faces changed. They had feared something otherworldly in her, but now they did not. They had decided she was a charlatan. It relieved their minds.

Mercor's face held a lingering intensity. She could see that he was still in awe of her. He had experienced her skill, 'foolish entertainment' though it had once been. She attempted to answer his question in a different way. "Not with any accuracy," she offered gently. "I am sorry for your king."

His face transformed. Even in the firelight he seemed to turn pale, then red. His brow and jaw were tight again.

Cemirowl tried to relieve his mind. "Sir, there isn't much I can do, but I will help put her spirit to rest if that will ease the king. I suspect that his priest will have it in hand, but it is probably the only thing I can offer," she said.

"Great Gates, Cemirowl, you don't understand!" he exclaimed. "If you don't tell him what he needs to know, he's going to charge you with treason! He'll do so in any case because you did not warn him of the queen's danger. He'll hang you!"

Her brows knit together. "Why, Caballier?" she asked, bewildered.

"Because he believes that you can do this!"

"But why does he believe this? I've never met the king. I cannot believe that my skills are of such note that..." She gestured wildly.

Mercor gripped her wrist. "I told him of your predictions."

She twisted her arm to free herself, but his grip was too strong. "All of it?"

"No, only of your predictions about Llora, that I would end my betrothal to her. You were dead on about her! She was packed up and taken off by her father after I told him I didn't want her anymore. I was trying to make light of the situation and the court found the tale diverting."

Diverting, Cemirowl thought, disgusted, and stared into the fire. The stew roiled in her stomach. The small thread she could see became a glittering tapestry for them. Cemirowl only saw or heard vague echoes in the Bones, but for this young caballier, with events coming to fruition... it would probably look as if she'd given Mercor the time and date of the events that had transpired.

"You told the story after my predictions seemed to come true?" she asked, but knew the answer. Cemirowl had already gone numb.

Mercor nodded. "When I found out about the queen I remembered what you'd said and blurted out 'She knew!' The king asked me what I meant and I told him about the other part of the reading."

She put her head in her hands. A vague reading made even more obscure... *No, 'Obscure' is the wrong word,* Cemirowl thought. Rising from a nebulous truth, fiction arose in a tale boasting of her accuracy. It had muddled the situation. *No... Made it dangerous.* Dangerous to her.

What drew her mind was the yawning gap that had suddenly become crystal clear: the difference between how other people understood her vision of the world locked with the realm of the dead. It was their misunderstanding of her perceptions that had bred this distressing circumstance. They could only guess at what she could see, imagine and build hope on the false impression of her reality. Her whole landscape was as foreign to them as theirs was foreign to her.

One did not need to go mad like Ferioul to wreak havoc, obviously. The landscape of Cemirowl's village was still scarred with the pain her mother had brought, speaking of the dead to those who had lost a child, a husband, a wife, or sister. Speaking of things the living should never hear. Clearly, even sane, Cemirowl's gift could generate a great deal of hurt and frustration.

It was difficult to accept that others might interpret her own abilities far more wildly than she'd wish or even know. Staring at the fire, her head in her hands, she remembered how the villagers had looked askance and whispered about her. She'd seen it all her life, but had not understood that it might be for her own vision, not her mother's.

Alcon had once told her, "They just don't understand your ability. They know it and respect it, but there are uncanny things about you."

She was damned by her gift.

The queen's death had put her dilemma into high relief. It had not altered it one stone, except by a threat of execution. The situation fit admirably in her own odd sense of humor. If she laughed, she would then truly cry in front of these strange men.

Cibran looked truly concerned, Tadeo surprised and

Mercor looked bewildered. While three men watched her, Cemirowl closed her eyes tight, stopping tears from spilling. With more effort, she bit back the bark of wry laughter.

She'd always hoped it was only the specter of her mother that the villagers had feared in her. That eventually they would stop waiting for her to go mad. That they would accept her, love her, and include her in their lives. Living apart from the village was her payment toward an acceptance that she now knew would never happen.

She shook her head, pained by the thoughts that betrayed two true friends. She was now even more grateful than ever for Toggas and Alcon's friendship.

Yet, even so, sitting in the camp with armored caballiers beside her and the realm of the dead whispering and moving around her, Cemirowl was in two worlds and isolated between them, unable to communicate with either.

What do they think I see? It was not a question she could ask out loud. Not having been able to explain her gift to Meelac, how could she expect these three men to answer her?

Stumbling upright, Cemirowl went to her bedroll, lay down and turned her back to the fire. Silent tears ran down her cheeks.

CHAPTER SIX

---◊◊◊---

The three caballiers and Cemirowl broke camp before dawn and rode hard all day, taking few breaks to change the horses. Her horse was basically being led by Mercor with a long rein, and she focused on staying on, and clutching the saddle bow with both hands.

Mercor had been right: riding a galloping horse all day was not at all similar to riding a slow, old nag for an hour at the most. They had thundered on rutted roads and crashed through fields as they bypassed villages and towns.

It was late afternoon when they paused briefly on a hilltop above the city of Elbyrge, letting their horses catch their wind, as they switched to the horses they hadn't ridden for a while.

"It looks as if the world ends beyond the palace!" Cemirowl said, as they looked down at the vast expanse of the king's city and the castle beyond.

Mercor nodded. "The buildings of Ilturir sit on the edge of cliffs overlooking the sea. It was expanded and rebuilt from older palace buildings, which began soon after the treaty was signed, and was finished as King Larthor prepared for marriage."

He pointed and she could see where the land sloped down

to a better display of the ocean. Whatever other emotion that had ridden his features for the past few days, Cemirowl did not miss the pride. A younger son who had earned his title. "Did you fight in the war?"

"Briefly," he said with a quick, dismissive shrug. "I'd also traveled and studied in lands to the south and east of Hergila, near enough to learn the language." He flashed a quick, wry grin at her. "So however I fought in the war, I helped pen the treaty that built that palace!"

As he said it, he rolled his shoulder in a way that told Cemirowl he must have been wounded and had worked on the treaty during his recuperation. *Pure speculation,* she thought. But she knew it was true. *Unimportant,* she added. And that was true as well.

"King Larthor worked hard to create that peace," Mercor said. "He could have won, you know."

"What?" Cemirowl asked.

"The war," he said, and his eyes grew hard. "He built peace and trade instead of destroying Hergila. He married from that country when he knew the peace was no lie."

"And you were part of that?"

"Yes," he said, and the bitterness returned to his voice. "And it is in meeting a fortuneteller I might lose all I gained despite all my prior fealty." He said nothing more, but set his horse in motion, jerking the lead rein of her horse.

Cemirowl sighed. There was little she could do about it now. For most of the ride it still looked as if the world ended just beyond all the king had built—not just a palace, but the peace with a land across the sea, and the queen who was now dead.

The sparkling deep blue went on forever, fading into haze.

She was glad Mercor was leading her horse, for her mind was stunned by all she saw. The city was noise and bustle as people went into or out of shops and inns and houses. Some of the streets were narrow. Cibran explained that this was the quickest route to the city plaza where the gates stood. Their progress was slowed by donkey carts, pigs, goats, one lowing cow, many dogs and more people. It was too much. She only had the energy to stifle an overwhelming urge to cry like a tired child, or laugh hysterically.

They came to a wide plaza with high walls that went along the river. Men were walking along the walls, and archers stood ready at the towers above the gate. It looked sturdy, but there were ornate additions for the entrance to the tunneled archway that spoke of the palace's promise.

Cibran said, "This is one of the entrances. There's two more, one for the western fields, and then another for the king's dockyard, and that part of the city that sprawls down to the sea."

"It's formidable," Cemirowl said.

"That's the idea."

Mercor stopped his horse in the middle of the wide plaza. The others straggled to a stop. The consternation on his face was plain.

"Do you think he's still angry?" Tadeo asked Mercor, looking back at him, steadying his horse.

Mercor glared at him. "What do *you* think?"

Tadeo shook his head and raised his hands, but Cibran said, "Well, the heat has passed, surely. It will be cold logic now." He moved up from behind them.

Caballier Mercor pulled on the lead rope of her horse again. She clutched the pommel with a start.

Dusane once told her that a good portion of a city, or town—

depending on the size of a keep—could, in theory, withdraw into the bailey and castle at need. It was the whole point of even the old motte-and-bailey, which had worked fine while Sir Thade's home was still at Soft Water, and made of wood. It had not worked well when he had attempted to renovate in stone—thus renaming the remaining village when he moved his revised motte-and-bailey upriver to a more solid foundation. The raised motte, or mound, would give the townsmen a better view of their attackers scrambling in the ditch below. The moat, which had once just been a bare ditch, was a new innovation. All her life, many of her father's talks had shown hints at a life beyond a peasant hut with an overly elaborate kitchen. Clearly he knew about castles and palaces.

But this palace went far beyond the descriptions in her father's talks. The palace was ten times as grand as anything she'd imagined—Sir Thade's keep being her only standard of comparison. Even from the view from the fields above the city, it was clear the palace—walled as it was—was as vast as a city. Within minutes she'd be passing through the gates and meeting a king.

Tadeo called out their greeting as they were approaching the gate, "Errant caballiers returning to the king!"

"Ho caballiers!" someone called. They went through the archway, and into another small court. There were guards here as well, and more towers to loom over them. Another passageway through the building. Cemirowl looked up. There were holes in the ceiling high above them.

Tadeo noticed her looking as they passed.

"They can drop hot oil or pitch from there."

She shuddered.

"No need to throw good weapons away, or bloody your dagger if boiling pitch can do the job," he said.

The bridge was the first real indication of the splendor to come. Though the walls of the building on either side of the bridge appeared solid, the ornate archway they approached was proof of both beauty and skill. Cemirowl knew of some houses of the village that could fit within these passageways. Carriages would easily move through them, and have little trouble over the bridge. To her left the river had been dammed, and made a small lake. The walls of the palace compound rose out of the waters, without giving anyone room or purchase to climb up them.

They went through another of these wide, well defended passageways, and into a rotunda that was large enough to fit a good portion of her village. It was balconied with pillars showing grace and elegance. While it was clear horses had been here, even the floor was patterned with brick work. Servants and pages came to help them, taking the free horses from their leads, to holding the horses steady.

The men slid off their horses. Cemirowl trembled. Having once thought her rank made her equal to the three men she'd ridden with, she could no longer doubt why they looked down on her. Rank might be one thing, but clearly wealth—and probably consequence—was quite another. The proof? Seeing the glory of this rotunda, and the wealth of the servants' clothing, even for those who were cleaning up after the horses. Cemirowl knew quite well how incredible her next few moments would be. She was about to meet a king. A king who might hang her for treason.

She was shaking so badly, she could not move. With a grim smile, Cibran helped her down off her horse, even as a page brought her a little set of stairs to step down.

As the horses and their travel gear were taken from them, a man came from the southern entrance. There were people, women and men, walking along the covered balcony above, as well as the gallery that surrounded the paved courtyard, and many of them stopped to watch.

The man approached them as the horses were led through the western archway. He had the dark blond hair of the coastal regions, and was well dressed. The three caballiers bowed. Cemirowl attempted a curtsey.

"Caballier Mercor. Well met! I believe this is your fortuneteller?" the man said.

"Yes, Lord Arthan," Mercor said.

Cemirowl realized this was the king's brother, Prince Arthan, and tried to curtsey deeply—but she was incredibly stiff from unaccustomed riding.

"Your name, lass?"

"Priest Cemirowl Dusane of Soft Water."

"I see." He turned to Mercor again. "Come, my brother will want to know you've arrived."

They followed the prince through the ornate archway into a small garden, where another building bridged the great rotunda building to another, with a well decorated portico. Four buildings walled in a garden in a misshapen square. It was teeming with herbs and narrow trees that towered over the buildings. They went through another building's archway.

"This is new, built for Larthor and his queen," Mercor said to her softly.

Cemirowl nodded. "It's beautiful."

It was more than that. It became difficult to see it as a place of her death if she could not prove her innocence, though that was why she had been brought here.

The intricate detail in the passageways, and the gallery walks surrounding the inner courtyard were ornate. Cemirowl had never seen a fountain that burbled up water. It spilled into a rectangular pool that reflected the pale stone and the sky. It was as if the building itself was a part of another world. Short shrubs, that looked like some form of myrtle, lined the pool. Large pots at flanking corners of the courtyard were filled with small orange and lemon trees that seemed to emphasize the entrance the pool pointed them toward. The court was alive with birds. The entrance they were walking through gave view to an ornate entrance to a furnished gallery. Archway opened to more archways with more scrollwork. The lines and arabesques illuminated a sense of delicacy and richness.

The gallery was filled with chairs and couches, but only a few servants attended a man pacing in the deeper shadows of the room.

"This is the king's sitting room. The audience chamber is beyond," Mercor said.

Cemirowl's mouth was dry. She could only nod.

The man, a taller, darker version of the prince was pacing. And as they approached, Cemirowl could see that while the hall looked furnished for leisure, the king's movements were driven by deep and powerful feelings. None happy. If Mercor had shown his grief with a short temper on their journey, she could guess there was more here. He did not walk with any grace. His limbs seemed bound by tension. When he finally saw them, he almost jerked in pain before moving towards them. He was dark haired, and strong, bigger than his brother, his dark beard jutted out, a forerunner to fury.

Mercor bowed, and she did her best to curtsey deeply. When she tried to rise, she could not stifle a groan; Lord Arthan helped her rise.

"The Bone Reader, Cemirowl," Mercor stated.

She glared at Sir Mercor.

Prince Arthan spoke. "She is an ordained priest, brother. After hearing about Mercor's tale, I took the trouble to confirm this. She was ordained by a Priest Meelac who was ordained in the school of Elbyrge."

The heat of her anger at Mercor shifted. Her surprise at the prince's knowledge brought a flush to her face, though the question of treason still loomed.

The king had been silent till now. His beard quivered. Cemirowl was alive to every nuance of his posture and his expression, and could see his jaw clench despite the full beard. "You predicted Her Majesty's death?" he asked.

She tasted bile, and shaking so badly, she could only gather her courage to speak the truth. She had to swallow to reply. "No, Your Majesty. I merely stated someone close to the caballier would die. I had no idea it would be my queen."

"The tale he told tells how you knew how brief his engagement would be, how you predicted its demise. Now you tell an opposite tale?"

She shook her head. "Your Majesty, I do not know how to answer you. I was not present when he told the tale of that reading. All I can tell you is that my reading gave few details." Her gaze went down to his shoes. It was not the time or place for the discussion. He was in pain and she wanted to speak to him as a priest, not a fortuneteller. Or not at all, since he had a priest within the court, no doubt preparing for the state funeral.

She was forcing herself to breathe steadily, trying to keep the bile from rising again. Could her ordination even matter to them if what she said contrasted with what Caballier Mercor had told them?

"I want you to read for my Tidyri tonight," the king growled low. "If you can find out who killed her before my men do..." he trailed off not wanting to offer her, a peasant, anything. His stance, his face, his anger said she could still die for treason. He might sacrifice her to the funeral pyre of his anger. She knew some people would rather lash out in anger than grieve. Terror warred with her compassion.

"Brother, that will not be possible. You have duties to perform."

"You are right, but I want this solved! By any means possible."

"I understand. As she is an ordained priest, I have arranged with Lord Marshal Buce that she will be a guest of my house, as being more appropriate even than a guest of Ferran in the chapel compound."

"That is good of you. And you are right, and far better than the dungeon I wanted Buce to give her!"

Cemirowl was pale. He was not speaking with any lightness.

"It is nearly dinner time, and I will let her share the meal in my household," Arthan stated.

The words seemed to spark something in the king. "Ah, I must go get ready," and without another word, he turned and left, disappearing through a doorway in a passageway between the long gallery room and his audience chamber.

When the king was gone, the prince turned to Mercor and

said, "He's been like this the past two days. I'd watch your step. It looks to him now as if there was, indeed, foul play. If you knew of it, then his threat to you and this..." he gestured to Cemirowl, "priest still stands. It may seem ludicrous, but the people in Hergila often rely on fortunetelling—even nobility. It will be a disaster if they could believe it had been predicted, and not prevented. If he finds any evidence you did know—either of you, then...."

"Your Highness, has anyone come close to discovering who killed Her Majesty?" Mercor asked.

"No," Prince Arthan growled. His brows moved together and his lips became a tight, white line.

Mercor broke the prince's brooding silence and said, "Maybe Priest Cemirowl can gain some wisdom from her bone basket. Something to comfort the king at least."

Prince Arthan looked down at Cemirowl. She had the distinct impression that he'd thought the suggestion amusing. Humor cleared some of the tension from his face. Her cheeks grew hot, and she rolled her eyes, shaking her head as she turned her face away. She was thankful that Mercor was looking at the stairs, but Lord Arthan probably hadn't missed her expression. She grew hot again. It was unfortunate that she was the joke. It was humor she could appreciate, more so because clearly the caballier apparently missed the irony. She was glad to find one spark of humor. She might be hanged tomorrow.

A lady came down another set of stairs. The tension in her face did not diminish the fact that she glittered with gems and lush fabric. Cemirowl's clothing itched and stank of horse and sweat. *Oh, let me just die right here, so that I can just take my rightful place in the dirt,* she thought. She pictured this woman's dainty satin embroidered slippers lightly stepping over her. This was what ladies of any rank should look like in a castle. The woman stopped and curtsied, her eyes intent on the prince for too many beats, but she then looked at Mercor and Cemirowl.

"Lady Harlyn," said Mercor, taking both of the lady's hands in his. "How are you and the other ladies?"

"We all do poorly," she said, bowing her head.

Mercor then turned to introduce her. Cemirowl gave a bob as low as Lady Harlyn's had been, but with less grace.

Lady Harlyn wore a dark golden tunic under a dark blue overdress embroidered in black and gold, circled by a belt worked in a matching pattern. As she bowed her head, her black braid fell upon her breast. It made a very pretty picture.

"Miss Cemirowl, please be well come to this castle."

Cemirowl curtsied again. "Thank you," she murmured, wondering when all the formalities would be over.

"Harlyn, I'm sure the priest is exhausted," Prince Arthan said, his voice tight. He refused to look at her. "She rode hard, and she has had little knowledge of horses or time to rest. Will you please convey her to her rooms. She will be in the southwest corner of the Lion Court. Mercor and I have other duties to attend to. That is, if you've nothing better to do. I can send her off with a page."

"I'm happy to help," she said, and bowed her head.

Arthan turned to Cemirowl. "I will have a page inform you when it's time to dine."

"Thank you, my lord," Cemirowl said, and bowed.

"Come, Miss Cemirowl...."

"Forgive me, but it is Priest Cemirowl," she explained, clinging to the only title she deserved, the one thing they might respect rather than what had brought her here.

"Oh, forgive me!" murmured Lady Harlyn, stopping for just one moment. She gave a wavering smile and then started moving again. "You must be tired, wishing to wash and refresh yourself. Let me take you to your room now."

Cemirowl feared she'd quickly lose herself along the way. They walked through a large hall, up some stairs, down a passageway that apparently linked three buildings together. And if she had any illusion that while she was nominally a guest of the prince, it became clear that Lord Marshal Buce's rooms were part of the Lion Court—but to the east. She was clearly well guarded.

They walked down a hallway that was given light only through what Harlyn called lanterns in the ceiling, but was a fretwork of openings that lit the covered gallery to pierce the gloom, along with a well-lit room that shared light that gleamed in the passageway. But it was a shiver, an echo, like a touch upon her skin that caught her attention. She hesitated, blinked away the brief sense of vertigo, and tried to get a better sense of the spirit lurking nearby.

Harlyn said a little sharply, "That is the entrance to Prince Arthan's sitting room. I would not enter, unless invited."

Cemirowl looked. The room was ablaze with light reflecting off pale, almost white marble, and illuminated the richness of the fabric of the furniture.

She still felt unsteady with the sharp presence of the ghost. "Oh, forgive me. A moment's dizziness. I'm very tired." She felt cold, the nausea rising again. She wondered if she looked as pale as she felt.

"It is not far now," said Harlyn.

Cemirowl had needed no warning about disturbing the

prince, and the ghost lingering near his doorway was not a matter she needed to take in hand.

"This will be your room during your stay," said Lady Harlyn.

Cemirowl nodded as Lady Harlyn gestured to two servants who lurked nearby. She introduced a young servant girl named Les, and a rather grubby groom called Ewan bowed to both women. From all of her father's tales of court life, Cemirowl was glad, not only of the servants, but also what this indicated. They wore neither the colors of the prince's household, nor—what she had guessed seeing pages, servants, and well-armed guards as they passed those halls —of Lord Buce's household. They were lower than that. She was being treated like a guest, but cautiously.

"Les will help you dress, and Ewan can guide you through the palace when you are called upon. Or take messages to anyone who you wish."

"Thank you, Lady Harlyn, this place is a maze. Thank you for guiding me," Cemirowl said.

"You are most welcome. I'll admit, after hearing Mercor's story, I wanted to get to see a bit more of you." There was a flash of a grin, but it was overruled quickly by tension. "I must go, there is actually a great deal I must attend to as well."

"Thank you again, then, for helping me."

Les began to unpack the clothing sack. Cemirowl was still shaking, holding onto her composure with all she had. She picked up and shook out her vestments, glad that she'd had the foresight to bring them. It was more suitable than her best dress, and if she was to join the prince's household, she had better wear something that gave indication of her rank. She ran the cloth through her fingers for a moment.

"Is that what you will wear, Priest?" Les asked.

"Yes, it's appropriate, I think."

Another servant brought in a fresh ewer of hot water to pour in a basin behind a screen.

"Will you be needing any help with your bathing?" Les asked. "The tub is ready."

"No, I'm fine," Cemirowl said.

"May I go fetch something?"

"Of course," Cemirowl said, almost letting her composure slip.

Les ran off on her mysterious errand. Cemirowl was finally alone in her room.

She tried to steady her breath, but she barely reached the chamber pot in time. She vomited so hard her intestines seemed to twist inside her. She was still shaking, trying not to weep in the deep gratitude she'd not thrown up on either the king or the prince's shoes, or Lady Harlyn's dress.

She had to focus on something other than the gallows. She sat down and stared out the window into the garden below, taking many deep breaths.

She could see the pale stone of the chapel rising from the garden. She was amazed at the verdant beauty embracing a riot of color next to it, and the sight of the sea gleaming beyond. The smell of salt—such a precious seasoning!—permeated the air, but without diminishing the giddy scents of flowers and fruits from below. But as she looked in the garden, she could see people pacing among the shrubberies and trees. Though they could not see her unless they looked up, the garden terraces rose to meet the landscape in her window, it was still low enough for her privacy. The scent of orchard flowers came on a breeze from the south.

So many people! She'd never seen so many in such close surroundings. A king. A prince. Caballiers, all glittering with a wealth of weapons. Ladies. Gentlemen. Servants. And those were only the people everyone could see. She knew how vast the palace was. Somewhere amid all this glory, there was a place of execution.

Somehow the prince had prevented her from being put in the dungeon that seemed an impossibility with all that she saw. She was being treated like a guest, so she had better join that public illusion.

Cemirowl rinsed her mouth, and then took off her filthy clothes. Reaching into her herb pouch, she took out a cloth sprinkled with scented oil, and used it to scrub herself, grateful for the large tub of water. She luxuriated in a bath much deeper than the one she had at home. She scrubbed her scalp, and her body, glad of the soap Les had left her. It was much finer than any Cemirowl had used before. There was far less stinging lye in it, and it was scented with oils much more pure than Cemirowl could get. But she did not linger; she had no idea when she'd be called to dine.

When she was dry, and had her shift on, she rummaged in her pouch and made herself a quick sachet of lemon grace-herb and put it in a pocket of her undertunic. She then pulled on her red vestment. She had chosen a red that did not clash with her hair, a brownish red, except around the cuffs that matched the faint, lingering funereal stains on her hands. She'd had one funeral since Meelac's death and had been unable to avoid staining the sleeves, though the stain had merged into the cloth as it had slowly wicked its way up. She was grateful that the black stole was unstained. Both were crumpled from the sack, but they would have to do. As a priest she was a guardian or guide of change —and the black was necessary. The black, being new, was still lush to her untrained eye, even while it felt poor next to the clothes of some of the servants she'd seen.

She combed out her damp hair and pulled it into a thick ponytail. Les knocked on the door and came in as Cemirowl pulled her hair from its binding in frustration. She was trembling. She could only pretend so much. She might die for treason, it seemed foolish to be cowed by the glittering ladies she'd seen, especially Lady Harlyn, and the memory of Mercor's gaze. She felt very shabby. How could it matter? But it did.

"Let me help you," Les said. "We can make this better. Would you like that?"

"Yes, please," said Cemirowl, grateful for the gesture of kindness.

Les had her undress to her shift, then took the dress and stole and laid it on the bed. She took an iron heated by the fire, one of three, and ironed out the vestments, switching out the irons when they cooled.

"See? Much better," Les said, as she helped Cemirowl dress again. "And look, I've got a ribbon close to the color of your dress, and it matches your unusual hair. Auburn is it?"

"I believe it's called that. My father told me that his mother had hair even more fiery red than this. The color is not uncommon with his own people, I gathered." She paused for a moment, wondering, again, who his people actually were.

"Well, I will do what I can to make my lady look her best."

Les explained that she'd never had the chance to work on a real lady before and she was eager to help. Les wound and braided the hair on either side of Cemirowl's face, finishing with a loose braid that fell down her back.

Just as Les was finishing the final bow, a knock sounded at the door.

"Yes?" Cemirowl called out, surprised.

It was a page in the prince's colors ready to take her to dinner. Les and Ewan bowed and left.

"Will they find dinner? Should I do something for them?"

"They will dine with the general servants in the kitchen. They are part of the king's household; they are well taken care of, Priest."

"Thank you."

The page led Cemirowl to that glittering white room, where lights that Cemirowl knew as lanterns were being hung as the evening twilight slowly began to settle in. Looking up at the ceiling, the dome was lit with the early evening light. The room was lush, and already people were standing, or sitting in chairs or couches. They did not approach her. The only one that tried to catch her attention—anyone's attention—was a vague specter rising from the floor. Cemirowl refused to make a spectacle of herself by reaching out to a ghost in such a public setting, so she resolutely ignored it as being just another one of the company. It would certainly not help her. Instead, she decided to feast her eyes with the details of the room till someone told her what to do.

She'd not known what to expect. In Thade's manor, everyone sat at tables in his great hall. There was a canopy above his table to protect his meal from birds trapped inside when he closed his shutters. Among the number of things she noticed that elevated the palace far above Caballier Thade's small castle were the windows! While glass was certainly something Pyrann had manufactured before, it was not the quality seen here. There was one precious and small pane of Hergilan glass in Thade's household chapel, a small room facing the morning sun. Here, glass was everywhere. The palace glittered with the wealth of their foreign connection.

And they were lighting lanterns with candles that seemed smokeless in Prince Arthan's sitting room. She could not see any sign of smoke on the walls or ceilings! More: there were no torches. In poor weather, and in winter, the torches spread throughout Thade's keep left everyone breathing in the smoke that left black smuts under the noses of even the prettiest of ladies in the manor. This was a reason most women dined apart there; no woman can impress anyone with little mustachios of smoke smuts. She wondered what winter would be like in this palace. Clean burning candles would be yet another sign of wealth.

The prince's room was filled with carpets, not rushes and herbs. Cemirowl hated walking on them, even while knowing her shoes had been cleaned by Les not ten minutes before. But even in the rotunda, there were servants cleaning up horse droppings, and all the garden pathways she'd seen were not muddy, but lined with gravel or flat stone.

Prince Arthan's sitting room had a rather ornate entrance from the lion court's building, but also a pillared entrance that led to the garden. There were couches throughout the room, with low tables beside them. As well as high tables with plates and platters. Servants were bringing in trays from some hidden kitchen, and put them on tables.

Up through the northern entrance pavilion came a man who was obviously a priest. He was framed by pillars and torches and the upper portions of the garden. He hesitated at the last archway, and then noticed her. He approached. She curtsied.

"You are the Priest Cemirowl? I remember your mentor Meelac. He was ordained the year I entered the school as a boy."

"I am, and you are the Honorable Ferran?"

"Indeed. Prince Arthan invited me to join him for dinner, so you might feel more comfortable."

Cemirowl guessed that as the body was being prepared, Ferran was not needed for the moment. She knew that the fortification of food would sustain Ferran during his vigil through the night. Even if the king chose to rest, the priest could not. As he was here, Cemirowl guessed he must have a huge staff.

"Your hands are stained red," he noticed.

"We do our best in Soft Water. Though there were three of us for our small village, now two. I did the wrapping for those who could not afford to hire women. So... I did most of it."

"Currently the palace has only you and myself, as ordained priests. Unusual enough, but one has left for the city's church, and another recently took vows to remove herself from open practice for a time. I notice you are looking at the architecture."

"I'm overwhelmed," she admitted, grateful for the neutral topic. "Every building seems different from another."

"Yes. Some of the buildings to the east, as well as the chapel are old. This building was built on an older one, and considered one of the newer ones. It was originally built by the king and prince for their late mother, but she never lived to occupy it. The architecture reflects a style that comes from further west, and some of the weaving styles of the upholstery and rugs are from that area as well. The rest are by the late Lady Boduscia."

"And the rotunda?"

"That was built by the king's late great-grandfather, though the king has added details to it, and other improvements that build upon its mighty theme. Larthor built his new palace closer to the sea, and in a style to reflect a new age. The queen's suite, which are above an old building and bathhouse—reflect a Pyrannian perspective of her homeland. You will note, when you see them, that those structures have a wealth of Hergilan glass!"

"Hergilan buildings," said the prince as he approached them, "rarely use as much glass as they add to the heat and glare of their arid countryside. My brother's purchase helped bring that industry into international attention, and improved the trade for Hergila, and helped ease their debt of war."

Cemirowl noticed by his stance that Prince Arthan did not like Ferran. And she watched the muscles of his cheek—he must be clenching his jaw as if he regretted his choice in inviting Ferran to dine.

Ferran said, "You are here on an errand of divination. It poses some question as to the suitability of your dress."

Apparently the respite of neutral topics was over.

"I am here because I would not disobey the summons of my king," she said. "To attempt such disobedience would be disloyal as well as foolish. But as you noted yourself, that you knew of my mentor and my ordination."

To her surprise, the expression on his face told her he was ready for discussion and not antagonism, and she was relieved.

"Come," Prince Arthan said, "let us sit and eat."

As they sat down, Cemirowl noticed that more of the women in his household sat mostly to one side of the room, and the men in another. They were not alone, but surrounded by men of note. She'd spent most of her life in the company of Meelac and Alcon and did not think to be shy.

Cupbearers came forward to the high table and knelt by

the diners. Cemirowl watched and saw that the others held out their hands. The cupbearer kneeling beside her poured water from one bowl over her hands into another bowl. A soft, aromatic scent rose from her wet hands. Another server came forward and helped her dry her hands on a towel.

"What is your reply to the priest," the prince asked, as they finished washing their hands. He was clearly curious. Cemirowl wondered if he'd had them sit so that her answer could be long.

"My lord, I would ask the honored priest if he recalled that our predecessors, including those at the former High Temple, practiced the art of lottery? In some of the earlier texts priests would employ that art for their king before battle or before the signing of treaties." Cemirowl used the most formal of language. Her father would have been proud.

"I believe what I do is similar," she continued. "I admit I cannot claim more than that. I began reading bones when I was learning to accept some of my other... abilities. I was not aware that the priesthood was allowed to only practice the duties for which they were ordained, if divination is truly outside those vows. My mentor would not have been able to farm, or be the villager's unofficial librarian and storyteller if that had been the case. He would have starved to death in our small village, and been very bored. His asparagus and squash were quite excellent. The only restriction for both priest and person that I was taught would be if those actions conflicted with the hope of the peace of the Guardian of the Great Gates."

Priest Ferran smiled. "Your argument is a good one. Lottery is still employed and I can see how it could be considered divination by some, even if I still adjudge your arts suspect. Very well, I am sanguine that your arts do not conflict with our role to guard the gates. If it is good to enquire by these arts is another question."

"I cannot admit that I am sanguine about that point either," she said wryly. "I know at least *one* case when reading bones has perhaps brought more conflict than peace."

The prince's mouth quirked in a smile as if he had caught her joke. None of the others listening had.

"Rarely, Priest," Prince Arthan said lightly, "does one disparage a gift such as yours. Your abilities have created great note in the court. Though I was away when Caballier Mercor told the tale, I have heard of your reading for him. Did you not predict the demise of the caballier's engagement, as well as the queen's death?"

Cemirowl felt the danger in his question, but remained calm; surely he'd invited her here to ask that very question. Answering carefully might mean her life.

"I read in the bones that the caballier would make his decision based on behavior of the lady to another. I also read that someone close to him would die—not a surprising prediction in a large palace as this—and that Caballier Mercor would experience confusion and distress, and that he would be pressed with many duties at that time. Also not a very staggering prediction. In my experience, confusion and distress upon someone's death is not uncommon." She paused and looked straight at the prince. "As to who would die, and under what circumstances, I had not a clue."

She hoped that her honesty would impress him; she was fully aware he had no measure of her truthfulness.

There seemed little to say. Ferran, who had not eaten much, was recalled to his duties in the chapel, by a young page.

"You may go to your duties, Ferran," Prince Arthan said.

Ferran rose, and said to Cemirowl, "I must go and attend those who would sit vigil in the chapel. Priest, I hope we will talk more. My lord," he said, rising and then bowing to Arthan.

There was a pause, and then Arthan took up the thread of conversation.

"You believe you did not predict all that clearly came to pass?" Arthan asked.

"Yes, my lord. I am very serious. I am not that skilled. I would, however, venture a guess that the caballier is a very skilled storyteller. Would it not be his duty to make the tale as entertaining as possible? My vague reading would not make a great story."

Arthan was intent, and leaned forward. "From his tale, shared many times since he told it, you knew that the baron would be giving Caballier Mercor his approval and that he would already have found the Lady Llora in another's arms. The tale also claims you had connected the two with a wolf on the baron's banner. He told me more details not two hours ago."

Cemirowl wondered if she had properly assessed the threat to the caballier. Why would he support the evidence of detail in her fortunetelling? The more obscure—and real—the better for them both, surely. She shook her head.

"Sir Mercor added details from better, personal knowledge of the situation as well as what transpired in his experience. I never knew that he was returning home from visiting a *baron*. I knew the wolf, but only suggested that it *could* be in his banner. I did not know. Nor did I know that he would find the lady, I believe I said, 'who sings well', in someone else's arms. If I remember correctly, I only said that her behavior to another would clarify the situation. I did not know her name."

Arthan contemplated her words for a moment. "If I remember correctly, she does sing well."

He seemed somehow satisfied by the discussion. He turned to one of the other men in a chair nearby, letting Cemirowl eat more of the food. Her mouth tasted bitter again, and the food like sawdust.

"How are the present envoys coping with being forced to stay, as well as not being invited to any royal household for meals while we are in mourning?"

"All are well, except for the envoy from Gastren," said the man, smiling. "Lord Steward Bartemo is entertaining him tonight, with constant attendance by Caballier Reg, the guard marshal's attendant. When I saw him earlier, he did not look as if he's having any fun."

"Perhaps not, but his arrival was poorly timed," Prince Arthan said dryly.

"Surely not his fault. He could not know that Her Majesty..."

There was a difficult pause, and everyone nearby looked uncomfortable. After a few moments Prince Arthan turned the conversation toward politics and other court topics that Cemirowl could not follow. She had not been given permission to leave, as he had with Ferran, and she did not know how else to remove herself from the conversation that could not involve her with any kind of politeness. Rudeness might sway any positive light she'd earned herself back toward the gallows. She did her best to pretend, but it was heavy going.

The only thing of any interest was a phrase, murmured low, the prince said to the other man, "You can thank the fact that the Ambassador Itrizeu's man was present, and actually alone in the room with her, that is keeping us from a renewal of war. Even they can't deny that he is suspect in this."

It was enough to make her feel incredibly embarrassed to be present, wondering if she—a person who might hang for treason —ought to hear that kind of thing.

A few moments later, the man replied to another whispered comment Cemirowl could not make out, "Yes, your brother has had word that her parents will be here. They are willing to be patient till they know who is at fault."

Apparently this was a normal place for discussing palace and political business, and so well understood that they did not think anything of her being there. The others joined in with considerably more energy than they had previously. They weren't being loud. It was clear that they were also being given space by the others in the room. Feeling more out of place than ever, she was no longer able to eat and picked through the rest of the meal.

Prince Arthan turned to make a comment to someone, noted her. "Forgive me, surely you are not interested in these politics."

How could she not be? Her life was tied to the matters they discussed, but not in any way that might help her. There was quite a deal she could not have followed had she tried. With as much dignity as she could muster she said, "I am more familiar with religion, but these matters must be pressing to you." Her heart pounded as she said it, and he seemed a little surprised by her speech.

He smiled, a small smile. "You may go," he said. She felt released, but somehow as if she'd passed some test of his—was she really a peasant, perhaps?

Not knowing what else to say, she said, "Good evening,

Your Highness."

Her thoughts revolved around her predicament and the conversation. She wished passionately that her Bone Readings were as clear as these people believed them to be. She'd love some advice. Cemirowl waited for the ordeal to end. When everyone rose, she felt a little lost as to what she would do next. The prince had clearly left her to her own devices, only excusing himself as he must get ready for the vigil.

She turned to go back to her room, not having any idea what else to do. She was relieved to see Mercor appear in the northern archway.

"Caballier, would you guide me so I can be present for the mourning?" she asked.

"I don't think that Ferran would let you read the body now, if that's what you intended. Probably you'll be able to do so in the morning."

"Caballier, whatever you think of my abilities in divination, dealing with death is part of my duties for which I was ordained. I have no doubt that Ferran has the job well in hand, but she was my queen. I would like to honor her." She did not say, *I might die tomorrow, but that will not stop me from doing my sworn duty!*

Mercor admitted he had planned to pay his respects as well. He led her down a corridor that led to a wide covered balcony. "This gallery leads to the queen's solar," he said. He pointed to a building beyond the garden below. "There is the chapel where Ferran will be holding vigil, and where she will be laid to rest."

The sun was beginning its sunset display. It lit the chapel's southern wall with a golden glow that slowly deepened. Even as people were clearly leaving either past them, or going down some stairs past the entrance to the solar, and then into the garden, the queue was slow in moving. As they waited in the queue with other mourners, Mercor murmured that the queen had been found in the solar.

Most of the people did not venture far into the room, bowing or curtseying to where the body was still being wrapped, then leaving either through the door on the other side of the room, or retreating the way they had come.

The solar was a beautiful room. It looked out onto the ocean, with windows along the full length of the outer wall. Where the walls had not been paneled in whitewashed wood, the stone was pale. There were elaborate tapestries that glittered in the sunset, fire, and candlelight. Cemirowl suspected that the view was breathtaking during the day. But she did not give them much attention. The windows framed the body of the queen in a sunset blaze.

The body had been laid upon a table near the windows. The table was covered in a rich cloth of purple and blues, stitched in gold. A crest of the queen's rampant dragon of her homeland on a field of white, green and gold bordered in purple was blazoned on the cloth as well. On either side of her crest, embroidered into the pattern, was the king's white tusked and crowned boar, rampant and guardant.

The cloth draped to the floor, gleaming in candle and firelight along with jars of scented oil, flecked with powdered gold and open bowls filled with crushed herbs, spices and minerals used in preparing bodies for burial.

Two women, robed in black, rocked the body back and forth as they wrapped it. They were nearly done. As they worked on the queen, they pulled long bands of specially woven cloth from a basket beside the table.

At the head of the figure lay Queen Tidyri's crown, flail and keys. Cemirowl did not see the knife showing that the soul had been severed—though she did not sense a soul tied to the body, trapped beneath the bonds. She wondered at this.

As they edged their way to one side of the mourners, Mercor explained that Ferran would keep vigil in the chapel, where mourners could go to offer prayers. The king would remain with the queen till he wished to leave. The room would remain open for the people to pay their respects, unless the king wished for privacy.

Cemirowl nodded, but was surprised. Meelac, Alcon and she had never divided their forces so widely. Wrapping the body was one of those tasks in the office of the priest. It was, however, one that could be hired out, or done by a woman mourner. Poor women, old women, or widows often did the work in larger towns. She had taken many of the duties involved with wrapping upon herself, as the village was too small to hire wrappers from Thadetown, and even some in Thadetown were too poor to hire them as well. Besides, she was the best wrapper in the area.

There had been times Meelac or Alcon had helped her with the body, if it were too large for her to move and wrap on her own. Sometimes one of the family members helped prepare the body. Wrapping did not take long, if the body had been prepared. But her role was not exclusive to wrapping and preparing the body. She had done her share of pastoral care. The village priests had always worked together, and with the family of the deceased always nearby. They were the ones that needed the most support.

Now here was the body and her beloved husband, and yet the priest was in a completely different building. Moving farther into the room it was not the queen's body that took her attention, but the kneeling king.

Her heart pounded in her chest in a wave of trepidation, but then Cemirowl only saw a man who had lost his wife. Looking around the room she was doubly sorrowed. Ferran was nowhere to be seen, neither were there any of his staff present—excepting the wrappers of the body—nor did any friend approach. He knelt alone.

Cemirowl could not stifle the moan of pity. In the village someone *always* remained near the ones hardest struck by the passing of a loved one, be it a close friend, Alcon, or even herself. She had held the hands of the grieving often enough in the years of Meelac's training. She knew all too well the hard pain of being alone at such times.

Cemirowl's heart clenched. She waited. No one approached him. No one even stood near him. He was surrounded by people who lived in his palace, even if they had their own households, and shared in the work of running the household and country.

He knelt alone.

No one comforted the man as he watched the body of his wife being barred from him by strips of ornate, red cloth and death.

With all necessary formalities and practices required of her office, her first duty was *always* to the grieving person. Ignoring Mercor's sharp intake of breath, Cemirowl went and stood close to the king. She did not impose her presence upon him. She merely stood quietly where he might notice he was not alone. The color of her robes would let him know that a person of the cloth was nearby. If necessary, Cemirowl would stand there all night. Even if he never reached out to her, he would not be alone. Even with his threat of death she could not have moved away.

Chapter Seven

❮❮•❯❯

Arthan made his way to the solar through the narrow passage. He strode past people waiting to pay their respects. It was a duty he would rather wish not to perform. His chest seemed too full of air, and his brow felt heavy over the grimace he could not erase from his face. He could not, however, ignore Tidyri or his brother. He would pay his respects and then go and pray in the chapel.

When he entered the room, he noticed the fortuneteller priest approaching his brother. Caballier Mercor quietly, but desperately gestured for her to return to his side. She ignored the caballier. Arthan took reign of his anger only because she was close enough to the king that his interference could possibly make her imposition worse.

She'd surprised him at dinner. Her tone of honesty had puzzled him. But now she was provoking his prejudices by approaching her king.

As Arthan watched he paused his judgment. His jaw relaxed. The peasant priest did not move closer or impose herself further on his brother. Standing nearby in her rustic vestments, she merely stood where Larthor could see her, but without making any further movement. Arthan expected that even this might make his brother angry.

He could feel his own anger broil with memory. He had knelt in the same place as Larthor, in a different part of the palace, for both wife and stillborn heir. Grief, which he had not yet conquered even now, rose to his eyes. He remembered what Ferran had counseled then: *Comfort yourself in your duty.*

He clenched his jaw on the memory and glared at the woman. She was just standing there, looking content to just wait there through the night's vigil. Perhaps she'd not ruin these proceedings with her village ignorance. It was not long before Larthor inclined his head toward the waiting priest and murmured something to her.

Cemirowl reached forward and touched the king's shoulder; her movements were slow and gentle. Arthan wondered what she would say to her king. Passing Mercor, he moved close enough to listen. If she said anything hurtful, he hoped he could repair the damage later.

While Arthan moved closer, Cemirowl knelt beside the king.

Larthor spoke to the priest, his voice tight and low. "She was so happy that morning! I still expect to see her happy as I have every moment since. Everyone has been so... damned cautious. What am I to do? I'm living in some nightmare."

Arthan knew that his brother would be dry-eyed. When their mother and their sister had died he'd been much the same, burying his grief behind a stony wall of duty and anger.

If he had been true to form, Ferran would have said, "You will move on. You cannot allow your grief to meddle in your role as a prince of state." What would this woman he associated with folly say in response to Larthor's question? Cemirowl looked up at the table. Arthan could see her eyes move as if she were watching someone moving around the room.

She took a deep breath then said, "I could say, 'let her go,' or 'move on' but I think that an injustice. You must grieve."

The words were said gently and Arthan caught himself smiling.

"And what am I doing, woman?" the king snorted out. "What would you have me do different?"

Arthan almost stepped forward, but the priest laid a gentle hand upon the king's arm.

"Your Majesty, I have seen many people grieve. I know what it looks like. I have seen people smash things, break things, wail and even laugh hysterically for they did not know how else to grieve. But I have also seen people unable to function, unable to move, and still others who refuse to do anything but go through the motions of living. I have seen people unable to let out their sorrow... and it wounds them."

"Why should I forget her? I had married her for a treaty and did not expect to love her! Respect and like, perhaps, yes. But I *loved* her!" His words seethed through clenched teeth.

Arthan looked at Mercor, who also recognized the tone of voice. A shared glance, they were both waiting for the explosion. Then, Cemirowl spoke. Her voice was gentle.

"Your Majesty! Why would you think that? Why do you think mourning means 'forget'? Grieving does not say we must forget our loved ones, but that we *remember* them."

Arthan recoiled as from the sting of a slap—though her voice had been soft and compassionate and not even directed at him. He did not stagger, struck against the fortress of his grief and the folly of the past. He stepped back and could not breathe. For a moment, the room swirled. After swallowing, Arthan began to breathe harshly. He had tried to not think of Boduscia and hurting either way.

"I do not have time to grieve!" his brother growled at Cemirowl, throwing up yet another stone for that wall he was still building. "I am the king!" Arthan almost heard the slap of mortar on stone. He was not aware of moving even one half step further, nor leaning toward the pair.

"Your Majesty," Cemirowl said, "now is a good time to grieve. In fact this time has been set aside for mourning and I promise that there will be more time to think of her as well. You must think of her, of your joys and your life together. You will burn. Grief will rain on your soul night and day. You will want to go to her, to find her. You must remember her *and live*."

Arthan could have walked upon the ache in her voice, soft as it was. It was real. He could see the faded red on her hands, the red stain on the edge of her sleeve, a different red than the rest of her dress. Death had touched this woman. And she shared the knowledge of that pain with the man beside her.

The king began to tremble. Arthan knew Larthor would throw up walls to his grief: worrying about his duties, the repercussions to the treaties and wanting to crush Tidyri's murderer. Ferran had probably, with the best of intentions, already told Larthor much the same thing as he had Arthan.

Hearing this village priest' words, he set aside his anger at Ferran, which he'd held for so long. He understood the advice now, but he did not want his brother to wait two years to hear it, because here it was offered in the soft words and hands of this small fortuneteller. Arthan ached, hoped, and held his breath.

Cemirowl looked at her king and took his large hand in hers. Arthan could see that she did not care if she were to die tomorrow. The focus of her being was in that one touch. His brother was so strong, that his clothing betrayed that muscular strength beneath it. She looked so small beside him. He saw Larthor's mustache quiver and his hair hang in his face.

For a long moment Arthan just looked at the village priest' hand holding his brother's, but then—even Arthan could see it—something inside that mighty man let go.

With his head bowed, King Larthor gripped her hand. As his trembling grew more pronounced, as he began to weep quietly, his hold became tighter. Arthan watched Cemirowl's hand turn white in Larthor's grip. But Cemirowl allowed it. She made no sound, merely bent her head to his shoulder—sharing, supporting.

It was one of the most tender gestures Arthan had ever witnessed.

His brother, his king wept. And Arthan wept. He felt his own sorrow wash over him, wanting to drown him again. He knew that Larthor was being allowed to grieve, but he would not drown with this woman holding his hand. Arthan wished that he could share the moment, holding onto that hand as a lifeline. He stayed back, weeping silently alone.

After a time, Arthan realized that the doors had been closed so the king could grieve without being watched. He waited even longer as Larthor's shuddering grew softer and his grip on Cemirowl's hand lessened. As his brother's shoulders grew still, Larthor murmured something to the priest.

She bent her head to the hand holding hers then stood, touching his shoulder briefly and left his side. She looked up, saw Arthan and went up to him.

"Will you stay with him?" she asked him, softly.

"I had planned to stand vigil in the chapel," he murmured, but turned to look at her.

"I'm not who he needs at the moment. Not a stranger. He needs someone who knows him. No one should grieve alone," she murmured softly. "I will stay, if you cannot," she said.

He saw in her eyes that she knew that she, shabby in her cheap vestments in this glittering room, and with the threat of the noose around her throat was a lesser option. But she would stay. She would stand nearby for the grieving man, even if she thought there were countless better choices. She would not leave him. She would do what, clearly, no one else had—not even his brother.

"I will stay," he said.

Something in her eyes glimmered in the candlelight, as if she noticed something in his face she'd not seen before. It was more than his grief stained face. She considered him for a moment, looking deep into his eyes, as she had done in his sitting room.

"When a man loses a beloved wife, there is shock and loss," she said softly. "If a man does not fully grieve he will only remember her in sorrow. Stay with him. Grieve with him, Your Highness. In time you will be able to remember her with joy as well as with sorrow."

She laid her hand on his arm for a moment and then quickly turned to Mercor and left.

As Arthan watched her leave the room and turned to the king, he realized that the last "her" might not have been Tidyri, but Boduscia.

He turned from the closing door and knelt beside his brother. Arthan could only think of how Cemirowl had held

Larthor's hand. Slowly, Arthan reached out and took his brother's hand in his own. Their hands tightened together.

Chapter Eight

⫷•⫸

Cemirowl followed Mercor to the gallery, away from the prince, the king and the ghost of the queen. She stopped. His grip on her arm tightened a fraction, but he turned and looked at her.

"I need some fresh air," she said, nearly gasping from a sense of loss.

"Very well," Mercor said after a moment. "Come this way."

By the grip of his hand and tone of his voice, he was angry with her. He pulled her down the stairs. His face was hidden in the shadows of the lanterns in the stairwell open to the deep night sky. It was then she realized she'd missed the sunset while sitting with the king. Mercor nodded and the tension in his shoulders shifted.

"The queen's gallery looks down upon these gardens," he murmured once they were outside. She knew he must still be tense, as he'd mentioned the fact earlier.

But his voice was lighter than before. Cemirowl was grateful. The grip of his long, strong fingers showed control over fraught emotions. The garden was lit with lanterns and torches along various pathways to the chapel.

She still wanted to sit vigil with the grieving husband, but when he'd released her hand, she could no longer impose upon the king. Reluctantly she had left, only knowing that his brother was a far better choice to sit vigil with him than a stranger. She could not, also, impose her care without insulting the office of the priest sitting vigil in a chapel little more than fifty yards or so away. She forced herself to be not a priest, but a peasant, even if a titled peasant.

"I can't believe you did that," Mercor said, leading her away from the chapel, deeper into the garden toward the wall. "If Ferran thought the king needed a hand to hold, he'd be there!"

Cemirowl said nothing. It was clear that the caballier was blind to what had happened. He was only alive to the apparent presumption on her part. *Obviously, vestment or no vestment, I am only a fortuneteller in his eyes,* she thought. By the furrow in his brow, the tension almost visibly quivering in his shoulders—even in the low lights of the garden at night. *I'm also the source of a potential doom, ruining all he's built up as a younger son. Poor man.*

"That sound—is it the surf?" she asked him to break the growing silence.

"Indeed," he answered, and led her up stairs to the walkway patrolled by armed guards. She looked over the wall.

The air was crisp. Underneath the smell of fish was a pervasive scent of salt. Her father and Meelac had hoarded salt, when they could afford to buy it. And the air even tasted of it! It felt like proof of the king's wealth.

"I have never seen the ocean," she murmured, looking down at the surf pounding at the base of the cliff.

"I'm surprised. I could imagine you were well travelled, if not well educated. From what I heard, you do not eat like a peasant." He noted her surprise. "Yes, I asked," he said. "I was fearful you'd somehow insult the prince and his household."

She shook her head, not wanting to respond.

"Your father, did he study medicine, then?"

"Yes," she said, wondering at his questions.

"And your skill is more mystical than medical?"

"I am proficient with the arts of an apothecary, but, yes, caballier, my skills tend toward the mystical. I *have* been ordained."

"You seem... You did not embarrass yourself dining tonight, and the servant said you spoke intelligently with the Honorable Ferran."

"My father had one of the better libraries in the area, and clearly he had an excellent education in his youth. He spoke..." She stopped. With a shrug she turned away, biting down on the words, *He spoke like a gentleman.* She shook her head. "Caballier, it's not my father that must concern us."

Yes, Cemirowl had been curious about her father's past, but those questions had long been futile. There were better questions to ask in the current crisis. Mercor turned away and stared at the ocean.

"Did you learn anything from the body?" he asked her intently.

She gave him a withering glance. "That was not why I went to view the queen."

"I am worried about you."

"Why?" What would be the point of entertaining those fears now that she was quite firmly stuck here? She was sure he was more worried about his own neck. He turned, shaking his head, biting his lip. Guilt seemed to shadow his brow more than the night. It was an odd expression on a man who clearly had not even been near when the queen was murdered. What did he have to feel guilty about?

"The king expects you to find how and why the queen died from reading your bone basket or her body! Is that not ample reason?"

In the moonlight, his eyes covered her intently. Cemirowl thought, *He must find it exasperating to have to rely on a fortuneteller to protect him when he's so used to working to build up his career on his own.*

Cemirowl looked down and watched the waves pound the rocks of the cliff wall and then recede. She looked up to the brilliance of the stars and the light of the moon making a path across the waves. She turned to him. He was the closest thing she had to a friend in the palace. The closest to an ally. And she needed one. One who could help her.

"It has been a long day, but I cannot sleep during the wake," she said. "Can you tell me about the queen?"

"She is from Hergila," Mercor said. "On a clear day you can see the queen's country. There! Do you see some dark shadows on the horizon? That is Hergila," he said.

"So close!"

"Our lands stare at each other across the strait between the Einterinne sea and Novish ocean," he said. "The treaty between Pyrann and Hergila was confirmed by the marriage of Larthor and Tidyri. Both countries now divide equally any tolls charged for passage between the sea and the ocean. Because of the treaty we have exports that travel through Hergila and countries beyond. Part of my appointment in Larthor's court is to write or translate trade agreements and drafts."

"Does Queen Tidyri's death affect that treaty?" Cemirowl asked.

Mercor shrugged. "I am sure that this is part of the king's worry. If they can prove that she died by force and we cannot exterminate the perpetrator, then Hergila may very well bring the treaty into question. That strait has been contested for at least four generations. If the Hergilan king chooses to believe that the treaty was a ruse to gain control, even partial, he might re-engage old disputes."

"King Larthor worked so hard for this alliance. Even I learned of that in some backwater village. Would not his obvious affection and grief prove his integrity?"

"Any lies can be told for political gain. The nobility of Hergila do not live here except the ambassador. It would be easy to tell them that his affections were only a tale. We cannot prove that affection unless they had children. Doubt can be created in many different ways. For political reasons any of our, or even their, nobles could choose a politically convenient suspicion. I do not think Ambassador Itrizeu would support such a story, but others in the Hergilan High Council might, if they thought there was something to gain."

She thought about what she'd heard earlier in the evening. Apparently the ambassador had a man who might be suspect in the murder. That couldn't make for easy politics. From what she heard tonight, that suspicion enforced some manner of patience for any kind of Hergilan response.

A guard approached. While he wore a short sword, his main weapon was a crossbow. She'd only heard about them. She'd never seen one. The guard held it at the ready.

Mercor leaned closer to speak more quietly as the man

walked past. His arm brushed her shoulder. He looked toward Hergila and said quietly, "It is bad timing."

Again, Cemirowl felt as if he was holding something back. Guilt rode his brow. The pain in his face as he looked towards Hergila was strong. She wanted to brush it away.

"Could anyone of this court gain advantage from a return to the dispute?" she asked him.

"It took a lot of work to bring the treaty to completion. The benefits were increasing. The duchies to the north were finally beginning to feel as if some attention might be paid them, and this will aggravate tensions that were beginning to ease."

"Does her death help anyone at court?"

Mercor tensed briefly, as his eyes glittered in the moonlight. "The prince is securely the heir apparent, but he was that before the queen's passing. Only the birth of the king's child would change that. He might be the designated regent, unless something happened to the king as the queen was foreign. Clearly she had not yet given the king that joy."

He turned to Cemirowl again, his eyes soft in the starlight.

"Is he the only one?" she asked.

"There are some nobles of both countries who might be able to gain a stronger alliance with the king, now that Queen Tidyri is dead," he told her. "The chances would be too slim to take such a hurtful, harmful action only to secure King Larthor for one of their daughters, however. Larthor could still choose anyone. If he doesn't choose from Hergila again, that Pruan princess might become a queen, rather than Arthan's intended."

"Who found the queen?" Cemirowl asked.

"Three of her ladies. They have been questioned—as they all had opportunity to poison the queen, if that is, indeed, how she was killed. The Ladies Terria, Soflia, and Harlyn, who you met earlier. From what I understand Harlyn was resting in their room, ill—and from what I know of her, she would be useless for most of the day with one of her headaches. I've seen her try, and then vomit because she moved too quickly. It is no wonder she keeps to her room when ill. The other ladies were running other errands. Even the pages had been sent out of the room. It is believed that she was alone when she died."

"Is that not unusual? Even Lady Thade is rarely alone."

"Apparently she was upset and wanted time alone. She'd had an argument with Ferran earlier in the day and was in need of some quiet."

"Do you know what the argument was about?"

"I have not had that much time since our arrival to find out many details."

He was silent as another guard walked past from the west. Mercor greeted him. The archer's return greeting was cool.

Mercor grinned in response. "They're still mad that I stabbed one of their friends."

"Excuse me?"

"Nothing."

Silence had grown between them. Turning to him, she realized with a start that he had been using the time to examine her.

"Tell me, Sir Mercor," she said, nervous again, "about the ladies of the queen's chamber. Are they married?"

Mercor flashed her one of his smiles. "No, not yet, but that is just the fault of time. Ladies-in-waiting are sometimes married; there were a couple from Hergila for a while, but one returned to her husband and the other returned to finally marry. The queen was sometimes aided by women of Ambassador Itrizeu's court. The ladies of Pyrann who attended her were of an age as the queen. The prince's wife attended her court, but she died in childbirth. Many ladies come to court and find a match to their advantage. Some remain as ladies after marriage if they are near enough at court. Soflia would have stayed, as she is marrying a rich nobleman who lives in a northern section of Elbyrge."

And the Ladies Terria and Harlyn are not yet engaged to be married?"

"Lady Terria might soon be, from what I understand. Lady Harlyn has already rejected one suitor. I think she agreed to come to court, but her overlord's choice would have removed her from the city."

"And... your lady?"

"Yes, she was one of the queen's attendants," he said. "She was disgraced; though I doubt that there would have been quite such an event if the discovery of her actions had not been quite so public. My fault, really. I lost my temper."

"Oh," she said; there was really little else she could say.

A wave of exhaustion ran through her. Mercor caught her arm and steadied her. It was the first real concern she'd felt from him.

"Are you all right?"

"I'm sorry, but I need to make myself a restorative infusion. I find that I cannot maintain myself this night. Do you know where there are cooking pots I can use, or do I need to go to the kitchen?"

"There is usually something left in the guest rooms," Mercor said. "Check the table near the fire. There should be an infusion pot, as well as boxes of herbs marked either for restoratives or sedatives—there was, at least, when my family came. It was something that the queen began providing for guests, an old Hergilan custom I believe. My family did not know what to make of it. Perhaps you will." He gave her a wry smile. "You may feel obliged to stay awake, but I'm desperately in need of sleep."

Slowly, and in silence they walked down the narrow stairs that led from the walk of the wall back to the garden. As they descended, Cemirowl could see the stairs and small courtyard that led to the prince's apartments. Lanterns lit the pavilion. Rising above the building, the dome above his main court was lit from within.

Mercor saw her gaze, and steadied her on the narrow steps. "Steady now. You can easily fall from here." He helped her down to the garden. "He calls it the Lantern Court. His sitting room is lit during the day with architectural 'lanterns' made in the dome. He often needs no light from the southern entrance."

"This whole palace, all I've seen, is astonishing! If it weren't for the circumstances that called me here, I'd be grateful for you bringing me."

He laughed. "It is among the most beautiful places I've ever seen."

For all that, Cemirowl was grateful. She could not imagine that she would ever see the like again, and if she died, at least she got to see something of true beauty before she was hanged.

They walked through the gardens with the lights leading the way to the chapel, and the gallery along the queen's apartments and other buildings. Cemirowl realized that this could be considered a romantic moment. Maybe, somewhere on these grounds it was. The night loomed with death, the queen's and the threat of her own, and that of the man walking beside her.

Mercor led her to the northern end of the gallery, and up some stairs. He led her through the maze of passageways that brought her to her rooms. The grand entrance to Prince Arthan's rooms bridging the passage in the Lion Court was firmly shut. She hoped he and the king were comforting each other in grief.

CHAPTER NINE

―――――――――― «‹•›» ――――――――――

Cemirowl's room was lit by candles and warmed by a fire. The candles were still tall, but would have to be replaced before the night was over. For a moment she needed assurance that this was, indeed, her room. The arched casements to her windows were still unfamiliar, and she'd seen too many expensive pieces of furniture to remember any in her room. On a table she saw her bone basket, and stepping past the screen, her clothes were arranged near the bed.

She sighed, and took comfort in the attention given her. Her travelling clothes were clean and pressed, as was her nicest dress. The servant girl, Les, had apparently remembered that Cemirowl was clergy and would be staying up all night. She had left some additional candles beside the tea boxes on the table, along with an assortment of delicate looking ceramic cups. The kettle was on the stone mantel above the fire.

Cemirowl ignored the flask of wine, and poured water into the pot for her infusion. Though using wine was more traditional, experience had taught her that wine made her sleepy, no matter what herbs she used. She decided to use the queen's herbs from the carved boxes rather than anything from her own herb satchel.

It was an appropriate gesture of remembrance. Beyond seeing her ghost, briefly, it was the only thing she really knew of her queen. She opened the box marked 'stimulant.' Instead of loose leaf, the herbs were in small, cloth pouches, lying on top of each other.

Cemirowl picked up the top bag and brought it to her face and smelled the brisk scent of spire. It had probably been used for taste. She had done much the same when creating a mixture and wanted to disguise the taste, or help calm the stomach.

The scent brought back a memory. A year before her mother had died, Ferioul had been lucid enough to join in the taming of some spire menthe in their garden. Dusane, Ferioul and Cemirowl had playfully pulled up the invasive, square stemmed spire. Laughing, they forbade the weedy plant to invade the purple wands, clary and bur golds.

The image of Ferioul's rare smile, framed by dancing wands of purple flowers, brought tears to Cemirowl's eyes. Her mother had paid for that moment of enjoyment, that moment of living and playing with husband and daughter. Before they had finished tying up the herbs they'd picked to dry, Ferioul became trapped again in the realm of the dead. Or rather the limbo in between.

Cemirowl snapped the box shut, shutting out the memory.

It was the queen she wanted to remember, not her mother. She set the water closer to the fire to boil. She put the bag in one of the delicate cups—probably more often used for ale than for an infusion. The herbs needed to steep and cool enough for her to drink.

Rolling the hot cup through her hands, Cemirowl thought about her conversation with Mercor. She set the cup down and thought of the most pressing problem. It was wrong to speculate on who could have killed the queen—she had little enough information. It was also doubtful that her bones would tell her anything of value, but instead of idling, she decided to pull them out anyway.

Figuring out what to ask was always the difficulty. Her first question, "Who killed the queen," gave too confusing a reading. The only image that came to mind, echoing off the bones, were four women and a man, and a flare of anger on all sides. Two of the women seemed divided by it—with the added influence of two other men. She could only guess that one was the queen.

"That's not helpful," Cemirowl said out loud to the ghost that had come to sit at another chair. It was one she believed to be somehow related to her. Cemirowl tried the infusion, but it was still too hot.

She tried the basket again. "Are there people they suspect?"

This time the lay was a bit more interesting.

There seemed to be slightly separate piles of bones. She looked at the lay of bones and wondered if they represented some of the women in the earlier, unhelpful reading.

Assumptions defeat intuition, she scolded herself. Yet one pile continued to make her think of what Mercor had said, that the Honorable Ferran had argued with the queen. She wondered about the others, surprised at five feminine piles. Delicate bones, with energy that rose up and swirled like Harlyn's skirts, as well as those of the other ladies of court she had seen. Only three men, with sturdier bones and robust energy she'd always associated with men.

"Who are they?" she wondered. Neither her ghostly pets nor the ghost across the table deigned to reply. The lay of bones certainly offered no definitive answers. "They're only bones!" Cemirowl said, shaking her head.

The ghost seemed to convey something, and she could only guess at what was being 'said.'

"Well, I knew it was futile before I started!" she replied.

She stood up, and took her cup to sit by the wide western window, and gazed at the torch lit chapel where occasionally people were still entering or leaving. By the moon it was not terribly late. It felt as if it should be further on into the night, perhaps because the hours before were tense and eventful. Her hand still hurt. She thought of the king and prince in a room barely in view of her room's southern window.

Contemplating Prince Arthan's actions, his gestures, the way his face moved during different conversations, Cemirowl thought, *He restrains a great deal of powerful emotions behind those eyes. His eyes brood, yes, but he controls...* suppresses *a great deal of passion, anger and sorrow.* The fine crinkles at the corners of his eyes hid sorrow. *He still mourns his wife Boduscia.*

The queen's death must remind him of his wife and child's death. That grief would, naturally, renew itself. This new grief would not change Prince Arthan's situation over much. He was still the heir presumptive. Queen Tidyri's death only made that rank more secure for the moment—for it might be some time before Larthor married again.

"That could be motive," Cemirowl murmured to herself. She could not know if he was a suspect. Surely no one would tell her if he was.

Guessing her tea had steeped enough, she pulled the tea bag out and set it on a small plate. It looked fat, and plump as a dead mouse. *Do people at court need a great amount of energy?*

she wondered and took a sip. The taste of spire was not as strong as she would have supposed. There was an underlying taste that reminded her of metal. It was not *too* unpleasant.

She drank absently and pondered the grief of the king. She wanted to help him more than she had, even though it had been folly that had brought her here. Her stomach churned as she thought of her task.

She had to convince the king that her skill in fortunetelling was not of great note—prove something contrary to the tales told by someone he trusted: Caballier Mercor. She would have to prove something even the closest of her friends did not believe. Of course she saw something they did not. That she could not deny. She merely did not see what they thought she did!

She put the tea down with a face; despite the spire she was not really enjoying it. It reminded her of something she'd made a long while ago. With her fingers on the rim, Cemirowl turned the cup around and around, wondering what the herbs had been. It did not come to mind readily, so she dismissed the infusion and focused on her current predicament.

Is it possible for me to just admit that I cannot reveal the killer through a reading and accept the result of that confession? She had tried to convey that to the prince at dinner. She had little idea that he believed her. Mercor had come to the defense of her accuracy, apparently, before the dinner—which seemed foolish to her. Perhaps he felt as if his storytelling had been attacked. Wouldn't he need for her to be proved a charlatan to save his skin?

Something else was disconcerting. A source of discomfort beyond a change of environment. She focused to the other realm.

Except for the more ethereal than usual ghost of her kinswoman, the dead she knew were not near. Her animals had followed her to the palace. Her ability to perceive was intact. But overall—for the first time in her life, the blanket awareness of the otherworld was gone, un-peopled by the dead she knew, the dead of her village. Those she had buried and those who had died before.

For a moment she panicked. Her stomach roiled, and she tasted bile. But then she laughed wryly. It was a reprieve. And they were not wholly gone. A few of her family remained close, and she sensed the dead of the palace and town nearby. They had not yet come to pay their respects, nor had she called upon them.

Her mind turned to the ghost in the hallway, who had also been in Prince Arthan's sitting room. It was the only ghost she had really noticed. The only one who had seemed...? Cemirowl reached for the idea. It had been searching, calling for something? She tried to find a sense of it, but she did not know the ghost well enough. Cemirowl shrugged and turned to her grandmother, or rather the spirit she assumed was her father's mother, a woman she had never met in life. It could have been a great aunt or someone else entirely.

Rarely did Cemirowl look for the spirits of people in her life, voluntarily—she always feared that she would see her mother. But Cemirowl felt lonely inside this vast palace. She had no true friends, no allies except Mercor, who was as dubious of their connection as she. Dead pets were not comfort enough, at the moment.

Her grandmother—if it was her—was never a clear spirit. The impression of long, graying copper tresses and a sense of steady strength was as clear as it ever got. Even the spirit's rare 'advice' was only a vague nudge toward a certain direction. She threw a great deal of attention her way.

"Would I want someone tried for murder only on my say so?" Cemirowl asked her grandmother.

"No!" She answered her own question immediately.

Her grandmother seemed to agree, being apparently equally perturbed. The little fox pup crawled up onto her lap, crouching, nervous, as if stealing into the privilege of her lap. Her hawk perched on the chair back, trying to peck at the cup in her hands.

"Even if I believed a reading to be true, I would want material evidence," Cemirowl replied, running one hand over the cub as best she could, and then put the cup down. "How else would they believe? And look at the trouble I'm in for one reading in the first place."

It was not a tempting idea that she might have an 'out' in fortunetelling or post-telling the identity of the murderer. She did not think the king was a man would take a village fortuneteller's words for truth, ordained priest or not. Indeed, if he did he was not sensible.

Stroking the trembling pup, Cemirowl laughed at the idea.

"Even if I could find the murderer, I'd still have to get proof," Cemirowl murmured after a moment. She twirled the infusion cup on the table, with a roll and a clunk. She wanted to know who had killed the queen.

In an odd way, I have been given leave to find out. She ignored the vague sense that her grandmother thought her young and foolish. Cemirowl wanted to do what she could. The puppy nuzzled into her shoulder, whimpering, and so insistent, Cemirowl could almost feel the real physical pressure of its nose on her arm.

"Helping might mean just staying out of the way?"

Cemirowl sighed. One could not sit, having one's hand

crushed by a grieving man and not be touched by compassion or a desire to be useful. But the funeral was most likely well in hand. There was little more she could offer.

Cemirowl stopped spinning the cup and took a sip of tea, swallowed as she stood. She choked on the bitter taste, then looked at her grandmother and said angrily, "After so many deaths that I've attended, *this* should not be!"

Cemirowl slammed the cup down on the table, the contents sloshed inside, spilling onto the table.

"If the queen had died, it would be difficult; the country would still mourn. I could accept that! But not this murder. It is not fair! Death... why would anyone want to *cause* such grief? We are not at war!" she growled in a low murmur to her grandmother, who also seemed quite agitated.

Cemirowl's stomach felt almost as if it was burning. The sensation had been going on for only a short while. But as she was not prone to stomach complaints, she clenched her teeth, knowing it must be tension. The past few days had not been easy.

Clutching her belly, Cemirowl was startled. Her father appeared and reached for the cup, but could not lift it. He gestured angrily, trying to signal to her. She could almost hear an echo of his voice, but no distinct word. She realized both ghosts and pets were agitated. She looked at the tea bag and at her father's spirit. She knew the stance, the gesture.

Was there something in the tea?

The spire had been obvious. Underlying that taste was something that tasted slightly of metal or bark.

She picked up the cup again. Critically, she took a sip and let it rest in her mouth. The taste, even disguised by spire, reminded her of a light colored bark. She spit it back into the cup.

There was an almost dark, numbing aftertaste. It faded after a moment, but she'd been a fool to miss it before.

She was reminded of the emmenagogue button bloom, which she'd once given a young woman whose menstrual cycle was preceded with debilitating pain. The cycle would not begin and she'd finally sent for Cemirowl, who had given the girl this herb in small doses. Mixed with spire, actually. It had been effective for the young woman whose cycle had become less painful and more regular till she was able to take other, less dangerous tonics. In small doses, button bloom was good for beginning menstrual cycles—and getting rid of worms from the digestive tract. In large doses, or continued use, it could eat into the stomach lining and, eventually, kill.

It wasn't a stimulant.

Someone had attempted to poison her! Cemirowl was horrified. There was absolutely no cause to put button bloom into any stimulant herbal mixture. It was a stupid attempt and badly done. Cemirowl could not imagine why anyone would need or want to give a guest button bloom without their knowledge. Except to rid a person of worms, or start menses, it was not good for anything else. It wasn't even a culinary herb.

Looking at the cup, Cemirowl saw that there was only a quarter of the cup remaining. She looked at the tea bag, attempting to gauge the amounts. Spire, being a rather aromatic herb, large amounts were not necessary. If the infusion was mostly button bloom, the least she could fear was a painful stomach for the next few hours and the possible start of her menstrual cycle. Her stomach would also be quite delicate for a while. The worst possibility was that she could be dead in two hours as the herb burned out her stomach.

Cemirowl had no way of knowing if the person had known how much would kill her, but clearly it was not something that should have been in the box marked 'stimulants.' How could Cemirowl know of the dose? Yet, unless the person had added extracts or oils, she seriously doubted that there was enough in the bag to kill her. It might incapacitate her for a while, perhaps.

"Why not wait for my execution?" she wondered.

The ghosts gave no response.

Hoping that she would only have a tender tummy—as some sort of petty punishment—it would be stupid if the dose had been greater than she'd believed. However, Cemirowl had to assume death was intended.

What did Dusane tell me about button bloom? Cemirowl asked herself nervously.

Looking at the anxious ghost of her father, memory brought her his voice.

"I remember a man of my acquaintance, Frelon," he'd said. "He was a nervous type and not inclined to listen to advice. Our teacher had told us of button bloom, or button blow as she called it, and the cautions. Frelon heard the first part of the instruction, but ignored the rest... obviously. Sometime later, he thought he had worms. Frelon was always thinking something was wrong with him: that week it was worms. He took two teaspoons of the extract and died two hours later in a rather painful death."

"Would a purgative have helped him?" Cemirowl had asked her father.

"I suspect it would have hurt as much as helped. While the stomach's being burned, it is not in a condition to accept any inducement for violent purging. The action of vomiting would do more harm than good. With a small dose, I would have the patient drink the milk of a cow or goat."

"What if you didn't have that?" she had wondered and received a pat on the head.

"Good question, Cemi. In that case I'd give charcoal mixed with an egg, or, at the very least, boiled water. It would probably help with a large dose too. But I would keep an eye on the sufferer for at least two hours, and dose him with the remedy at least once more, that is, if the dose of button blow was large."

The ache in her stomach brought the memory to a close, reminding Cemirowl of the necessity for action.

Not having milk on hand, she went to the fire and using one of the fire tools, scraped out some cooled charcoal. She blew most of the ashes off the largest, warm, black piece. She dashed the contents of her cup into the chamber pot and rinsed it. She then put the charcoal into the cup, poured the boiled water over this and then mashed it. She drank the vile contents quickly, drinking more water to rinse out her mouth.

She no longer needed something to keep her awake. As the pain in her stomach slowly calmed, her anger grew. *Good thing I used water, not wine. It would have disguised the taste even more,* she thought.

Her knowledge of herbs had saved Cemirowl, but she was still appalled. She had not been here long enough to make enemies. *Granted, people can be twitchy.* At least they were around her.

The situation had a macabre sense of ludicrousness. Even though she was the sufferer, she was not unamused. The dead had kept her from dying, and a skill that had gotten her into considerable trouble had been there to save her. As yet, she still had not heard voices as clearly as her mother apparently had.

Cemirowl did not *want* the clarity which might risk her own sanity, though her stomach might have suffered less if she had.

She stopped short. *How had the queen died? With what? A knife or an herb?*

All Cemirowl knew was that she'd been found in the solar, apparently alone, three days ago. She had been brought all this way and had no more information than this. Even if the dose of button bloom Cemirowl had been given had been intended as a warning to frighten her away, she could not leave without the king's permission.

Had someone attempted to hurt her, possibly kill her because they feared her abilities? There was no other reason she could think of. As Cemirowl gazed at the flickering light on a tapestry, she found herself breathing harshly. Laid open now was a fear she'd been hiding from for a long time.

In the dark room of a castle, and feeling the grit of crushed charcoal in her mouth, Cemirowl could no longer avoid that fear. How else could Cemirowl deal with her own fear that she was uncanny? It was more than fearing that she would die like her mother, incapable of knowing one realm from the other. She learned things she might not otherwise. There was rarely much detail, and much of it was quite useless, no matter what anyone thought. But know she did.

Her throat went dry and ached at the thought of how much of her ability she had not yet explored. In the dark room with the quiet murmur of a low fire, Cemirowl closed her eyes. She could feel the expanse of the other realm, reaching out past the walls of her room. She knew that she could touch any of the dead nearby, or call any from far away.

There was a great deal, Cemirowl guessed, that was

possible for her—possibilities that both terrified and tempted her. What had frightened her was the ease she knew could be hers—that had to be tempered with control.

She shook her head. It could, of course, be very easy to reach those things, but there was no purpose in those abilities, and they had driven her mother mad. Greater skill would not make her fortunetelling any easier! Or more clear. It would not help her put the dead to rest any better. Yet it was possible someone else believed in those untapped abilities more than Cemirowl did.

Someone had tried to hurt her, possibly kill her because of those abilities. Someone had said by a—possibly—silly gesture, that they were afraid of her.

The division between herself and the rest of the world became sharp and harsh. *And yet she asked, if I take any steps toward any of those possibilities what would I become?*

The rest of the night was very bitter and unfortunately without relief, even while a second dose of charcoal calmed her stomach even further. There was no way Cemirowl could change her alienation from most people without losing her gift. Besides, the dead had been her companions for a long time. She spent the night struggling to find her center and it was very, very hard.

CHAPTER TEN

C emirowl rested at dawn, after laying her vestments carefully so they would not wrinkle. After different physical and emotional stresses, having ridden hard for most of two days and staying up all night, sleep was a blessing. Unfortunately at midmorning she rose from her bed no longer able to sleep. Her eyes felt heavy, but her body pounded with a strange numb and yet nervous energy.

Cemirowl considered changing into one of the better dresses she'd owned in her life. Much of the money Caballier Mercor had given her for his reading had paid for material for two dresses, thread, and two extravagant new needles. She could rarely treat herself, but Cemirowl had fallen in love with the cloth's color and texture. The clerical robes were not as lovely, but there had been no cloth in the proper colors that met with the same quality. Neither, of course, matched the finery she'd seen in the castle. She loved the dress all the same.

The tunic was of a dark bronze color. She'd spent the spring months embroidering the sleeves in a simple pattern of leaves with a gold colored thread. Cemirowl always felt better when she used her hands. Her mother had taught her the rudimentary elements of sewing, but encouraged by her father in the calming pursuit she had experimented and learned.

Bringing the sleeve to her face, she still smelled the compass, purple wands and arbor vitae she used when storing her clothes at home. *With the smell of home,* Cemirowl thought, *this work on the dress, I know I did well. I have something I can be proud of.*

The light bronze overdress had cost her some pains. It was something like what she had seen other ladies wearing, with large and embroidered openings for arms. It was warm and allowed her to work with her hands. This she had worked with a vine, bursting with leaves, twining all along the edge and the collar. She longed to wear it, but she knew she must still do the work of a priest.

She put her vestments back on after a quick wash. She made her way back to the long gallery walk to the solar. A guard stood there. Cemirowl knew she should have expected this. What was she to do? What could she say? She hoped her vestments would be entry enough.

"I've come to see if there is anything needed for the body before the funeral," she said. She knew that she had been asked to read the body—as if that was how her power worked. It was still a bold enough question, as she'd not been given direct leave to do the work at that very moment.

"Yes, Priest," the guard said. He shook his head. "It's a shame the wrapping is so plain for the queen, blessed be her memory."

"Oh?" Cemirowl's heart pounded.

"I guess I could understand it. In Hergila they aren't wrapped, and only wear their clothes, with a cloth over their head. But she married Pyrann, as you know, my lady priest." He seemed genuinely sad.

She lifted her stained hands, mostly faded, and grabbed at a chance. "Perhaps I can do something about that, if you give me time?"

"Indeed! Can you work quickly though?"

Cemirowl's heart was pounding so much she felt dizzy with a sense of relief. "Yes. Before coming here, I have wrapped many a body. She is slight. It will not take me long. An hour, little more."

"She will not be needed for another two hours, ma'am. And thank you."

Cemirowl went inside, the guard following to speak to the guard at the other door. He only mentioned as he passed back to his post, that the ladies were not in their room, but housed elsewhere in the palace till after the funeral, so they could have time to gather their things and move to their new homes. "And the king rests. You will not be disturbed."

Cemirowl smiled and thanked him. She wished she did not feel like a fraud. *Being thought of as a charlatan is much easier.* She had never felt so brazen in her life, not even when she stood next to the king of her country!

She might very well be insulting everyone—Ferran, the women who had wrapped the queen, the king... anyone—but her life was on the line, from the king and some unknown person as well. She'd been bold enough to be free to comfort the king, hold his hand with its bruising pressure.

There were four jars with symbolic lids beside the table. They were of different sizes. She did not recognize the symbols. When she opened one, it seemed filled with linen and what looked like sand. She touched a wet finger to it, and tasted it. It was acrid. It did not taste of dirt, but strongly of salt. A richer, more dense salt than she knew. Curious. This was not a Pyrannian part of burial. She guessed it was Hergilan.

Cemirowl wondered how the Hergilan death rites would affect Pyrannian symbolism that affirmed the finality of death. Meelac had taught her that the whole process was not merely for the soul's benefit—the part that only she could see—but also for those experiencing the loss as well. Cemirowl could hear her mentor's voice in her memory: "If they cannot call their beloved back, then they can grieve cleanly—and their loss can heal as well. Your job is to help make the grieving process clean."

How could she have told Meelac that, even if the cutting of the soul was effective, she could still see the dead? Though some did come back to visit her, ever since her mother's death Cemirowl usually pushed the dead far away from her. For her, the grieving process was not 'clean' the way Meelac imagined.

Looking at the red, glittering and oil soaked wrappings, Cemirowl altered her focus. Sensing the otherworld, she had to accept that she could not find any attachment of spirit to the body, though the queen's spirit was certainly still present in the room.

She called her animals to her. These spirits she had never needed to cut away from her. She bit back sorrows better left untouched and took comfort in their presence. Calmer, she focused on the body that lay upon the table and touched the wrappings.

Despite the comforting presence of her pets, anger returned to Cemirowl. This death had not been 'clean'. Not only did the mourners have to contend with their own sense of loss, but they also had to contend with the horror of how the queen had died. They did not know if she had suffered, or if she had died in peace. They could not equate the love they felt for this woman with the willful violence done to her.

Knowing she had to find the murderer for the king's sake, if not her own, Cemirowl wanted to see the physical body. Even if all the preparing unguents had been used, there might be evidence that could tell her what had killed the queen. Some herbs, poisons rather, left marks on the body. The body, smelling of decay, sweet gold flecked oils, pungent herbs, balsam-bowl resin and olibanum, the body no longer betrayed any scent that could indicate a poison.

It was not merely curiosity. Professional pride also stirred in Cemirowl. She wanted to do a better job with the wrapping. She knew she could. Honor done to the body was one way to 'clean' the process of mourning.

It was a fiction, and she knew it, that she'd been called to do more than read the body. It wasn't anger or pettiness that made her want to set her skills against the women who had already wrapped the queen, or anything else. The whole reason she was there was almost an insult to the queen, as well as herself. There was one thing she could do to make peace with both the queen and herself.

"I might still die tomorrow, but I'll do my best for the one who needs it the most," she said to herself.

Cemirowl turned to her work.

"My queen, there is not much else I can do to change the nature of your death but I hope that this office that I perform honors you," she murmured.

Cemirowl unwrapped the body, working carefully but quickly. When the body lay revealed before her, even oiled and packed with herbs, smelling of spices, she could see that the queen had been beautiful. Very few adult women had hair that fair; the lightest hair she had ever seen had been the same dark shades of the king and his brother. Her hair must have intrigued men.

Recalling some of Meelac's stories, Cemirowl looked hopefully under the table. Though villagers could not afford to waste burial wrappings, the rich, the nobility would save some of the extra for remembrances, destroying or burying the rest. These winding cloths had been woven for the royal family. No one else could use it. She needed to begin re-wrapping, as she was going to use the most elaborate herringbone wrap that she knew. It would require extra binding. She lifted the baskets to the table.

The weave she intended to do was one that had four angled points running side by side up the body. She'd practiced it on a number of smaller animals she'd not used with her basket, using almost thread thin strips of cloth. It was too elaborate to perform for anyone she'd known, even Meelac, as it required plenty of cloth, but wrapping was something she did well, be it for a small animal or human. She was glad to gift her skill to the queen.

She quieted her mind and began at the head. While she let her fingers work, she could examine the body as well.

Working on the wrapping, she allowed details of the queen's body to rest in the back of her mind to be reviewed later. The first surprise was the hair. It had been hacked short, which surprised Cemirowl as it had been commonly understood that the queen had left it long, choosing to uphold a more Hergilan custom. She decided that long hair would have suited the queen; this hacked cut was an insult to Tidyri and added a depth of sorrow to Cemirowl's task.

The second shock was a line that incised the queen below the breast to her navel. It was sewn back together with red thread. She paused. Was this the murderous wound? It might not be. She saw the same salt from the four jars peeping out of the wound. Salt, especially this intense mineral used here, she guessed, would halt some of the messy, wet decaying process. She believed this was to ensure that her body could last the long days before she could be buried, beyond the few things she'd read about that would help delay decay. The liver, lungs, stomach, and intestines were among the first to decompose. Cemirowl knew that these internal organs caused bloating, which would not make for a pleasant body a few days later. But if she was killed with a knife, it may have been disguised by this incision.

The third, found later, was the cord of light greens of new life around her waist. One was light, almost yellow—for hope?—and one tiny thread of protective red. A cord like this bound new life within a mother. Would a Hergilan woman wear such a Pyrannian symbol of hope under her shift? Most Pyrannian wore a thicker version outside their clothes to gain the goodwill of all who could see. This, then, had been secret.

After a moment's hesitation, Cemirowl cut a knot from one of the ends of the cord that prevented fraying, and put it aside. She retied it, knowing it was too late for the cord to do its job. She shook her head, and went on with the final part of the wrapping. She began the other part of her work.

While working on finishing the wrapping and allowing the physical details to be stored in her memory, Cemirowl looked to the realm of the dead, focusing on the queen. Cemirowl had the sense that one thought, idea or communication from Tidyri's spirit pressed on her mind, yet it continued to elude her. She could gain no clear concept of this echo except that there *was* one.

Her hands worked, slick with golden oil and resins that saturated the cloth, as she tried to listen to what the elusive thought might be.

Assumptions are the demise of intuition, she reminded herself as she finished the wrapping at the queen's feet. There was an art to finishing the wrap so that it would not unravel. If she did it well, then others would find it difficult to unwrap the body as easily as she had unwrapped their earlier effort. She would challenge any well-paid wrapper to find where she began and where she'd ended. She exulted in a skill she could be proud of.

She bowed her head. *I honor you my queen,* she thought and knelt beside the table.

She closed her eyes. Laying her hands on the wrapped body of the queen, Cemirowl breathed slowly and concentrated, focusing and centering. When she felt ready she allowed the thought to come.

There was the queen, raging in grief. Tidyri's spirit did not know what had killed her. The strongest impression Cemirowl received was that Tidyri felt betrayed by someone she'd trusted, and had been humiliated while dying. Cemirowl perceived that the humiliation had been driven by revenge, and not only at Tidyri. The queen remained close to the realm of the living because she wanted to protect someone or something. The sense of frustration in being unable to communicate, even to Cemirowl who could obviously see her, hammered itself forcibly in the Bone Reader's head. *That, at least, is clear! Shared too, my queen.*

Cemirowl took a deep breath, ignored her trembling, and went one step deeper in focus. She cleared her mind. After a moment she began to hear more. The ringing words inside Cemirowl's head were still unclear, but she could hear voices. She refused to feel fear and made herself remain calm. Trying hard to hear Tidyri, one word came through: "Child."

The word was more of a concept, the image of a child, the pulsing of a new heartbeat. It was surrounded by the queen's own grief as well as the horror of her own death. Cemirowl shuddered out of that depth of focus, appalled. She staggered back from the body. There had not been one death, but two.

Having seen the secret cord around the queen's slim waist, she should have known!

Taking deep breaths, she realized that she was crying. Trembling as she had when she'd cut her mother's spirit from her body, Cemirowl reached for her curved soul knife she'd put in an inner pocket of her vestments.

The spirits she could sense were not attached to the body in front of her, yet she knew they remained. The child would not find another home if Cemirowl did not do what she did now. It was a priestly mystery and rarely used. Meelac had done it once long before he'd come to her village, admitting that it had been more symbolic than real, at least for him.

She could feel the realm of the dead upon her skin, under her feet like the pressure of air within the lungs of a deep breath. Severing a soul from the body, Cemirowl used both knife and mind upon something she didn't see as much as feel.

Sensing the realm and the 'veil' or boundaries within it, she cut a doorway that led deeper into the shadow realm. The two could find their way to this deeper mystery on their own eventually, but the child was so young and needed help. With Cemirowl's prayers and the same type of pushing away she'd instinctually forced upon her mother, the two went through the opening.

Heart hurting, Cemirowl then closed the opening and sat back on her heels. She forced herself to calm. She did not want the guard to know how shocked she had been, how much she wanted to sob. She brushed tears from her face and noticed her hands. She stared at them for a long time. They were not stained by the dye from the burial windings, which must be the difference between village dyes and castle dyes. But the last time her hands had been clear of stain had been shortly after her mother's death.

Quietly she rose and went to the gallery.

"I'm done," she told the guard. "I would like to walk in some fresh air." Cemirowl wanted to get away from the room and the disturbing news she'd just learned. Had the killer known about the baby so young inside its mother?

She made her way down to the gardens beside the queen's apartments. After a moment she decided she ought to find Mercor and ask him a few questions. She went back to her room to see if Ewan could guide her, if either he or Les were nearby. He was, and waiting by the door with some breakfast.

While Cemirowl ate a sweet, dense roll, and some fruit, she tried to talk with Ewan. She noted his reserve. Yet, he called her priest and did what he could to ensure her comfort. When the servant boy bowed, she realized there was a quiet respect in the tone of his voice and face, matched by his willingness to help her. It was a surprise, and it lifted her heart.

When she was done, Ewan guided her to Mercor's rooms. He was not there and so she gave up that plan. It was possible he was at the chapel to sit in some vigil for the queen. "Ewan, can you tell me how to get to the chapel? I'm guessing you need to return the dishes to the kitchen. I will be well enough at the chapel."

He gave her directions that seemed easy enough.

The passageways were empty, and she guessed that people who had kept vigil in the night were still in bed. Most of the doors

158

to various rooms were closed. She was lost almost as soon as Ewan left her. She stumbled by a half open door that led, clearly, to a hot, steaming bathhouse. She backed away quickly.

She heard Mercor's voice, but in a clearly foreign language.

Another man spoke up. "I will not speak to you in my language here!" The bathhouse carried it easily to her ears. A room in which they expected privacy clearly gave less than what they wished.

"But you need my help," Mercor said.

The foreign man snorted. "You would betray your king?"

"I will not betray King Larthor, but had your father allowed it, you would have been my brother."

"My sister married to a rude, impulsive Pyrannian? Never."

"Your sister wanted to marry me. No matter how much you've come to hate me, we were once friends, and might have been brothers. I won't let you hang for a crime some say you committed on a woman who was your liege's cousin."

There was a snort. "Everyone talks! Even my Lord Itrizeu," the man said in pain even Cemirowl could hear, though they were trying to speak softly. She guessed they would never have had this conversation if they hadn't believed everyone would be abed. "And I was there, or near enough, when she died!"

Mercor said something, again in Hergilan.

"Pyrann!" the other man snarled.

"Amec, please let me help you."

"For the love of my sister you persist—even though it is hopeless?"

"Yes!" said Mercor.

"And my Lord Itrizeu has asked me if I have done this

thing!" Amec paused. "The thing I hate about your people will save me. I will accept your help, whatever you can give."

There was a noise of water splashing over stones, as a small waterfall in a creek. Cemirowl fled. This time she found her way to the garden. She passed one sleepy page, and asked that if he could, would he find Caballier Mercor and let him know she would be in the garden, below the chapel.

So, there is a foreigner who is a suspect in the crime? She wondered if that was what Mercor had held back the night before. She knew that now she had to find out who the suspects were!

She paced through the garden, feeling pensive and out of sorts. She pondered what she'd overheard, and felt very guilty for having eavesdropped. When Mercor found her, his hair was still damp from his bath.

"Did you get any rest?" he asked her.

"Not much. I woke early."

"You seem upset," he said, after they had been strolling in the dawn lights for a few moments.

"I went to see the queen. The king was right, she'd had great joy for the day. It was a sad thing for her to be taken out of life at this time," Cemirowl said.

He said nothing. She wondered if he'd heard. He did not ask more. She was glad he was not curious, and wondered if she'd said too much, if he was helping one of the suspects. To her sorrow, she still needed this caballier. She knew, however, that his loyalty must lay with his foreign friend, and not with her. She would have to practice at reserve—which she had already done poorly at. Still she required information. There would be time to put up a better reserve.

Hesitant, she asked, "Can you tell me... how was the queen

killed? Except for what was necessary for this burial..." she paused. He had been to war; surely he knew what happened to bodies left too long unburied. "I would like to know, was she poisoned?"

"From what I understand, that is the best guess. We do not know with what poison, however."

Cemirowl nodded. She thought about the queen's body and the hair. Questions were all that she had at the moment, and Mercor's good will. Hopefully he still needed her. "Caballier, I understood that the queen chose to keep her hair long. Was it cut for the burial?"

"No, she was found that way. At least, I remember seeing her that way."

Thinking on the past hour, Cemirowl decided that the queen's spirit had been attempting to convey that the hacking off of her hair had been the disturbing humiliation she'd experienced. Cemirowl wondered why it had been an attempt at revenge.

The two continued to walk along the winding path of the garden. Now that he was here, she did not know what to ask him. Cemirowl scraped fingernails on the pads of her thumbs. It added a soft rasping and flicking sound to the crunching of feet upon gravel while her thoughts revolved around the many questions in her mind.

Mercor only walked beside her and waited for her to speak, yawning from time to time.

Before Cemirowl considered how and which poison had been administered to the queen, she wanted to know why someone would have thought that hacking Tidyri's hair would be important enough to risk discovery. It had been the return of the ladies that had led to the discovery of the body. If the Ladies

Terria and Soflia or even Lady Harlyn had returned sooner, they would have seen Tidyri's hair being cut. Even dying, the queen must have put up some sort of struggle to prevent it, unless symptoms of the poison had stopped her.

Cemirowl stopped walking and put a hand toward the knight, "Caballier Mercor, would you do me a favor? I need help."

He stopped and turned toward her. "Of course. I'll try. I was wondering if you'd had any questions."

"Would you find out what the queen and Priest Ferran argued about before her death?"

Cemirowl, from her experience of the man, believed that the Honorable Ferran preferred philosophical discussion, even heated ones, but she had a general idea that others were not as sanguine.

"Of course," he said, and seemed surprised that she had not asked anything more difficult.

"Thank you. I have slept little. I would like to return to my room and rest. No doubt you also have preparations to make for tonight's burial. I must not keep you. I am not good company. I'd wanted to ask more, but now... I feel merely foolish and slow."

"The company is fine," he said with a smile. "But indeed, I do need to consult with the king's office and that of the ambassador and prepare for the burial. I will do as you ask at the earliest convenience," he said with a graceful nod.

Cemirowl could see that he wanted to say more but Cemirowl stepped back. He subsided, bowed, turned and left. His right hand gripped the pommel of his sword tightly, gravel flew from his brisk feet.

She made her way back to her room, guided by directions from different pages, valets and grooms.

As she was passing the doorway to Arthan's chambers, she stopped short. Again Cemirowl felt the presence of a ghost calling out. Her mouth felt strange, and she felt a sudden rush of cold as if she were about to be ill. Unlike Tidyri's spirit this one was still tied to its body. It was in the hall, but when she focused she could not follow it for it had disappeared. In the lingering echo brushing against her, Cemirowl sensed that the spirit was searching for someone or calling out for help as if lost. As it faded further, she paused, trying to see if there was anything else she could discover about it.

A lady walked past, moving down the hall toward her room. She was speaking to her servant. "We will only be here a little longer. My father has rented us a villa above town, where we can finalize the wedding. I think it is Harlyn, only, who is more pleased to go home than I. She misses her friends from the northeast, and whatever hopes she'd had are all gone."

Cemirowl followed behind, with less guilt as she was headed in the same direction.

"Did she hope much here, my lady?"

The woman shook her head. "No, despite declining the marriage offered her, she did miss her friends. After each letter from her friends, that's all we'd hear about... or another maudlin song!"

"Sad songs are well, for mourning, are they not, my lady?"

"Of course, though not the love ones."

Cemirowl reached her door, and noticed that the lady went to the room next door. She went inside, and shut her door. She wondered if this was Terria or Soflia, and if so, had they put the button bloom in her box of tea? The more she thought of it, how would the person who put it there know she'd be making tea for herself? It was a chancy thing to do.

There was a knock. It was Ewan. "Is there anything you need, my lady?"

"Ewan, tell me about the barracks-like room I saw in this court. The guards have rooms there, correct?"

"There's one here, but there are barracks throughout the palace, and even more to the east. Guards, and archers and other defenders of the keep under the marshal of the guard's orders live in them, unless their rank allows them private chambers."

She saw the gleam in his eye. "I think you'd like to be a caballier!" she teased.

"Perhaps." He grinned at her. "But if I'm lucky I can become an archer," he said, looking wistful. It was unlikely, but not impossible for a peasant to rise in rank due to service.

"I know they must practice the arts needed for war... do you know if they fight amongst themselves?"

"Of course! Lord Marshal has had to break up at least two fist fights this past month, already! I still think that Sir Gorran had the upper hand of Sir Plausen, no matter what my friend Tellen thinks!"

"Where did they fight?"

"Oh, by the stables."

"Has anyone fought inside, near here?"

"Oh, years back, I think."

She paused, thinking gloomily. Trying to identify the ghost wasn't as easy as she'd hoped. As Meelac had been fond of saying: *Well, then, fish never jumped onto a hook either.* "Perhaps my thoughts are gloomy this day," she said aloud. "Do you know if anyone died in those fights?"

Ewan shrugged. "I think Sir Ruge's page Elern died

cleaning the wrong end of a crossbow, but that was long ago, and I also heard he died from a bad case of itch-spot," the boy offered.

Well, it was an answer. Even though she believed that the spirit might be that of a woman, it was good to know that. She could rule out other possibilities.

He asked if she needed anything, and she asked for a pitcher of clean water and some more food. He ran off as Les came with her arms full of clothing.

"I brought you these, ma'am. Privileges of a guest and in honor of your being clergy," she said with a smile.

Cemirowl was surprised. "How kind! Who am I to thank?" she asked as she added the knot from the queen's cord to her bone basket and covered it back up.

Les shrugged her shoulder. "The lord or ladyship probably asked their lord or lady, who asked their gentleman, who asked their valet, then their valet, who in turn asked their servant, and then the groom who came to find me and let me know I could bring these to you," Les said laughing. "I was given thread and needle to help you fit into them."

Cemirowl sighed. She'd wanted solitude, but looked at the piles of clothing in the girl's arms. The dresses were in colors suited to the clergy and more ornate than any she'd ever worn. One by one, Les showed them to her. Among one or two were some garments Les called day dresses she could never imagine working in. She looked ruefully at her best gown, and then at her sleeves of her vestments showing signs of the oils in that morning's wrapping. At least they weren't stained red. The glittering vestments in Les' arms had never met funerary oils or cheap dyes.

"Where did you get all these?"

"Storage rooms here and in the chapel building. The seamstresses and ladies make clothing throughout the year to give to the servants at festival time or need. The palace takes care of the chapel, as clergy women are often too busy to do women's work. There are some that didn't fit the person they'd been made for because they'd grown too large, but they'll probably fit you. They always make extra so that the servants are well dressed. We've had some priestesses serving with Ferran but they have since moved to other churches or cloisters."

"I feel privileged. We can work on fitting them later."

"But I'm to get you fitted for the burial. I was to give you a message that you're to attend."

"By whose request? I thought only those closest to the queen would be allowed."

"I believe the Lord Steward Bartemo requested your presence. At least, his valet Nathe himself told me to pass on the request."

She sighed. "Les, I really need time to think."

"Well, let me pick out a dress for you and we'll fit it to you. You can think while I mark the fitting, then I can leave you in peace till you're needed. Ewan will wait outside and let you know when you need to meet the others as well as tend to any errand you wish."

Cemirowl murmured thanks. The girl helped her off with her clothes till Cemirowl was in her shift. She sat on one of the chairs near the fire, and let Les tend to the job of choosing the dress while she thought of her own tasks.

Cemirowl knew that the queen had not cut her hair. Was the reason Queen Tidyri's hair had been hacked due to any reasons a woman here might have? Or were there other implications in the queen's former country suggested by the cut hair? Honored Ferran, she understood, might have wished for the queen to do so for conservative religious reasons in honoring marriage. Would not such a gesture be silly *now*, either by choice or by force?

Even Cemirowl could see that by not cutting her hair when she'd married, the queen maintained ties to Hergila. Of course Cemirowl could not say how politically important that might be. Sir Mercor might be able to tell her.

Either way it was possible that cutting the queen's hair was an act of breaking those ties, religiously or politically. There might have been more to the act or possibly even less. Revenge or humiliation? The revenge to hurt the king? She was a queen, and a child did not change it as an act against the state. Even the baby was a political entity who would one day act with little thought to his own pleasure, but of his country. But what did Cemirowl know?

Cemirowl felt her ignorance keenly. She had not spoken to the king, except in pastoral care, and did not know how much of her own fate hung on her ability to find the queen's killer. It seemed preposterous. *You're just a village Bone Reader and Priest not marshal of the guard and horse!* She could entertain herself with speculation like everyone else in the palace was probably doing. She had nothing better to do except wait for the king to judge her with treason and execute her.

Watching Les take her time choosing the gown only added to Cemirowl's exasperation. *Just pick one!* Cemirowl wanted to shout, but it would have been unkind. Les was clearly enthralled and eager to help. So Cemirowl returned to her thoughts, biting a fingernail.

She did not think that merely having an opportunity to cut Her Majesty's hair a motive for murder. It was too silly. But could the cutting be a clue to the motive? Was it secondary? Had the symptoms of the poison created the opportunity to merely add to the degradation of the queen's death?

Les finally picked the dress, and brought it over, but though Cemirowl allowed Les to put the dress over her head, she was too distracted to examine it. She stared at the cup on the table, now cleaned from the grit of charcoal.

Whoever had attempted to poison her last night had not done a skillful job. If murder had been intended last night then how would the person know that Cemirowl would be the recipient of that particular infusion? It was possible that the person knew little of dosing, or measurement. What if the murder was a mistake? Which meant that the killer was incompetent? Of course, death was an obvious symptom of the poison, but Cemirowl knew that many poisons did not cause death instantaneously. Had she finished the button bloom she would have been writhing in pain for hours before she finally died—if the dose was large enough.

Needing to stand still she asked Les to bring her the box and show her the other restorative infusion bags. They all looked a normal size, but that meant little.

Cemirowl smelled each bag. Carefully she opened each one and drew out herbs to smell. None smelled like button bloom. They did smell like epitonin and another tonic she knew of, but could not recall the name.

"Has anyone else come to my room, besides you and Ewan?" she asked.

"The Caballier Mercor's valet and a groom with a message about your attendance. The Priest Ferran sent a servant who left you a book, there, on the shelf. Lady Harlyn also came and waited for you, but has gone to rest. She said that she and the queen's ladies might come and see you later. That is all I know of. I was gone to eat."

Cemirowl nodded; it wasn't exactly helpful. Anyone could have put the herbs in the box, even before she'd arrived at the castle, or while Les and Ewan were away. She asked to look at the book. It was Reverend Tonn's *Treaties on the Offices for the Dead*. There was a note inside, sealed in wax. She opened it.

Priest, Wrapping was once only the offices of the clergy, not that of old wives. I had not known you had been so well taught. You do great credit to your mentor in the honor you have done our queen. I understand that you also comforted the king last night. As my duties kept me in the chapel, I thank you for the succor you tended to our liege as well.

Forgive my words of yesterday evening. Though I believe divination to still be an error, you show that your ordination was not misplaced. Perhaps we may speak further on this at a later date, after the funeral? As you have already performed sacred duties for our Royal Highnesses, I request your help with the funeral. Despite the sad circumstance, I will be glad to see you perform your ordained duties during this function.

The book is yours if you do not yet own it, with my thanks:

Ferran, Honorable Priest.

She was touched by the letter and surprised. She had not guessed that Ferran would have made such a gesture, certainly not to *her*. Trembling, she struggled to be grateful. She'd wanted to earn his respect. Now she had it—much earlier than expected—and did not know what to do with it. She handed the book to Les who put it on the table. She still had much thinking to do.

Would pregnancy soften the queen's disposition to hair cutting? Had Tidyri cut it herself as symbolic of finally carrying a child that the country and her husband wanted? It seemed unlikely. The job had been too badly done. And the queen was dead. And no one had spoken of the queen's pregnancy. It could not have been a secret for long. Certainly the women wrapping the body would know of the cord—would they assume it was to help her be fertile, or to protect the baby only Cemirowl had seen? The baby had been old enough to begin showing. Surely the death of a possible future heir would have been mentioned. Who could have known besides Queen Tidyri and her ladies? A midwife, surely, and one who might use button bloom!

It was well known that the queen and king were married with great affection. Any prior difficulties with childbearing may have argued for keeping the matter quiet till proof of being out of danger could be given. Who would tell a village priest except a ghost? Had the king known of his child?

Les helped Cemirowl struggle out of the dress. They talked about the rest of the morning, then Cemirowl sat in her chair and thought about the body that had been packed with herbs, spices, and fully soaked with the sweet oils gleaming with gold dust. *Don't even bother about what scents you might have missed,* she told herself. *You weren't there when she died and you already know that it is impossible to hope on that score!* The scent of olibanum—reminding her of the lacquer her father had used on his carvings—came to mind. That alone would have buried any lingering scent besides death and decay.

Next thing: physical symptoms.

Before wrapping the forehead, Cemirowl had checked the

face. The eyes had not been fully closed and the face had looked a little anxious. Opening one eye she had seen that it was also fully dilated. She recalled the other signs that might indicate a poison or means of death. Cemirowl had found neither bruising due to convulsions nor any marks of irritated skin. With all the plants in the country, from flowers, leaf, stem and root—it would be hard to determine only one from the distinct evidence of dilated eyes.

It was little to go on. Cemirowl decided to review her herb lore, center and rest. She slept a good portion of the day, exhausted from hard riding the day before and little sleep.

Les brought her an early dinner. "I hope it's not too early. Many of the greater houses have their dinner later, but the main kitchen is preparing a feast. The queen's parents have arrived by boat."

Clearly Cemirowl was not invited, which suited her quite well. She'd participated in too many events far and away above her rank. It was too much!

"That's fine. I don't mind eating now."

She ate, and wondered what else she could do. There seemed little to do but read the treatise and wait. While the book was interesting, especially the passages describing royal funerals, Cemirowl was tired, and fell asleep on the open book.

CHAPTER ELEVEN

──────────◀◆▶──────────

Cemirowl dreamt of a forest in which her ghostly animals roamed. They hunted and searched for something, and scattered at unseen fears then coalesced into a pack and returned to their hunt. She was dragged with them, their growing tensions ringing like a bell, louder and alarming as the animals' searching grew more frantic.

She awoke with a start. Someone was knocking on the door.

Heart pounding in the shock of coming awake, Cemirowl took a deep breath, went to the door and opened it. Lady Harlyn, and two other ladies, including her new neighbor, stood outside. Harlyn glared at Ewan snoring beside the door.

"May we come in?" Harlyn leaned forward, whispering.

She noticed the slight tremor in Harlyn's hands, the blush on her face and the eager light in her eyes. Harlyn wanted a reading. As did the others, apparently.

"Of course," Cemirowl said.

Lady Harlyn introduced the Lady Terria, who wore golds and browns, and Lady Soflia in a rich green. They wore sachets of various flowers. It was as if a bouquet of flowers entered the room.

"Does your room meet your needs?" Soflia asked.

"Yes. Thank you." Of course it did. It was grander than her cottage.

Harlyn moved toward the table. Scent from a sachet wafted from glittering blue skirts. Cemirowl realized in some surprise Harlyn smelled of yellow creeper flowers. It was certainly a common enough plant, and it did have a lovely smell used in many perfumes, but its root was among many herbs that might have been used to kill the queen. Cemirowl would need to know more about the state of the body when it had been found: what it smelled like, its color and how clammy the queen's skin had been. Even if it had been early spring, when most women wore crowns of the flower in their hair, under the circumstances it was not a flower Cemirowl wanted to smell rising from the gown of a lady.

But there were plenty of other choices for the poison that might have killed the queen. As she began to list them in her mind, Cemirowl gestured toward the table and chairs.

"Please be seated," she said, remembering that at the moment they were her guests.

Despite the confident movement with which Harlyn had entered the room and possessed the chair, her hand trembled on the tablecloth and her eyes glittered with need. Cemirowl was still groggy, unhappy, and did not want company. However, giving the ladies readings might offer her an opportunity to learn more about the queen's day. If readings were best understood by a questioner's context, so might a murder be.

Already knowing the answer, Cemirowl asked, "Is there something that you need?"

Harlyn leaned forward on the chair, looking both determined and scared. "I was wondering, I mean would you... I understand that you're here on another errand, but I wanted to know if you would give us a reading from your bone basket? You did bring it?"

"Certainly, if you are willing to exonerate me and give payment. But readings are usually private. Do you want your friends to hear what the Bones might tell you?"

By the way they looked at each other, this thought had crossed their mind.

"We can wait in my rooms; they're only next door," Soflia said, clearly relieved.

"Very well, ladies, who will be first?"

Terria stood. "I'd like to try."

Harlyn and Soflia left.

Terria came to sit at the table, where Cemirowl gestured, bringing the bone basket as she sat down.

"Please, don't think us as frivolous. We have little to do, and we're all uprooted. The queen's parents are resting before the funeral. We need distraction... and frankly a sense of peace before the burial—not only from having been questioned by Marshal Buce, but..." she paused, and wrung her hands. "For my part, I know that the queen and I parted on sad terms. I want to know she's at peace."

Cemirowl nodded. It wasn't the first time people made such a request—though in the village they had a far better idea that she might be able to see their loved ones and wouldn't bother asking for a reading from her bone basket. It was one reason why she tended to leave as quietly as she could at most of the village funerals, as she normally denied those requests. This time, Cemirowl wanted answers.

She brought the bone basket out, humming her little tune

to call the spirits of the animals from the basket. She watched them gather round her, swirling around her skirts.

Terria gave her money and her exoneration. As she moved, Cemirowl smelled a lemon-like herb. More, Terria just seemed clean. She was not dismayed by the bones, and threw them onto the table.

"I want to know if the queen is at peace, despite our argument?"

Cemirowl looked at the bones, but also noticing that her animals were mostly standoffish to Lady Terria, except the dog, who lay down at her feet. The bones themselves seemed far more positive, and yet, looking at an array of various teeth, there was a source of tension—an argument. There was the knot from the queen's protective baby braid that added to the source of tension. Cemirowl wondered about this, and thought about what to do. One thing she knew about the bone basket, and presumably any fortunetelling, was that the questioner often shared more than they planned. Sometimes so much that Cemirowl felt called upon to give pastoral care. Still, Cemirowl decided to push the truth a little.

"I gather you feel a burden about your argument, and a source of sorrow with your queen. A secret you may have been keeping."

"You see that? I'm amazed. Yes, I was keeping a secret for her, or rather keeping her secret. We did not discuss it, and I understood, but... it would have been happy news."

"I gather that it adds teeth to the argument that you had with her," Cemirowl said, pointing out the teeth.

"Yes, we argued not hours before she died. Lady Kahina, of the ambassador's household, loaned me a Hergilan dress to wear at that night's dainty. I wanted to show Sir Quormen as well as our queen my respect for their homeland. Instead of pleasing her, she grew angry."

"I see that. A source of sorrow for her," Cemirowl said. "She felt... out of place?"

"Yes, she still struggled though I hadn't realized how much as she was coping better, and speaking so very well. She said I was not Hergilan, and that I was pretending, as if I were wearing a stage player's costume. But I wasn't! I'd learned how to dress her in her country's clothing—though she often wears Pyrannian dress, here, of late. But after her Hergilan ladies married and returned home, she could not rely on Lady Kahina, or other women of that household, because it might look..."

"As if she were siding too much with her homeland?"

"Yes," said Terria. "She did not want me to learn her language, even when it became clear that Quormen was courting me."

"And the dress?" Cemirowl gestured to the bones, as if it was represented there.

"She asked me to return it."

By the slight tension in the lady's jaw, Cemirowl guessed that it had felt like an order.

"Did the other ladies side with your queen?"

Terria shook her head. "Lady Harlyn was getting another of her headaches. She'd been writing letters to friends back home at the queen's writing and work table. She always had plenty of paper and Harlyn had none. Soflia had been using the other table to lay out cloth for her wedding dress. She hadn't finished, as Ferran had come to speak with her about the ceremonies to prepare her for her marriage."

Cemirowl nodded. She knew in the high church this could get elaborate and involved. The look on Terria's face made her guess that this was added tension.

"There does seem to be more than one man involved." Cemirowl pointed out the one part of the lay she'd already guessed was Sir Quormen. She would, at least, have something positive to say about it.

"Tidyri was already upset with me. I think it added to her anger. Sometimes her understanding of our customs amused her. She laughed at them."

Cemirowl asked, "Are Hergilan ceremonies that different?"

"Yes. Hergilans conduct relations between married men and women very privately. Women often do not eat with men, as their eating habits, using a kind of flatbread to pick up various foods, is a bit messy."

"I've noticed men and women sitting at opposite ends of a room, here."

"Yes, but there, apparently, they will often eat in different rooms. Also they do not discuss relations with men they are not betrothed to."

"Relations?" Cemirowl asked.

Terria blushed. "What they do in private."

"Oh!" Cemirowl blushed as well.

"And Soflia being told what the ceremonies would be by a man... it was too much for her! She laughed, and they all began to argue. Harlyn cried out in pain, finally, and Tidyri shushed everyone. She sent Harlyn off to bed with her potion to help ease her. Harlyn would have been asleep within minutes, and hard to wake, but she would have been able to be at the dainty later. Knowing Harlyn needed sleep, hating that the arguments had gotten too much, and too loud, she ordered us away. I left to take the dress back to Lady Kahina, Soflia went off with her dress cloth to the seamstress, and Ferran stormed off to the chapel. I heard her sending even the pages away."

Cemirowl looked at the bones.

"There is a protective energy about her part of the argument with you."

"Is there?"

"Indeed." And this was true. She waited. And she was rewarded.

"It is difficult at times for Tidyri... was difficult. I know that her anger with me was not only about a perceived pretense on my part. She wanted to spare me the pain she feels all too often here, being far from home and everything she knew."

Cemirowl pointed to the part that she believed to be Sir Quormen. "If it is of any consolation, what I read in the bones does have you discovering a new life and new lands—if you make that choice. There is love there, and you will not be unhappy."

Beyond what she read and added to the reading, Cemirowl knew that Terria was one of those women who would always look to the positive—as she had with the argument. She was too sanguine of mind to be much daunted.

"Thank you," Terria said.

There was a knock at the door, and it opened. It was Harlyn. "May I have my turn? It's getting late, and if we're not careful, we'll run out of time."

Terria stood. "We're done. Thank you, priest."

Cemirowl gathered up the bones, and began to stir the basket.

"Thank you for seeing us!" Harlyn said. "I'll admit, we were all very curious to meet you. With luck you'll soon be sent home, but that would mean we would not have much chance to get a reading from you. Soflia will soon be leaving as will I, back to my friends near my property. Two weeks ago, I received an invitation to one of my best friends who now lives on the western coast! I've long wished to see her, so this is my first, and maybe last opportunity."

"I'm happy to do this for you," Cemirowl said.

"Caballier Mercor mentioned the exoneration. I gladly give it: you do not cause what you read. Here is some money." Lady Harlyn took Cemirowl's hand and put money in it with hasty, jerking movements as if she was afraid, but also eager and excited.

It was a great deal more than Mercor had given Cemirowl and there was something odd in the way Harlyn was offering the money to her. The dismissive flick of the wrist, the confident tilt of her head? No... the look that Harlyn knew exactly what she'd just paid for. Cemirowl didn't think that a reading was worth quite as much as the silver that lay in her hand.

She stirred the bones, and silently asked her animals if the basket was ready. They seemed to affirm, still present from the last reading.

Harlyn asked, "Caballier Mercor told us that he put his hands in the basket of bones. Will I have to do that?"

"The answer is usually more clear if you do." Cemirowl bit her lip. It wasn't true; it was a petty gesture and unfair. Harlyn had been kind to her so far.

Harlyn's lip curled in distaste. "Very well."

If the cant of Harlyn's shoulders, the way she wrung her hands and looked at the basket were any indication, it was a love question. Another one! The last one she'd given had gotten her in quite a lot of trouble. Something in the tension of Harlyn's shoulders told Cemirowl that the lady would not otherwise visit a fortuneteller. The woman was frightened, but whatever her costs the question was probably a 'live or die', 'vital to my happiness' type question of unrequited love. The idea was not as amusing to Cemirowl as it had been in the past.

"You will need to concentrate on the question you would like answered," Cemirowl said, as she straightened the cloth on the table in front of Harlyn. "When you're ready, stir the contents of the basket and then pick up some of them and throw them gently onto this cloth."

"Do I have to tell you my question?"

"No, that's up to you. Sometimes it can help me focus the reading, but it isn't really necessary."

"That's what I hoped," Harlyn said, and immediately began to think on how to word her question.

While Harlyn's face grew determined in her concentration, Cemirowl looked at her ghost animals. The rats didn't mind her, and the crow tried to poke at her ribbons and shiny decorations on her wrists and in her hair.

When Harlyn finished thinking of her question, she looked at the basket on the table, unable to meet Cemirowl's eye. Harlyn bit her lip, her face a little green. She hesitated, her hands trembling over the basket for a moment. Breathing out a short moan, Harlyn thrust her hands into the basket of bones. She stirred the contents. With both hands she picked up a good pile and then threw them onto the cloth.

"Is that sufficient?" Harlyn asked, rubbing her hands on her dress.

"Yes, indeed," Cemirowl replied, thinking that her petty

gesture had backfired, as many of them did. Harlyn had thrown with deliberation and intent despite her obvious distaste. Cemirowl leaned forward and examined the throw.

Well, well, well. It's nice to be right. A question about love. But it was also not hard for Cemirowl to read that this was not a happy throw. The whole reading seemed laced with the humors of melancholy and choler. There was hardly a sanguine moment in it, but for one bit of relief—and that of a man happy in his escape.

Cemirowl's diaphragm tightened. Personally, she would have stirred the bones again. Even the animals showed their discontent. The cat prowled. Cemirowl could even hear its growl. She wanted to bite her lip, push herself away. She swallowed as discreetly as she could. This reading would not be fun. She was quite prepared to lie again, pushing what she saw to a great degree to allow for entertainment rather than truth. Her stomach roiled, but she could not give the girl a happy reading.

"This is a love question. There is a man who has been led away from you because of duty."

"You can see that?"

"Yes, you see how these bones are laid out, this away from this pile?" Cemirowl pointed to a grouping with a vertebra she knew was from the neck of an adult blackbird that used to sing outside her cottage. Near it lay some bones from the paws of a dog and a raccoon. They all seemed scattered in a pattern flowing away from the pile of pack rat bones that Cemirowl knew represented Harlyn.

What she didn't tell Harlyn was that though duty divided the two, the dog rib curled protectively around the grouping showed that duty was a relief to this unnamed, passionate, vocal man who'd needed touch.

"I believe you wish to know if he's coming back to you?" Cemirowl asked. The way Harlyn was gripping the table and leaning forward, it was the most obvious question.

"I do. I need to know if he loves another, and that's why he's stayed away. I want to know how he feels about me!"

"He's not coming back." To Cemirowl's relief, the man's duty gave Cemirowl an opening to fudge the truth. "Duty prevents him."

"Then he loves me, despite duty?"

It was not merely looking at the bones, but Cemirowl could also see the whole affair written plain on her face. Despite the desperate hope etched on Harlyn's face, Cemirowl could only think, *There is no comfort in these bones,* and felt the weight of it on her shoulders. Her own face crumpled in sympathy.

She looked at the bones, at their echoes of feeling and action. Harlyn wanted a declaration of his affections or even intentions. Not getting them from the object of her affection, she wanted them in the bones, which was foolish. Cemirowl could not tell her some of what she read in the bones. They were far too contrary to the lady's obvious hopes. Instead she looked up and said, "Even if he has not said a word, what do his actions tell you?"

"Oh! That he does! I know what he has done for me! He has gone to great lengths to subdue his own honor for me."

No help there. The bones said there were ties of foolishness and desperation—on both sides. Cemirowl could see by Harlyn's face that it was not just the actions of the man which might have encouraged this belief. Harlyn needed to examine other actions. "And what of other signs. What actions has he not done that a lover should?"

The rims of Harlyn's eyes pinked up, and her eyes glittered

with tears in the flickering light. Otherwise, the lady controlled any further signs of emotion.

Cemirowl asked, "I take it you met here, at court?"

"Yes," Harlyn said, hesitant and nervous again.

Cemirowl smiled as encouragingly as possible. "Perhaps I'm wrong, but I imagine that court life gave you plenty of time to meet?"

The look on Harlyn's face made Cemirowl realize how sensitive a topic she'd touched upon. She ought not to have mentioned it for the same reasons she wouldn't tell Harlyn that the man was relieved.

"Naturally," Harlyn said slowly.

Cemirowl nodded, feeling clueless, grasping for information. "What are the duties of a lady?"

Harlyn shifted regally. "There are a good deal of duties! I kept the queen's room in order, supervised valets who tended her room, kept her dresses clean. We were her companions and helped teach the castle children, embroidered, read, and hunted together." The words came out clipped and short. "I was not long enough in her service to work with the treasurer for her jewels, or as her wardrober." Harlyn's eyes slid away. "Tidyri chose to have Soflia perform that duty when Lady Amaris returned to Hergila."

Cemirowl nodded, looking at the bones. Harlyn's proud words had turned bitter, but there was a great deal of grieving swirled into the mess of the throw. Choler was often a normal response for people who'd lost a loved one and this would no doubt be true for the one that had been murdered. As Tidyri was still unburied, there was still a great deal of grieving Harlyn would have to do.

Well, better not mention the grieving, Cemirowl thought,

the death, or the child in this reading. Why is the child in there? Did Harlyn know the queen was pregnant? But the green knot from the cord was not there. *And the frozen quality makes me think on the symptoms of the body. But wasn't Harlyn there when the body was found? And this is about her own sorrows, not that of the queen's murder.* Cemirowl reproved herself. She was confusing a possible physical symptom of poison with Harlyn's reading. She drew her focus back to Harlyn's reading. *This must be the grieving. And perhaps not being able to let go of a love who not only cannot have her, but will not.*

"What do my duties to the queen have to do with the reading?" Harlyn asked, interrupting Cemirowl's thoughts.

"Oh! Forgive me. I'm just trying to understand about court life. It's foreign to me. It might help give me the... the words to make the reading more clear. For instance, in the village we don't have water that runs inside a courtyard or building. I've never seen a fountain."

Indicating two parallel small leg bones that were obscured by a mole's pelvic bone, she added, "Or like this. A passage, I'd call this, or a hallway. If we were in my village I'd probably think this was a bridge of some sort. Or an alleyway. There are few in Sir Thade's town near my village."

"Passage?" Harlyn's voice was light, but she leaned forward, eyes intent, to look at the bones.

"That's what it looks like."

"So what does it have to do with Ar..." she stopped, coughed and began again, "with my reading?" she asked, wiping her eyes.

"Well, it's metaphoric, I imagine." She pointed to a grouping that was not the pack rat bones, but part of a small rabbit's pelvis. "It shows a woman that moves through a passage. It could be a hallway, which seems a bit silly, or not actually as dramatic as the sense of this reading, so I'd say it was probably a rite of passage to something...?"

"And those might be?" Harlyn breathed.

"Grief. But the grief could be there merely because of what you and the court have just gone through. I'll admit that readings do not often have a time line."

The look on Harlyn's face said that it wasn't enough. Frustrated, Cemirowl thought, *I see mercenary motives through here.* She said to Harlyn, "The passage is part of it perhaps compelled by this man's duty."

Cemirowl really wanted to focus on this reading. There was so much in there that she'd love to get further into, but Harlyn was not in the right state of mind. Cemirowl would have to do it alone. That small, intense pile representing the man hid so much intriguing information: grief, anger, denial and this need for comfort all bound together in one man. Who was he?

"Duty keeps him away? To whom? The king or the queen?" Harlyn spat out the words. "I'm so glad I was going to visit my friend, regardless. To get away from here. Now it's all terrible."

Surprised by this burst of emotion, Cemirowl looked up, feeling guilty. She wasn't saying as much as she usually did for a reading. Harlyn was looking away, her jaw and shoulder tight with tension. Cemirowl could see she was ready to cry. She felt she had to give her something. "Perhaps it was your duty to the queen that kept him away?" she asked, knowing that it wasn't true. It was *his* duty, not Harlyn's that drove the wedge. "Or perhaps duty to the king?"

Cemirowl bit her lip. The words had slid out of her mouth,

despite knowing it would be painful. *And she's only been kind to me!*

"You say that there is no chance he's coming back? After all..." Harlyn waved her hand, shaking her head.

Harlyn had exonerated her. "Forgive me. No." Had it been someone else, Cemirowl might have touched her glittering, embroidered sleeve in a gesture of comfort.

"Even after all the time spent in making him *prove* that he loves me? The other actions, even lack of actions...? They cannot matter. So you are saying that even had the path been cleared, he would not come back?" Harlyn asked, leaning forward, her hand gripping the table, wrinkling the red cloth on which the bones were laid. There were tears glistening in Harlyn's eyes, but her face was determined.

Cemirowl took a deep breath and looked at the bones. It wasn't there. Love was completely lacking. On both sides. Passion, grief, need were there. *Rat-bones; I'd be relieved too.*

"No. I'm sorry." There was no glimmer of hope to offer.

Harlyn turned to her, her lips a line of white, her eyes hard. Then Harlyn suddenly relaxed. Clearly some internal decision had been made. Cemirowl hoped that it was acceptance, though the line of her mouth was still bitter.

"So is there anything else you want to know about court life?" Harlyn said. "You must be feeling very out of place."

"Yes. You mentioned your duties, I'd like to know more about them. I understand that you were ill, but the queen herself, did she look unwell before you left? How long was she alone before she was found?"

"You're here to divine the cause as well as her murderer. Has not your art already told you this?" Harlyn asked, surprised.

She moved, her face turned away from Cemirowl, but Cemirowl still caught an amused look in her eyes.

As lightly as she could manage, Cemirowl said, "As I've said before, my art is not that clear."

Without turning to Cemirowl, Harlyn smiled. "Yes. That would be a problem for you."

"Your help might confirm some of my impressions."

Harlyn thought for a moment.

"The queen was feeling a little unwell, perhaps, but she had a tonic her midwife made for her to steady her courses. I don't know if she took it. The infusion I take often makes me sleep quite hard, but it's a relief from pain. I only woke when I heard Terria and Soflia screaming. But I gather that while Lord Marshal Buce has questioned us, Ferran and a few others, no one knows who was with her when she was actually dying."

Something nagged at Cemirowl. She looked at the bones scattered on the cloth. *The child!* There was this child, shown by the blue, speckled fragment of the eggshell and the rabbit's pelvis bones. She closed her eyes, thinking of what she'd learned just that morning.

She opened her eyes and asked, "Do you know the queen's midwife? I'd like to speak with her."

"Abenne? Why?" Harlyn asked. "Surely you do not need one!"

Shifting in her chair, Cemirowl responded, "Because I also work with herbs and healing. Having the larger libraries and broader education of the king's city, she may know of herbs I do not." It would be an interesting discussion, and she would not mind improving her knowledge of herbs. But Cemirowl's source for medicinal herbs was the woodland, and sufficient for being gathered fresh.

Cemirowl waved her hand over that poor broken egg fragment and the crushed skull of the baby mouse, with one of its ribs sticking out of it like a tiny cudgel. She could still see the queen's fetus's ghost in her mind, and clenched her jaw. It had nothing to do with the queen, but Harlyn's reading reminded her of questions best asked elsewhere.

"Yes," Cemirowl said. "I think the midwife might have some information for me." Such as: Did she carry button bloom? And other herbs that could be poisons?

"Actually we haven't seen her in days. Soflia was going to ask her about something that would ensure her fertility for when she got married. But perhaps you can ask Arthan."

"The prince? Why would he have need of a midwife? Isn't his wife deceased? I thought..."

Harlyn's smile was arch. "Abenne served his wife upon birth and on the deathbed, but a passionate man like that? I have reason to believe he's called upon her services since."

It was an uncomfortable moment, and Cemirowl felt a blush rising. By the archness of the lady's face, Harlyn could not have embarrassed Cemirowl more by showing off her undergarments. Under Harlyn's amused glare, Cemirowl dropped her gaze to the reading.

It occurred to Cemirowl that the ladies who served the queen would have access to the midwife—clearly as Soflia had wished to consult with her. She could guess that a murderer would not have as ready access to Abenne's herbs and potions, and would wish to keep their contact with her quiet.

Perhaps there was more to this reading, after all—perhaps not about the murder. If Harlyn could leave, then Cemirowl could look deeper into the reading and learn more. There was more to read, even in the emotions underlying what had already been noted.

Something banged against the door, and Harlyn gasped and leapt out of the chair.

"Please don't let anyone see my reading!"

Cemirowl was surprised. Harlyn seemed almost terrified. She was white, in fact.

"Certainly."

Cemirowl began to cover the bones with a cloth, but Harlyn stood and gathered up the bones and other delicate objects and tossed them in the basket. Defeated, Cemirowl put the basket back on the shelf. As soon as it was put away, Harlyn opened the door to Ewan and a few other pages. Soflia also stood at the door.

"I see that you are to be made ready for the funeral. Perhaps I can have my reading later?"

"Of course."

"I only want to know if she is at peace."

"I can tell you now. Yes. Whatever lingering fear or anger she had, she is at peace now."

Soflia smiled, her eyes grief laden still. "I'm glad. We fought, but we'd always made up and understood each other better after. I never had the chance to resolve our argument."

"Yes," said Harlyn, her eyes suddenly rimmed in red. "All arguments were resolved with Tidyri. It was, perhaps, one of her greatest gifts. She disliked her rooms being a place of upset."

The two ladies said goodbye, and left. Cemirowl understood the differences in the questions the women had asked. Of the three, Harlyn had not argued with Queen Tidyri before her sudden death. Instead Tidyri had shown her care and attention.

She, alone, was free to ask about love.

The pages began bringing in large copper ewers of hot water to fill her tub.

Les came in with a dress and said, "For your bath, before the funeral."

With her thoughts swirling in her head, Cemirowl let Les help her to prepare after the boys had left. Bathing before ceremony had never been this luxurious. Times before, even in winter, she'd washed in the stream near her house, freezing alone in the cold water, or in the hip bath when she could fill it with water. Les scrubbed her back, her hair, combing out the tangles. Together they tackled her fingernails. Rinsing herself with water kept warm beside the fire, Cemirowl realized that the water had been infused with balsam bowl and grace herb. She'd used the last of Meelac's precious supply of balsam at his funeral. She did not think he could ever have afforded a supply that could infuse *bathing* water.

Cemirowl was even more stunned when she finally noticed the dress. "I've never seen anything so lovely!"

"You did my lady, when I fitted it to you," Les said with a laugh.

"Oh. Perhaps I was a little distracted?" There had been so many dresses Les had shown her, but she'd not picked this one out of them!

Les laughed again. "We worked on it, and when you might have had more opportunity to notice it, I had reversed it so I could mark it for sewing."

"How would you have the robes of office for a priest, though? I doubt Ferran would wear something so clearly made for a woman."

"He had a cleric working with him here at the castle, as I mentioned before. She took vows of solitude and went to the cloister outside the city before this could be given her. I'm glad I found it. One of the chapel maids helped me find it. At the moment you and Honored Ferran are the only ordained priests in the castle. The rest of his staff are still in training. The others were the basic clergy gowns that even Ferran's current clerk, Roal, could wear but are certainly too dull for a queen's burial."

It was an astonishing thought as Cemirowl realized that the king's household actually spent time and money clothing those people under his roof. "But would clergy wear anything this... this... elaborate?" Cemirowl asked, nervously.

Les chuckled. "At high days and festivals, I've seen Honored Ferran wear vestments worked even more elaborately than this!"

The dress was the color of dried blood, almost a brown. It did not clash with her hair. A pattern was embroidered in the red cloth. The four circles of the different realms or the baser humors were worked in black. Thin lines of gold swirled through each circle. The center diamond was in raised gold threads. Around the wrists and collar these centers were sparkling with tiny gold beads. Along the forearms, three lines of tiny bright, red stones had been sewn over the gold thread at each corner.

"Sanguine, center, be at peace, be with the One," Cemirowl murmured to herself, and then something struck her.

"Gracious Gates!" Cemirowl said, shocked, realizing that these were not glass or painted. "She must have been well loved! Are these... these can't be..." she stuttered as Les laced the wrists. She tried not to tremble. *Charlatan. Fraud. Imposter.* It was hard to remember that she'd earned her ordination.

"I put those on today, as well as the gold beads, while the seamstress, Hen, shortened the gown and tightened the sleeves. They are real gold and real rubies. Oh! I forgot! I was supposed to tell you! They are a gift, in honor of your office, as well as this comb, but the deliverer forgot to tell me from whom they came— and I did not see any colors of any particular household. I had thought Lord Bartemo might have tended your invitation and the dresses, but I do not think so. I do not believe he keeps a collection of rubies. His lady would never wear such a comb. She tends toward silver and blue. No matter, you will look lovely in this," Les said, prattling as she worked.

Cemirowl's heart clenched. She would never be able to wear this in Soft Water. Perhaps she needed to move into town, but went pale at the thought. Surrounded by the noise of people and the murmur of spirits, she would go mad.

Tears pricked her eyes. She would wear it once, in honor of the queen.

"What are we going to do for the surcoat?" Cemirowl asked. "Mine will look wretched with this!"

Les laughed. "It comes with a gored overdress, much better for a lady than a man. If I have my way, I'll see that you never again wear that masculine surcoat you wore yesterday again!" She picked it up and put it over Cemirowl's head.

"It looks like a surcoat to me, or a more elaborate tunic!" said Cemirowl, seeing it laying across the end of her bed.

"Faw! This is much more suited to the female form than a belted tunic or surcoat!"

It did fit her better. "I imagine I look like both a woman and a priest, for once."

Les laughed.

The black overdress had also been worked with the four circles, but along the sides, done in gold thread. At her breast was a larger design symbolic of the four gates, with the center embroidered in gold. Four lines, starting at a ruby, rayed from the center, between the circles.

"And the gates are opened," said Les, catching Cemirowl's eyes away from the dress.

Les wound her hair in gold and black ribbons, bringing it up behind her head and binding it in a thick roll at the nape of her neck. She secured it with a comb decorated with the same symbol as on the front of the dress.

"I've never worn anything this fine," Cemirowl said, shaking. "Les, to be honest, I'm not nearly as rich as even you! At the very least you are fed better than I am. What am I doing here? I've never been this... honored! I'm a village priest that reads bones to make spare money."

She sat down on the bed, shaking her head.

"My lady, you must be more than that. You comforted the king, and honored the queen. Hen's sister is one of the castle wrappers. She said that you did a much better job than they had, and in a shorter time. She'll probably come looking for you when the king has finished his business with you. I think Hen said that Fenna wanted to know where you started and where you finished, or something about 'How did she hide the closure?' or something like that," Les said, kneeling in front of Cemirowl, looking up into her face.

Cemirowl shrugged her shoulders and wiped her tears. "Don't you think I'm... uncanny?" she asked.

"I don't know you well enough. I may just be a daughter of a city varlet but I think that you are frightened of people."

193

Cemirowl snorted a bitter laugh. "I always thought that they were frightened of *me!*"

"I have only seen your kindness. You don't even want to burden me with work, though I am here to serve you," she laughed. "I suspect that even when you are doing acts of kindness or performing your office, you rarely look upon the recipient without fearing that they will hurt you. If you fear them why would they not fear you?"

"But I was called here because..."

"I know why you were called here. You see things that others do not. But I've lived and served ladies that can read, discuss philosophies, and talk about lands I'll never see. I could live my life in envy. Actually I'm rather wistful."

"Wistful?"

"Yes. I want to see what they see," Les said softly.

"If I'm here long enough, I'll teach you to read, if you like. My father taught me."

Les laughed. "I'd like that. But it is more than the reading, it is the understanding of things that are not in my hands."

Cemirowl looked at the girl for a long moment. "Les, I suspect that you see more than you give yourself credit for." She paused. "I wish I could afford to keep you with me, long enough— before you feared me."

"Why would you say that?" Les asked.

"My mother died mad. She saw the dead. She could hear them and see them, I suspect, as clearly as I see you. She couldn't tell the difference between the boundaries of one realm and another. Before I was eight I knew how much the villagers hated and feared her. I think she couldn't help it, but she would tell widows about seeing their dead husbands as if they hadn't died, or tell parents of their dead children running around—though their souls had been cut and their small bodies had been wrapped to veil them from ever returning.

"And they fear me, knowing I have that same gift, though I may be more discreet than my mother ever was. I may not tell them that I can see their dead, but they know it. They come to me to help them out of illness, but fear to do so no matter how bad it gets, how close to death they get and no matter how many times I heal them.

"They come to me to find answers Alcon cannot give them—wanting the easy path from what my bones might tell them." She snorted. "I wish I'd never shown Meelac what I was working on. It had started out as a game, using the bones of dead animals I'd found in the forest and had called to me. It was another way of talking to them—but different lays would help me clarify my thoughts."

Les was silent for a long moment, looking at Cemirowl's face. "Did you ever try to hurt the villagers?"

"Not really, no. I sometimes played with their heads—like telling Lady Harlyn that she had to touch the bones to get a good reading. It really isn't necessary."

Les smiled. "That's more mischievous than hurtful. I suspect that it adds to your mystique."

Cemirowl smiled. "I suspect that mystique I have plenty of, swirling around me at this very moment," she said, widening her eyes.

Les did not take the bait to look worriedly around herself, wondering what ghosts might be touching her. Cemirowl suddenly wondered if she could sell the dress and afford to take Les with her, but that would be taking her to a poorer place than this. Here

Les lived better than any of the villagers at Soft Water.

There was a knock at the door. Les went to open it. Caballier Mercor stood outside and gave a quick bow. He told Cemirowl that it was time to go to the chapel.

Chapter Twleve

Arthan entered the chapel. There was pressure in his chest, and his throat and jaw ached. Had there been any other way, he would have avoided the whole scene. He looked at the bare walls and the empty sconces and knew that soon they would be filled with colorful banners. He could not bear to look at the figure lying on the pallet on top of the marble altar, and could not avoid the olibanum and other spices rising from the red-wrapped form. It was almost too much.

He looked at Larthor. There was nothing he could do there, for in ceremony Arthan had his own role to play. He moved near the front to wait. He leaned against the wall, nursing bitter thoughts as the room filled with people.

Though he was here to mourn Tidyri, Arthan took the time to notice the priest Cemirowl when she came in. His gifts had been received, he noticed, glinting on her gown. He watched as she looked around the chapel. He could almost smile. She still wore that stunned, almost fearful expression as her eyes took in the size and simple splendor of the room. As she turned, he saw the comb.

He had avoided looking at the body, to keep his composure. Seeing the comb, his eyes pricked with tears. He could see Boduscia's face framed with curls and combs. Even so, this comb fitted the Bone Reader better than it would have suited the one to whom he'd originally wanted to gift the comb. The sun gleamed against the blackened silver and the bright red of the stones. As the sun lit on her still damp hair, the priest blazed like a sunset moving into the depth of night.

He was glad to see her relax into her role. Tension eased from her small shoulders, and her focus and attention was all to her duty. She must have made a very good village priest.

Arthan allowed himself the smallest of smiles. *I wonder if she knows how much strength she displays when she allows herself to do her job,* he thought. He smiled more as he imagined how her fears and tension would temper that strength, which would surely be wasted on her, no doubt, tiny village.

Lord Curro approached, looking at him strangely. "My Prince, it is good to see you smile again even through your brooding looks, but remember yourself and what we are about this day."

Arthan looked at Curro, with whom he'd shared many an intense debate. He knew that something had changed since the previous night, for he realized that they'd fueled those debates with the hot coals of their individual bitterness. Where once it would have warmed him, now it was unbearable. As politely as he could, Arthan said, "Perhaps I have reason to now remember both wife and queen in joy."

"You are yet too cynical for that," Curro said, with a derisive snort.

"You have reasons to be right," he said, well aware of his former ill humor. He turned to watch Cemirowl bend her head to Ferran's young clerk.

He turned and looked toward the front of the chapel. Whatever Curro thought, Arthan was glad of the gift that the girl's thoughtful words had already given him.

The chapel was already filled with people when Mercor and Cemirowl entered into the vast main room of the church's building.

"I must go. I am to help translate for the queen's mother and father," Mercor said.

Cemirowl watched him leave, again feeling abandoned and out of place. He went to a group of people who were quite clearly foreign. Some of the women wore simple and yet lovely sheath dresses slightly tailored to show that they were women, with deceptively intricate embroidery. Others wore a dress that had what looked like a pleated skirt, with a wrap that covered the top, as well as their hair. Like the women here, hiding their tear stained faces, they also wore veils. The men wore loose pantaloons with long tunics. Distance could not hide the richness of the linen. Cemirowl remembered that while royal, none of the people here were in line to inherit the Hergilan throne, though they were members of that family.

Cemirowl could imagine what Queen Tidyri must have looked like in those style garments. She would have been lovely. As her sense of loss was not nearly that of the family, Cemirowl turned her face away. She wore no veil. Taking a deep breath, she wondered which of the foreign men might be the Amec she'd overheard talking with Mercor. If he was a suspect, would he be welcome here?

I must talk with Mercor, she thought. *It is unlikely that Amec would come to me for a reading. He has greater problems than wanting to know if the queen is at peace or if his love life will improve.*

A young man in plain but well-made robes of a clergyman came toward her. He bowed his head in greeting. "Priest Cemirowl?" he asked.

"Yes," she said.

"I am Clerk Roal. Honored Ferran requests that you stay close to the proceedings, as he would like you to share in the offices for our queen. If you will come with me, I will lead you to your place," the young man said.

She was stunned, but focused on the young man's whispered instructions. She could not deny the truth now; she *had* earned Ferran's respect. He was including her in the royal offices for the dead, the burial. *Good thing I read those passages in Tonn's treatise!* she thought, though part of her duties, according to Roal, were in respect to Hergila.

Cemirowl still felt woefully inadequate, standing near the head of the pallet, amongst the highest ranking in the land. She could even see the prince talking to some lord. Trembling and wanting to fidget, she took deep, slow breaths.

She calmed herself somewhat, for it was only a funeral and she had performed many. It was only that some of the ritual was different. Cemirowl found that the living company was not alone. She felt the ranks of the dead standing by. Even her father's spirit seemed proud and as rich as any of the nobles already displayed.

He was the only one she knew present. She could almost hear him say, "You will do fine, my girl."

Although Cemirowl did not exactly smile, she took comfort in his presence. She did not wish to miss one of the most important ceremonies of her life by concentrating on the dead. Funerals were for the living.

Ferran came through a door on one side of the altar. Much to Cemirowl's relief, his vestments were indeed more ornate than Cemirowl's. He bowed before a votive of the Four-faced Guardian, then moved to where the king knelt on the dais. The knave of the chapel rose up several steps, so that King Larthor could kneel and still look down upon the wrapped body of his queen resting on a marble altar.

On the other side of the queen from Cemirowl, Roal lifted a gold horn and sounded out three notes.

The gathered mourners grew silent.

Ferran opened his palms before the court and said, "We come to honor the life of Queen Tidyri of Pyrann, wife and consort of King Larthor, Princess of Hergila, daughter to the High House of Wrothan and Hailine. Who comes to witness the closing of her gate?"

Cemirowl was awed by Ferran's voice; he commanded the whole room. Meelac had had no need to teach either Alcon or herself how to be heard in the village's tiny chapel. She was impressed.

The ambassador and the queen's parents stood forward as two of their knights lifted banners. On one of the banners a dragon ran rampant upon a field of purple, white gold and green: The High House of Hergila's markings. The queen's mother, with a pale braid falling out of her white gold veil, turned and wept, clinging to one of the women near her.

Queen Tidyri's father spoke. "We to remember our daughter, and represent the High House of Hergila."

The other banner reflected the colors worn by Lord Itrizeu, with a bull reguardant. "I come representing my own house of Wade. I stand for those of her land of birth who could not be here this day." He bowed and stepped back. The two knights took the banners and placed them in sconces along the wall.

Prince Arthan stepped forward naming his house, his knight raising his banner of his couchant swan, collared by a crown, on purple, blue and white. As he bowed low, his knights set the banner in a sconce. Visiting dignitaries stepped forward to remember the queen as well.

The dukes and barons, either who lived in the palace, or who had come for the funeral, came forward and set their banners on the wall. These included the Lords Steward, Treasurer, Marshal of the Guard, and Hall Marshal. Caballiers also came forward representing their own lords or ladies or their own service. Only one name startled her, but she realized it had been Dusavan, not her father's name.

In his turn, Caballier Mercor lifted the banner of his father's land and his squire lifted his. Lady Soflia stood for her father and her house and Lady Harlyn stood for Lord Ross and her own land.

Ferran nodded to Roal, who took up the banner of the church: a red field, with the four circles, the center, and the rays of the open gates.

The Honored Priest Ferran said, "By the name of the church, I give honor, and the peace of the One. But I stand for myself and my own love for the queen, as do the clergy who perform these last offices for her this day." He tied his own small banner of gold and white, bordered in red marked with a buckle to the staff. He bowed toward Cemirowl and Roal, who were not ranked high enough in the church to deserve a banner, including them in the honor they performed. Roal took the banner and placed it beside the votive of the Guardian.

Only then did Cemirowl notice the king's banner on the other side of the statue. It too hung open for all to see. For the first time Cemirowl was able to see the royal rampant and guardant boar, on its field of purple, blue, gold and white: the banner of the king and country.

"Be at peace, be at center, be with the One," Ferran said bowing before the audience. Roal took the horn again and played three notes.

Three musicians moved forward into a gallery high behind Cemirowl. Craning her neck, and turning, she could see one man seated upon a stool, holding a vihuela on his lap, and standing on either side of him, were a flautist and a vielle player, who clutched his instrument to his neck and saluted the audience by touching his bow to his brow. They bowed to the company and proceeded to play a hauntingly simple song in honor of the queen.

The flute and the vielle harmonized in long lingering tones with the vihuela's harp-like chords. Without denying sorrow, there was a sense of celebration, which seemed wholly appropriate: Tidyri would find peace. There was silence when the musicians finished the funerary song.

After a moment, Ferran called to the Guardian of Sanguinity. He spoke in a baritone that echoed the last lingering notes of the flute.

"Four-faced Guardian of the Gates, remember that Queen

Tidyri was not often angry, she was never touched with languor and she brought joy to our king and our land, never sorrow. She worked to be at peace, despite leaving the only home, people and faith she'd ever known. She worked hard to overcome her sorrow, frustration and confusion, working valiantly for the peace of those around her. Let her come through your gates, in peace, at the center, and with the One."

Prince Arthan and the ambassador then came forward and lifted the pallet up. They carried the body down stairs to a tomb carved from bedrock on one side and then echoed in carved, set stone on the other. The king and the rest of the company followed. Mourners made their way to the sarcophagus, weaving through arched pillars that lifted the ceiling high above the crowd. Their hushed voices mingled with the muffled echoes as they moved through the tomb.

Roal had told Cemirowl that three different master carvers and their journeymen had worked night and day to finish the masterpiece of the lid. It represented the crowned queen lying in an ornate gown, with her hands held together upon her chest, and her face peaceful. The carvers had done an excellent job. It certainly looked more alive, resting and peaceful than the body Cemirowl had worked on.

She felt her nose fill. Her skin hummed; the spirits in the hall were also agitated.

More than Meelac's creaking cart, she would always remember the smell of cold stone, dust and the chill of the tomb as death. No longer 'harsh and inevitable,' but cold and final. With the body soon to be sealed into a dark emptiness, Cemirowl felt the vastness of the dead realm, peopled in the thousands, in infinite solitude.

Heart thudding in her chest, she worked to combat her rising hysteria. She took shuddering breaths and willed her legs to not move, to not run in a mad flight to the shadows and all the spirits hiding there. Or away. Running all the way back to her cottage, never to roam again.

"We bring her to the final gate," Ferran said softly, though his voice carried in odd echoes through the chamber.

He nodded to Cemirowl. Still trembling, she moved past Arthan and the ambassador. Her throat and eyes were full with the honor of being present, but also the deep regret that she had never met the queen in life, which she knew would not have been possible.

In the torchlight, the gold and rubies glittered from the sheet covering the body. Cemirowl was called on to honor the Hergilan in the queen. Only a woman could touch her body, if not her husband. A Hergilan woman helped her, as Tidyri's mother moaned. The poor queen was not heavy. They lifted the body into the sarcophagus over the pitch lined rim. She could smell the brazier, where another servant continued to stir the tar pot. The soft bubbling sound grew to fill the encroaching silence.

Cemirowl and Ferran moved to either side of the lid that lay at the foot of the stone coffin. Ferran stood by the chest of the stone carved queen and Cemirowl stood on the other side, by the carving's knees. Four strong knights came forward and together they lifted the lid. The six of them carried it over the sarcophagus and together covered the body of the queen.

There came a choking sound from Larthor, but nothing more. With her hands, still moving the lid, Cemirowl looked at him, but he was controlling his emotions with a clenched jaw. His brother's hand was on his shoulder. Cloth wrinkled under

Arthan's fingers, and his fingernails were white, and his face a bitter scowl. His eyes, when he looked toward Cemirowl, were grim, but he gave her the smallest of nods.

As they finished shifting the lid into place, Ferran said, "She is in the arms of the One."

Cemirowl turned to him. She was close enough to hear his whispered prayer, "Forgive me of my errors, my lady. I wish I had never argued with you on things so pointless! I will miss the sunlight gleaming on your hair," he said. Cemirowl saw that he wept. Silent tears ran down his face, he turned away, moving to the brazier. The servant moved away with a bow. Ferran, alone would finish sealing the queen's final resting place.

Everyone else had turned away, leaving, rising up the stairs to the chapel away from the body of the queen and the tomb.

Chapter Thirteen

⫷◆⫸

Emerging from the tombs, Cemirowl did not know what she would do next. She was tense with the lingering desire for flight. She knew there was to be a meal soon. The timing would be for a dainty, but Cemirowl doubted they would use the term for such a somber night. It would not happen immediately, giving family members time to compose themselves. She did not feel up to twiddling her fingers alone in her rooms.

Mercor was talking to Lady Harlyn, their heads bowed together. There was an intimacy between them Cemirowl did not wish to breach, no matter how much she still needed to speak to him. She looked around for anyone else she dared converse with, but she only knew names of some of the caballiers and the ladies. It did not matter. Even had they been villagers, she would not have attempted to impose herself on them. There was not even a hint in their body language that they needed her pastoral care.

She looked toward Mercor, the only person she felt any degree of comfort with, and watched as he squeezed Harlyn's arm before leaving the room. Cemirowl was about to follow, but was surprised when the prince came forward and spoke.

"Thank you, Priest, for the service you gave the queen," he

said.

She curtsied, feeling awkward, not knowing where to look. "You're welcome, Your Highness."

Her heart was beating rapidly. The pounding in her ears blocked out even the undertone of spirits murmuring around the room. She felt like a dingy sparrow with peacock feathers trapped in a chapel. Her cheeks felt like they blazed.

He inclined his head in response to her curtsey and said, "You were taught your office well in your village. Though I do not approve of the reasons you were brought here, you have carried yourself well despite those reasons, and in the company of people who outrank you. It has been an agreeable surprise within all our grief."

His voice was low, melodious, with a pleasant deepness. Cemirowl wondered if he ever sang. Briefly, she was lulled by the tone of his speech and even thought of lifting her face higher than his shoulder. But then felt the sting hidden in his words.

Cemirowl's nose filled up and her eyes burned with threatened tears. He had looked kind, even a bit hesitant and awkward. For a moment she had been unafraid. Her trepidation rose in a flood, though she could not in honesty say he'd intended to hurt her. Somehow it was the final straw, after two very difficult days.

She curtsied, stammered a "Thank you," and fled.

She pushed past a few gentlemen and ladies, including Terria and Harlyn, whose faces expressed a belief that Cemirowl's behavior was repugnant, which made things yet worse.

Cemirowl went blindly through a door and discovered herself outdoors and into the garden. The wall was nearby. By the light of the sunset she knew that she was on the opposite side of the chapel from the queen's garden. She turned her back to the chapel and went down the path, hiking up her skirts, and letting gravel fly from underfoot.

The path was hedged by evergreens and fruit trees. After a few minutes she saw a stone between in the evergreen hedge, as if another path turned down it. Instead of continuing her flight, she stepped into a nearly hidden garden. It was a circular garden of cooking herbs, ringed by a narrow foot path. She noticed a seat almost hidden in the wall of greenery surrounding the small garden, just to her right. She went to it and flung herself down, gripping the cold stone with her hands.

Cemirowl did her best to calm herself. It was too much: being in a building larger than her entire village, and continually surrounded by the murmur of people and unfamiliar ghosts. She had been handed a ludicrous responsibility and done little toward resolving it. Instead, she'd performed the offices for which she'd been ordained, but for people she'd only heard tales of. Till a few days ago they were almost more mythical to her than any hero in a story and more unreachable than the Guardian of the Gates would ever be.

A few times when the two realms of her sight had clashed, Cemirowl's vision had become blurry, swirling floors and ceilings. Her father had once described the symptoms as vertigo. This felt rather like that. The world she was walking in felt more unreal than the realm of the dead, clashing with the memory of her village life.

I am walking in three realms, she thought, quaking and shivering.

She felt the presence of her animals, swirling at her feet. Suddenly she felt as if the animals shackled her feet and that the ghosts were suffocating her, clinging like cobwebs and dreams. They would tie her to these gifts all her life. There was no escaping them, even if she were to die, there would be no peace from them. They would always be with her.

"Why can't you leave me alone?" she sobbed to herself, aloud, knowing that she'd bound those animals to her.

"Maybe they care about you," said a gentle voice.

She looked up and Prince Arthan stood near the entrance of the path to her left, holding out a large handkerchief embroidered with his crest.

After a moment of hesitation, Cemirowl took the handkerchief and wiped her face as he sat down.

Holding the cloth to her face, pressing it into her eyes with her fingers, Cemirowl could feel his warmth as he sat down beside her. *Oh Guardian, why does* he *have to sit here?* she wondered.

Cemirowl knew that she could not keep her face covered forever and slowly lowered her hands. She turned her head toward him only high enough to look at his knees.

"Who are 'they'?" he asked.

"Excuse me?" she said, looking up at him.

"When I approached you, you were wondering 'Why can't you leave me alone?' I inquire because you were alone at the time."

She was surprised. "What? You've not heard?"

He shook his head and raised one eyebrow; his dark eyes glinted in the evening sun. She realized that, excepting Les, no one in the palace knew that she did more than read bones.

"The dead. I see the dead. I have my dead animals from my bone basket lying at my feet and my father, and grandmother are sometimes nearby," she said, gesturing to them, lashing out at

210

Arthan with her words, daring him to reject her.

Arthan looked at her surprised for a moment, then his eyes grew sad and drifted away from her.

"Do you see more than them?" he asked softly. He turned to her, concerned. "I thought if their souls were cut and their bodies wrapped that they would not return. How is it that you still see them?"

Cemirowl was surprised, again, and gained some composure. "That is a question even my mentor never asked me. I think he assumed that I merely see into the realm of the dead, but not those who people it. Of course I never questioned it either. I see where we are connected in this world but for some reason I can also see into their realm. I don't see clearly, and I can almost hear them sometimes, but no more."

"And the animals?" he asked gently.

Her heart beat wildly, suddenly. She did not know why the words were suddenly so weighty, or even why she offered him the truth, or rather the seed of the truth... knowing it, hearing it herself for the first time, unable to stop.

"Because I don't have to cut them away from me," she replied as lightly as she could. Turning her head away, she tried to bury the words, deny that something had shifted inside of her forever.

His hands clutched the bench and straight-armed he leaned forward. Arthan frowned a little. "How long have you done that?"

The elusive, internal shifting seemed to slide precariously, even further. Heart pounding, Cemirowl could not stop. "A few months after... after my moth..." She hesitated. "After my mother died," she said, keeping her face turned away from him, choking on the sorrow she did not want to flow. She would drown if it did.

Her eyes brimmed and she clutched the bench, feeling the rough stone grate her palms and fingers. She had refused to say those things, feel those things, connect them together. *Why now?*

Arthan sat silently beside her, then asked, his voice gentle and cautious, "Why after your mother died?"

Trembling, she closed her eyes and shook her head. *No! I will not go there! I will not!* She had spent all the years since not thinking of these things.

"Did you have to cut her soul away?" Arthan asked after a moment, his voice low and gentle.

It was a blinding flash of pain. Vertigo hit her, even as she tried to stumble away from him. Arthan caught her and held her. She struggled for a moment, then crumpled into his arms. Arthan held her and rocked her, touching her hair, even when she pounded on the bench and called out for her mother. When her sobs subsided and she was able to sit up, he picked up the fallen handkerchief and gave it back to her, letting her compose herself. He sat back down.

"Tell me what happened," he asked softly, not touching her, but his presence was strong and reliable.

"I was eight. My mother could see more of the spirit realm than I do. Toward the end I'm not sure which world was more real to her. She could see and hear them so clearly. The last month she could only lie in her bed. She didn't even wail anymore. Father and I did our best to care for her, but she couldn't fight any longer. When her body died the priest came and performed the offices for her. It was only symbolic to him."

She paused and looked up toward the night sky.

"She didn't know she had died," Cemirowl said quietly.

Turning after a moment to face his knees she said, "Father had already taught me a lot about meditating and centering. He did a lot of that himself just walking in the woods looking for herbs and roots to help the villagers. He also told me about the funerals where he had come from.

"He didn't know that she was still there. He couldn't see or hear her. The priest, Meelac's predecessor, had already left us to sit vigil in the chapel. No one wanted to stay the night with us in our house." It was one reason she would never leave any person alone during a vigil, when they grieved. She took a deep breath and continued. "Well, so Mamma was still there, and father kept talking to me during the vigil, but I couldn't hear him. I could only see and hear Mamma crying again. I tried centering and meditating, but I couldn't escape the sound of her wailing. It's the only time I've heard anything that clear for that long. It was as if she were standing right there, as clearly as you are. Even the newly dead are more ghostly.

"I didn't know what to do, but I heard him talk about the soul cut. I had already started seeing what I believed to be spirits. I couldn't imagine listening to her wail for the rest of my life, knowing that she didn't know she was dead; so I told her she was dead, severed her ties and *pushed* her away. I wanted her to find peace."

Arthan had started gently caressing her back as the story came out. He was silent for a moment and then asked, "And did she?"

Cemirowl looked up into his grey-blue eyes, stunned.

"You know, I never asked," she admitted. She'd spent the years since she'd cut her mother's soul from her body, unable to ask that simple question.

"Can you now?" he asked, his voice gentle.

She thought for a moment. "It will not be easy, but I think I can."

His voice was a little rough as he asked, "Will you?"

She paused, wanting to be truthful, wondering if she really would. "Yes," she said, giving him a smile. "Why do you think that my mother's death hurt me more than any of the others? My father's or Meelac's?"

"Borrowing from your own wisdom, I suspect that it was because when the others had died, though it probably brought you pain, you could remember them with joy. You knew they were at peace."

She was thoughtful for a long moment.

"Do you sing?" she asked, surprising herself. She had not meant to ask that.

He laughed lightly and said, "Yes, why do you ask?"

She shook her head, embarrassed. "No reason." Her heart pounded again.

Smiling, he stood up and helped her to rise.

"This has been a more surprising conversation than I've had in a long time. I believe that it is nearly time for the funeral feast. You have time to wash your face," he said. "You will come?"

"Yes, My Lord," she said, now knowing she was invited.

They went back indoors, through the western archway of the Lion Court. He left her at her rooms and continued toward his own. As she washed her face she realized the interlude was over.

Having been asked to divine the queen's killer, her gorge rose at the thought that despite his kindness, Arthan might have been involved with the queen's death. Cemirowl knew that a midwife might have been involved—and he'd recently called upon her, unmarried as he was. Whatever might have happened in the garden, he still had motive; Cemirowl did not know about opportunity. *Stupid, village peasant caught up in things beyond her world.*

Her heart hurting, she clenched the handkerchief she still held in her hand and stuffed it inside a pocket within her overdress. She hoped that there would be no opportunity to give it back. Even as a symbol of his kindness, it also served as a bitter reminder of the swirling fates that surrounded her beyond her control.

Chapter Fourteen

E wan led her to the Myrtle Court, admitting that he would also be helping the servants with ensuring the comfort of the lords and ladies.

"So, I'll see you there?" she asked him.

Ewan laughed. "I doubt it. I will be bringing things up from the storerooms, or helping bring food from the kitchens. I'll be back to check on you, to see if you need anything, later."

"Thank you," Cemirowl said.

He disappeared down some stairwell, while they were in a narrow passageway between buildings, after pointing her to the king's sitting rooms. Despite the rich fabrics of the cushions on low couches and chairs, and the aroma of food that set Cemirowl's mouth to water, it was still a somber affair. There was no music, and voices were low. There were ladies who had lifted their veils so they could eat the small portioned pieces of dainties and savories. Their faces were pale, and many looked as if they'd been crying. Cemirowl wished to be anywhere else. She felt hungover from emotion, and did not know what to do with her hands and feet.

She soon realized she need not fear having another

emotional interview with the prince. She saw him through the large group of people pass into the audience chamber where, no doubt, the royal family must be. Ferran also went into that room. Cemirowl almost turned to leave. Whatever bravery she'd felt the night before, or this morning, had evaporated. She had only courage enough to stay. To give herself something to do she took a plate and sampled the food.

She ate a cured meat wrapped over a date, and thought she'd found a taste of the heavens. Among other foods, there were olives still warm from the oven, and cheeses of more varieties than she'd known existed. One was rimmed in red, and she realized had been soaked in wine. She realized that some of what filled the platters had been at the prince's dinner, but at the time she was so tense it had tasted of dust. This reminded her that she would still have to speak to the king or his marshal of the guard about why she hadn't warned them in time to prevent disaster. She gave her small plate to a servant and started to walk away.

There was a light touch on her arm, and Cemirowl turned to see Terria.

"Thank you so much for helping me know that my lady was at peace," she said.

"You are most welcome," Cemirowl replied.

The gentleman beside Terria, a man in Hergilan clothes, bowed his head and murmured something about his duty to his lord.

"Is this the man?" Cemirowl asked in a whisper.

Terria blushed. "Yes, Sir Quormen. I'm sorry; I should have introduced you."

"I'm not offended. I imagine many in these rooms are not themselves tonight. Is all of the ambassador's household here?"

"No," said Terria, "his servants are in his suite, and Sir Amec has been asked by Lord Itrizeu to stay away."

"I see," murmured Cemirowl.

"Oh! I should not have said that."

"Lady Terria, it is a difficult time for everyone," Cemirowl said gently.

It was clear that Terria was overwhelmed. "Let us take a turn around the court," Cemirowl said to give her time to compose herself. For a few steps they walked in silence, giving Cemirowl the opportunity to see through the gallery pillars how the stars were mirrored in the pool.

She waited a few moments, and then asked, "Lady Terria, I understand that you have lived in this city all your life?"

"Yes, my father is the king's steward, Baron Bartemo."

"Do you know the midwife that attended the queen?"

"Yes, midwife Abenne."

"Do you know where I can find her?"

"Do you need Abenne, or would another midwife serve?"

"Abenne, please. Unless there were others that served the queen, or came here?"

"No, I do not think so. Perhaps others came to other ladies at court, but I rather believe that we all used Abenne when she came. Where she lives, I do not know. Abenne came regularly to the castle, nearly every week, so there was rarely any need to send for her if we could not find our own needs from an herbal or by another lady's advice. Unfortunately, we have not seen her since before the queen passed."

Cemirowl exhaled in frustration. "Do you know *anyone* who might know where to find her? Lady Harlyn mentioned the prince."

Terria bit her lip in thought. "Lady Harlyn once hinted to me that the prince had cause to call upon the midwife in secret this past year. Harlyn does tend to find out some odd bits of news, some of which is impossible to test the truth of. It is possible to ask him, but I do not know how anyone of decency could broach the subject. I cannot imagine why she would even mention it. If it were a delicate situation he would not wish to have his connection known. Perhaps, instead, I can send a page to find Abenne, if you wish."

Cemirowl smiled. "I would be most grateful!" she said, squeezing the lady's hand.

Terria laughed lightly. "Surely you do not need one!"

Cemirowl shook her head with a smile. "No, indeed. I merely wished to consult her about herbs. There are a few questions my own herb lore cannot answer."

"I will send a page in the morning then, and fetch her to you," Terria said.

Cemirowl was struck by how much she liked Lady Terria. The lady was comfortable in herself and more at peace and center than many people Cemirowl had known, despite the grief she felt, or the worry that the queen's last memory of her was tainted by argument. She wished that she could get to know her in better circumstances.

Ferran found them as they returned to the sitting room. "Forgive me for taking her away from you, Lady Terria, but I thought she would like the opportunity to meet the clergy from Hergila that have come to condole with the family of our late queen, blessed be her memory."

Arthan was there, as well as Mercor. The king was sitting down and speaking to Tidyri's father nearby. Cemirowl shook hands with some of the most powerful people of Hergila, including their clergymen. She tried not to feel like a mouse with stolen gems. The conversation was slow going, and if Ferran had intended that she'd gain some sort of wisdom or debate theology with them it was clear it would not happen. It was mainly a show of polite noises and sympathy. They were there to comfort their people, and soon were called upon to do this duty—not attempt to converse with a visiting village priest. She withdrew politely as Tidyri's mother began to wail again, setting off the tears of the other ladies present.

A Hergilan lord approached her, and she recognized him as the ambassador. She curtsied again.

"You are a priest?" he asked in accented but good Pyrannian.

"Yes, my lord."

"Would..." He paused, looking over at the Hergilan priests and Ferran. "Would *you* be free to give some pastoral care to one of my household?"

"Of course, my lord."

To her surprise he led her toward the eastern side of the palace complex. He said, as they walked, "I do not wish to neglect any of my household, but it was best that he not join us this evening. I know that he is not as stoic about this tragedy as he claims. Will you help him?"

"Yes, as best I can."

Her heart pounded as she had the awful idea that she would soon meet Sir Amec, someone under suspicion for murdering the woman people were mourning not too far away. Ambassador Itrizeu led her into a court lit by only a few lanterns. The court did not reflect the austerity in Hergilan dress, or what she could see of Sir Amec's clothes. It was clear to her that he would be the most stoic of men in better circumstances.

"Amec, I have brought someone to counsel you," Itrizeu said, and gesturing to a chair near Amec's, he said, "Priest... I will leave you now. Thank you."

Amec and she both sat down.

"It is dark," he said. "I can have more lanterns lit for you if you'd like."

"I do not mind the dark."

He was silent a moment. "I know much of the palace. There are not any ordained women in the palace at present except one. You are the fortuneteller who did not warn the royal family of the doom over the queen's head?"

"I am, though I did not know it would be Queen Tidyri who would die. Your country, I gather, relies on fortunetellers more than my own. Perhaps they see more clearly than I do."

"I have never relied on them."

She nodded. "Even in my experience readings are never straightforward or very clear."

"What a strange country is this! Here we are under a credible threat of execution over our heads, but while I am not invited to mourn the queen, I am still fed with the excess notable in your country, and still in my rooms and no dungeon. A village priest—also threatened with doom—is given vestment covered in jewels!" He gestured to the glint of rubies and gold in her dress.

"Yes. I find it disconcerting and strange myself."

"My Lord Itrizeu must not have realized who you were, or why bring a priest to comfort me if she too is threatened?"

Cemirowl had no answer.

He leaned forward. "I was there. And being of noble

family, and a rich family, I know to have both knife or poison ready to kill those I find necessary to die."

His face was close to hers. She gripped the arm of her chair. He was not threatening. He seemed cold. His words were passionless. A statement of fact from a man used to ruling his emotions. For some reason it frightened her.

"More, Priest," he said, "I even opened the door and heard her weeping. Her ladies Terria and Soflia saw me as I closed the door to leave."

"Did you kill her?"

"I will let your arts tell you. So far it seems to me that it does not matter what I think. Even Itrizeu worries enough to forbid me now to leave these halls."

"Do you dislike the treaty?"

"Only in that it prevents me from going home while under obligation to my lord. I cannot, thus, resign myself of the duty to take a wife and give my family sons to continue our traditions. I fear the emotional excesses will also poison our country's northland and seep down to the south and destroy what my duty would inspire."

Something in that statement made him show more emotion than having witnessed, in some part, the last minutes of a dying woman. Cemirowl thought for a moment.

"Is your duty to your family onerous to you, then?"

He shrugged, but it was there: a tightening around his eyes, and breathing from a chest that had tightened a fraction more. "I have always known I must do this, without the freedom of my own inclination. I had one brief season of freedom," he said.

She was distracted, briefly, as her ghostly hawk flew up from his shoulders and over the roof, calling out in piercing tones to the south.

"You miss your homeland. What do you yearn for most there?"

"The horses. The desert. Days filled with quiet. The surprising beauty that the desert hides within itself."

"I think this is very much like you as well."

He gave her a smile that did not sit on his face well. She guessed Amec rarely smiled, but it went to his eyes and was genuine. "You see much."

"Sometimes."

He shook his head. "I feel the weight of doom upon my shoulders," he said. Cemirowl did not see his lithe strength being burdened, but she guessed that he was less calm than he appeared. "I must rely on the unruly passions of your countrymen."

Cemirowl remembered the thin thread that led from a woman back to Mercor and into the mess of murder. She realized the reading might have meant the sister who tied the two men together.

"Is murder rare in your land?" she asked him.

"No," he admitted.

"Then it is not a question of passion—ruled or otherwise. I believe that you have one friend here who would speak for you."

"You are a witch to know it."

"Considering I read the fortunes of this friend, and for that reason I am here, under a threat of doom as are you, perhaps that is the best word for me."

Amec grinned at her. He was another one who seemed to understand her humor. She liked him better for it, even though she believed she was sitting next to a killer, though maybe not the queen's killer. "Yes," he said. "Unruly passion personified. He made much of a small thing!"

"Why did you come to dislike him?"

There was a slight spasm of muscles at his jaw. "We traveled together for a time in the south of Hergila, and in countries beyond and to the east. We went to various tourneys there—though they are called something else there—and both fought and learned various forms of combat. Sometimes we even fought against each other. He would win, or I would. At first we did not travel together, but when it became clear we were traversing the same roads, we spent our days together."

"You respected him."

"Yes. He was a good man. His honor toward others was high, no matter the country. In this land, I do not think you would use this term between men, but I... loved him, respected him for strength I now only see when he is in tourney."

"Why do you hesitate over that word?" she asked him.

"Love for your people seems such an unruly thing! We understand it differently in the dry south of Hergila. Here love makes fools of men."

"And sometimes women as well," she said.

"When he met my sister, he lost his head. He was not the man I knew. With passions repugnant to our father, and distressing to our mother, he was blind to their feelings, only his own and my sister's. He was certainly blind to mine. He would have devolved our friendship into becoming mere brothers. When he was rebuffed by my father, he chose not to return to our wandering ways, but to return here, and no doubt drown himself in excess of emotion."

Cemirowl could only turn her head to give him the privacy

of his emotions the man clearly valued. She could see now, with some pain, how Amec must have felt flayed by the very things he trusted most and betrayed yet again by something that had taken his friend. His breathing had deepened, and even in the faint light Cemirowl had seen that his eyes were tighter than before. Only his sturdy self-control—at its lowest ebb—kept him from deflating and weeping like a boy. Something, she guessed, he would have despised in himself.

She took a few breaths as well. Betrayal was the very thing that had dismayed Tidyri's ghost.

"He never realized how..." she started to say.

"No. Of course not. And what would it have mattered? One day I will return home, if I am allowed to live, and take a wife. I never expected anything else." His voice was passionless again.

"Why did you despise his affection for your sister?"

"He was not the same man. He was unfeeling toward her family, only alive to her young, naïve and romantic wishes. The only time I now see him as he was is when he is on the tournament field. He is no longer an unruly pup. He is strong, focused, determined. He is careful with his thoughts, and feelings, ruling his passions."

"Good qualities in a man," she said.

"But it is the besotted puppy of a man who would stand for me in this trial!"

"And that is still unwelcome to you?"

Amec was clearly near to breaking again. "No," he said. "May the gods help me."

She put a hand on his shoulder.

"No, don't!" he said. He straightened, and brought himself under control with a speed she envied. "You forget, Priest: there is much you cannot comfort me in. The gallows loom, or the ax. But you have brought me comfort where you could."

Cemirowl almost asked, *I have?*

He continued. "You reminded me of friendship, and one I had lost. Go back to the funeral feast. There will, no doubt, be others who need your care. If you are to live and I to die, will you pray for me?"

"Indeed." This dismissal, however, was too abrupt for Cemirowl's liking. "Are you sure you would not want me to at least sit with you a moment longer?"

"No, Priest," he said, but his voice was less cold in the warm night. "I truly must think and rule myself for the days coming to me. Go. I am going to sit and pray to the old gods of my country."

She nodded and left him. As she walked she felt her shoulders relax, and her breath shuddered in her as she realized she'd almost been afraid to breathe. Sir Amec was not tormented by the queen's murder, and clearly would think nothing of killing someone he believed deserved death. He might share a strange sense of humor with her, but she could not be comfortable with him. Worse, she knew that she had not given him the pastoral care she was asked to by the ambassador. She had not ruled her own emotions, and so had not left him with any less pain than before. She may have, in fact, reminded him of pain more hopeless than that of his former friend.

As she followed the passageways back to the Myrtle Court, she realized that while his sorrow was real, it did not remove the fact—one he admitted—that he could have killed the queen. The reasons he'd confessed or implied were not ones she recognized as motives, but they were clearly real to him. She doubted that he'd trust *her* with the real reasons he might have murdered her. It occurred to her that he had betrayed himself in sharing his emotions with her, but they had little to do with any reason to kill the queen. In fact she would be the last person he would talk with about that, as she could use that information to save her own neck, sacrificing his.

With all honesty, she reminded herself that she would not have hesitated even were there no threat of execution bowing her neck as much as his!

It made her ill to realize that whoever had killed the queen had motives that however real to them would still never have the same power for her. There could never be reason enough in her mind to kill another person.

Near the court, she saw Mercor coming toward her.

"There you are. I've come to find you. The king wishes to speak to you before the night is over."

"I will need my herb bag and bone basket."

"I will guide you to your rooms."

She could not speak to him in the passageways. There were still too many people about. When they got to her rooms, she asked him.

"Caballier, tell me of Sir Amec, the foreign man some say had opportunity to—"

"How do you know about that?" he asked, cutting her off. He seemed angry. "Did your basket tell you that?"

"Mercor, if I had asked my basket they would hardly tell me height, age, weight, name or nationality. I know because I just came from speaking with him. Ambassador Itrizeu believed he needed pastoral care, and Ferran and the other clergy were busy comforting the royal family."

Mercor shook his head.

"There was, if you recall in your reading a thread tied to you from another woman. I'm guessing it is to this man."

"Yes."

"And he was there."

"Yes, with a letter from her father, but..."

She wondered how deep his friendship to Amec was. It did not change the odd sense of betrayal to the man she had just left in deep pain. She spoke anyway. "And you have information that could be important to the king and others? If you hold it back, it is your life or his. I do not doubt that if it was merely a choice of his life or mine you would side with him. Is he worth it?"

"Yes; and his sister is worth even more of a yes!"

"Even by his words he had opportunity. Do you believe he had motive?"

"I do not know about motive, except to harm the treaty. I do know that he has knowledge of poisons. I've known him to use some when we traveled together. It would not surprise me to learn he'd brought them here. Yet to kill the queen? I cannot believe that of him."

"Caballier, are you forgetting that someone indeed killed the queen? That she died and, if I'm right, suffered? Even Sir Amec told me she was weeping. Your love for this man, or his sister will not change that she died."

"Do your bones tell you he did it?"

"No. But if you know something that would help the king, you should share it. I may still hang for not warning him of something I could not know, but if you value honesty, then speak to those who should know."

"It is a terrible thing you ask, when I do not know anything enough to execute him. Even Ambassador Itrizeu doubts him—even though once he valued his opinion!"

"He brought a man who dislikes this country to advise him?"

"The ambassador wanted to ensure that he did not put his own opinions above that of his country and king—for those who accept or value the treaty, and even for those who still distrust it."

Cemirowl nodded. She thought of Amec's worn stoicism. "Interesting choice." She knew that she'd pushed the caballier. Now she wanted to know the answers to the real purpose of her questions. "If this man acted to destroy the treaty, and killed the queen, would you still hesitate?"

Mercor looked devastated. After a moment he asked in a near whisper, "No. How did she die?"

"I'm not sure. If I'm right, she was slowly paralyzed by the poison, so that her murderer could take the time to humiliate her. It may very well have been a gesture to say she was no longer Hergilan but of Pyrann. Unable to move, she would still have been in pain."

Mercor looked sick. "I understand." He paused. "I will speak to my king."

She laid a hand on his arm. "I am very sorry."

Mercor was white. "I was divided from her already, but had hopes to regain the friend. She must despise me now, if she hears of this!"

Cemirowl was not pleased with herself. If he was not the killer, Amec would be a man to befriend. But she could not trust him yet. Mercor saw the tears on her cheeks.

"You were right," he said. "I would have chosen him over you. And I am not choosing my life over his, but that of Queen

Tidyri. I forgot that she suffered. I only wanted to spare a love I could not have."

Cemirowl hugged herself. She wanted to stifle a strange, protective inclination—for all the suspects to be cleared. To not have a killer who humiliated a truly defenseless woman. But someone had taken her life, and that of her child. The pain of that act was spreading, and she had just helped to feed that pain. She thought, with grief, *I am not a priest tonight!*

CHAPTER FIFTEEN

―――――――――― «‹•›» ――――――――――

"**W**e should go back, if you have your bag and basket," Mercor said. "We can sit in my room for now. You do not look as if you want company," he said.

"Nor do you."

"I will let Rimmel know where we are when they need you."

They were both silent as they walked down the hall. At the open doors to the prince's court, Cemirowl paused, disturbed.

Standing in front of her was the mysterious spirit, desperate for attention. It stood almost as real as Caballier Mercor beside her. Mercor started to say something to her, but went silent after seeing her face.

Cemirowl shrank back from the specter, with a little gasp of horror. It was covered in something that moved. The shifting whiteness seemed to ripple against a figure so live looking, she could almost touch it. This was no ordinary pale shade. Heart pounding, Cemirowl stepped forward. She could hear an echo of a voice from the woman, but no words.

Coming up as close as she could without stepping through

her, Cemirowl could see hundreds of ghosts of crushed white spiders that faded, even as Cemirowl's mind and hand reached out to touch them. They faded, but the spirit did not, and she could see her clearly as if she had just died. The spiders returned to bury her again.

"What in the world?" she asked, but the spirit was drawn away back to her body, leaving only an echo of a wail fading in Cemirowl's head.

"What is it?" asked Mercor. "What do you see?"

She looked up at him in surprise, having almost forgotten that he was there. "I'm not sure. A ghost," she said, with a little shake of her head. Breaking her reverie, she said, "I'm sorry, we must go."

She did not speak to him about what she saw. It was a spirit in torment. There was no choice; she would have to deal with this ghost, later, when more immediate problems were resolved.

As they walked, Mercor, in low tones, gave her pointers on the etiquette required during an audience with the king. The main one was waiting to speak until after the king spoke. She also had to wait to be dismissed.

They did not get a chance to sit in Mercor's rooms, as another caballier gestured to him, and she was guided through the sitting room, to a stairwell between the two halls. They emerged into another small sitting room with two doors. One to the queen's solar, she recognized, as the door was wide open. Another was shut. Mercor knocked, waited, and when he heard a muffled, "Come!" he opened the door and they entered the king's office.

The room was smaller than the one Tidyri had used, though she taught palace children. It looked like a room that a rich and strong man might use.

"Your Majesty, the Priest Cemirowl," Mercor said with a bow.

He stood near another caballier who stood beside the door to guard it. Cemirowl waited.

Larthor sat at a dark wooden desk. It was intricately carved, despite the heaviness of the structure. It was a piece of furniture where a king might work on the day to day business required for tending his land. Cemirowl thought to herself, *a less sturdy desk would look rather breakable next to the king.* There were scrolls upon the desk and on the wall behind him there was a map of Pyrann, other lands along the coastline on either side of the strait. It was a huge screen of dyed or painted cloth and very detailed. Cemirowl presumed that one of the other lands across the strait was Hergila but that other countries were also represented.

King Larthor was studying her and after a moment said, "You may come forward, priest."

She did, curtsied and, not knowing what else to say, murmured, "Your Majesty."

He gestured to a chair in front of the desk, and then looked at the caballiers and other servants around him and said, "You may wait outside. I wish to speak in private with the priest."

As his servants and well-armed caballiers left, Larthor turned to her and smiled briefly. It was a sad little smile; sorrow deepened the shadows around his eyes. Cemirowl was surprised by both the privacy and the smile, but sat in the chair he'd pointed at and waited for him to speak. This imposing man had called her, a peasant fortuneteller, on an errand of folly rising from shock and bitterness. Since then, she'd been impertinent, and spoken to him… and let him crush her hand till it nearly broke. It was, in fact, still sore if she moved it wrong, a counterpoint to the continued ache from her long ride. She had also presumed to rewrap his wife and had helped lift her body into a sarcophagus and seal it shut. What would a normal man make of such a person? What would a king?

After a moment of thought, he leaned on his desk and spoke. "I know that you've seen Tidyri, more than during the vigil and burial. Ferran told me. He was impressed at how well you rewrapped her body after the other women finished, even with such a short time."

"Oh, Your Majesty, I hope you don't think that I…"

He lifted his hand. "I thank you for your honor. You performed the office well."

King Larthor paused again, then said, "Ferran is quite put out by not knowing what to do with you. Obviously you're more than merely competent at your duties as a priest, but he's at odds with what you will do for me now."

Knots twisted inside Cemirowl. "Your Majesty, I…"

He raised his hand, again. "He wanted to know if you were a charlatan or mad. I'd rather like to know myself, having ordered you here. I believe I said you'd die for treason if you failed in what I asked you. I said it in anger and shock; do not fear it. However, if you *can* help me, it would be added foolishness to send you away now."

Cemirowl nodded. "Thank you, Your Majesty."

She paused trying to gather her thoughts. For a moment she felt the room expand and her body shrink. It felt almost as if she were only a head, staring at a king looming over her across a desk. She took a deep breath and focused.

"Your Majesty, I do not know what Caballier Mercor implied about my gift. I gather that in telling an amusing tale he gave the impression that my gift is greater than it really is. What I *can* see is at your disposal, either as a priest or as a practitioner of divination."

The king looked down at his desk. "Priest, you've seen Tidyri's body. Did you read her?"

Cemirowl stood, and moved to the desk, putting the bone basket down upon it. "It is not how I usually practice divination, but I did."

His head shot up. "What did you learn?" he asked, his voice gruff.

"I did not learn the identity of the killer," she said, hesitant.

"You did learn something?"

"Your Majesty, if you would be so good as to humor me, I would like for you to consult my bone basket. It would help me know how to proceed."

His face underwent a few emotions, one of mild reproof. "How would this benefit me? I gather that you did learn something you are reluctant to tell me. Is this true?"

Cemirowl bit her lip. She nodded and said, "It is, Your Majesty." She paused in thought and then spoke. "Your Majesty, I haven't learned the identity of the killer. What I read of the physical clues of Her Majesty's body gave me some idea of pinpointing the probable use of poison."

She paused then looked at him. "The truth is that I am a humble villager and you are a king. I may be more educated than most peasants, because of my father and my mentor's love for books, but that doesn't change who I am. I *would* like to use the skills that I have, since you have consulted me. At the moment, reading the bones will help me organize the presentation of what I have learned in a way that would help you the most."

He raised his eyebrows. "I know nothing of these matters, but I am curious as to how you do these things. It will help me understand who you are better. What do I need to do?"

"All I ask, Your Majesty, is that you concentrate on our current situation then stir the bones in the basket, grab a handful and toss them out onto the cloth. I will read them and we will go from there."

He said nothing, but gave one nod.

She opened the cloth wrappings, calling her creatures to her. The ones that were clearest she could see crouching in wait on and around the table.

He stirred the basket, then looking at her, threw the contents of his huge fist upon the cloth.

She leaned forward.

"It tells me, Your Majesty, that you are a strong man. Your appearance deceives people as to your wisdom."

The king snorted with humor. "And?"

Cemirowl looked up and smiled. "I believe that you will not be instrumental in finding the name of the person you are seeking, but I do believe that you will learn soon. Within the week, I would guess," she looked up at him, "I will not guarantee that, Your Majesty. Bones cannot tell time that well."

A look of wry disbelief traveled along his eyebrows, softening into some humor with her last statement. The king leaned toward her, putting his arm on the table. "Is that all?"

"I could also say that your grief would last you some time, but that it is a healthy grief..."

"Grief? Healthy? How can grief be healthy?"

"If grief is suppressed, as you were doing last night, then it can harm the person keeping it. In privacy, I think that you will allow it to be as it should."

"You are a young girl to be telling me this. How have you learned this in such a short time?"

"I did my first cutting, Your Majesty, when I was eight. It was for my mother. I have seen a lot of death and a great deal of mourning since then."

"I see," he said. He looked at the bones. "You haven't told me what you learned about Tidyri."

"First I'd like to ask you a few questions, Your Majesty. When you found Her Majesty was her skin clammy and cold to the touch?"

"It was."

"I suspect that her upper eyelids were drooping, and her lower jaw seemed slack? I know that her eyes were dilated, but the rest I could not, of course, confirm."

"Indeed. They were."

She nodded thoughtfully, then pulled open her herb pouch. She brought out two small bags of waxed cloth and a small square of cloth. She dumped both bags onto the opened cloth. One was a pile of small dried flowers, and the other was a small piece of root.

"Was there any scent of either upon her, Your Majesty?"

The king looked curiously at Cemirowl for a moment. He then leaned forward and picked up a pinch of flowers, brought it to his nose, and then did the same with the root. "I think there was a little of the root on her lips."

Cemirowl nodded. "My father called poison creeper or climber. I believe that the same herb killed the queen. Depending on the dose, I've understood it can kill anywhere from one to seven hours after being administered."

"Why would she take it? Did someone force her to take it? Or could it have been added to something she drank or ate?" he asked.

Cemirowl took a deep breath. "You called me because of my ability to read bones... and see the dead. From what I understand, the person that killed her was someone she trusted. Poison creeper is known to be a sedative, used to calm the choleric humor of the body. I understand that she was angry with two of her ladies and Priest Ferran earlier in the day."

"Yes, and in fact he was seen at her gallery after that argument, after she'd sent him away. Why would she drink this?"

"I would rather use maythen, grace herb, or capon tail, myself, but it is possible that someone she trusted gave her poison creeper to calm her nerves. However, an overdose can kill. It might have been a mistake."

"Except someone cut her hair," said the king.

Cemirowl nodded in agreement. "She would have died relaxed and weak." Cemirowl did not add that while helpless Tidyri would have felt the full horror of the betrayal, unable to move. Depending on the dose, her nerves might also have been on fire. "The effect would have started at most half an hour after she'd taken it. She could have been given the potion before her ladies left her and no one would have been the wiser except for the person who had given it to her."

"So, widening the scope of suspects," he said with a groan.

"Possibly. It depends on who knows the use of poison creeper. From what I understand from Her Majesty's spirit, she was humiliated while she was dying, which I think was the act of cutting her hair. I suspect that her killer came back to the room while Harlyn was away."

Cemirowl paused.

"You wish to say more?" the king asked.

"I was also surprised to learn that she was not only angry, but grieving. Yes she was infuriated, but it wasn't for the death of herself." Cemirowl paused, not knowing how to proceed.

"If not for the death of herself, then why was she grieving? That doesn't make sense. Or was she grieving for me?"

Cemirowl swallowed. At the burial nothing had been said of the baby. She'd gotten the impression, through the conversation with Lady Harlyn, that there had been no one, except perhaps the midwife, who had any reason to suspect that the queen had been with child.

"She was with child, Your Majesty. I guess she'd been pregnant about three months or so, at most five."

King Larthor's face turned stony, his eyes lost focus. Clenching his hands into fists, he whispered, "Why would you want to hurt me?" Then forcefully asked, "Can you prove this?"

"Not yet, Your Majesty. I have asked about the midwife, but no one has seen her for days. Both Ladies Terria and Harlyn mentioned that she has not come to the castle since before the queen died. Lady Harlyn also gave me the impression that the Prince Arthan might know where I could find her, but Lady Terria has offered to send a page to bring her to me, instead. It is not unusual for a midwife to be gone for some time if there are births for her to attend. Some are, as you must know, not easy."

The king looked piercingly at Cemirowl. "You seem to be looking for more information than what your arts can tell you. Are you?"

"Yes, Your Majesty. Even if I had been able to tell you who had killed her, I have no doubt you would want proof. I certainly would!"

He nodded with a grim smile, and his eyes were lit with approval. "True. Have you any ideas as to whom the murderer might be?" he asked her.

"I have a few suspicions. The poison used on the queen is one that a midwife might know of, but not use, or possibly even carry with her. Despite that, I have reason to believe that there might be some connection between the midwife and the queen's murder. I'm trying to find the midwife so that I can see if she can tell me who might have known about the queen's pregnancy. If someone had talked to her about it besides the queen or yourself…"

"Yes, I see, that person might have been the one to kill the queen. If the child was the incentive."

There was a knock on the door and Prince Arthan came in.

"Your Majesty," he said and bowed.

"Brother," said the king, "the priest was telling me of her views on the possible identity of the murderer. I'd like you to come and sit with me and commiserate with us."

Arthan's right eyebrow raised. "Indeed, brother, if I can be of help," he said, and sat down. He was not covered in weaponry as Mercor tended to be, but wore sleek blades, which he moved to accommodate his chair. His brooding face was not the only ominous aspect about him.

"The midwife attending the queen was the same as your wife's, I understand?" the king asked his brother.

"Indeed she was," Arthan replied, and began tapping a finger on his thigh, as he leaned into his chair.

"Have you seen her, recently?"

"Not for some time," Arthan said, and took out a small glass vial and began playing with it.

The gesture caught Cemirowl's attention. She also fidgeted with her fingers when tense, but looking at the prince, she saw no other expression of tension. He seemed only to be focusing his thoughts.

"Priest Cemirowl has identified the poison and has some ideas on how it was administered. Please tell the prince what you have told me."

Heavy of heart, Cemirowl did.

Arthan leaned forward during her discourse of both material and immaterial impressions and clues she'd found.

"Is this plant common?" he asked.

Cemirowl nodded. "It is fairly common, Your Highness. Many women wear it in their hair during spring festivals. I would not even be surprised to know it was in your garden. Perhaps you know it by another name. The light yellow flower is relatively harmless, unless a child eats a great number of them. The scent is lovely, and commonly used in sachets and perfumes. The root is not harmless."

"Who would know of its use?"

"Most apothecaries would and a midwife might, if she was knowledgeable in herb lore, Your Highness. There may be references to it in herbals but it is not in the one my father left me, Ronson Lieve's *Apothocaric Companion*. He did leave me a book with his own study of herbs and anatomy."

The king looked curiously at her for a moment. "You made mention that you had thought that the murderer may have had some familiarity with herbs used by a midwife. Why would you narrow it down so much if any lady or scholar might find it in a book?" asked the king.

"The first night I was here, I was tired. I'd been on a long ride, and I needed to stay awake for the vigil. Caballier Mercor told me that I could make a restorative infusion from herbs left for my use in my room. I chose to use what was provided instead of concocting something from my own supply. From the taste, I'm fairly certain, the tea I took from the box was spire menthe heavily laced with button bloom. I drank enough in my distraction that I began to feel the symptoms."

"What does it do?" asked Arthan.

"Well, it would not help someone stay awake. It is an emmenagogue or even abortifacient when used in small doses. Large doses or extended use can burn and eat into the stomach enough to cause death. It was a clumsy attempt to hurt me. If the queen's murderer had given it to me, and I cannot say this for certain, of course, then I would suspect a connection to a midwife."

The prince leaned back. His jaw seemed hard, as he clenched the vial for a moment. Cemirowl's eyes drifted to the contents of the vial he began to twirl along the arm of his chair. The contents caught the light in an odd way, and it looked vaguely familiar to her.

"Your attention seems caught," said the king.

"Pardon me, Your Majesty?" she asked.

"You were staring at whatever my brother is fidgeting with," he said, and looked at his brother. "Have you lost that pendant you used to fiddle with?"

"No, brother," he said, and pulled out a chain from his shirt, bringing forth an odd silver pendant with a rough, but colorful stone.

"Ah," said his brother, "but, I've not seen this before, may I see it?"

Cemirowl noticed that Arthan hesitated, though briefly. "Surely," he said, and handed the vial to his brother.

The king looked at it, shrugged his shoulders and handed it back to the prince. "Odd little thing."

"May I look at it?" Cemirowl asked, her voice sounding weak.

The prince raised an eyebrow, but said nothing as he handed it over.

It was a white spider. Cemirowl frowned and her pulse quickened.

"Do you know of these?" the prince asked, surprised, but his voice more gentle than she felt was warranted.

"I... I have seen something like it before," she said, again not liking the weakness of her voice.

She handed the spider back to him, unable to look at his eyes, or the king's. She could feel their eyes weight her with their curiosity. She swallowed twice before she could speak.

"Tell me, Your Highness, what does the midwife look like?" she asked as strongly as she could.

"The midwife Abenne is an elderly woman, graying hair usually tied back in a barbette, I believe it is called, or sometimes merely wrapping her hair in a veil, but without any train, as that would interfere with her work."

"Does she walk with a stoop and have a burn scar along her left forearm?" she asked lightly, looking up, but she was unable to meet the prince's gaze.

"Indeed, yes. You have seen her?" He leaned forward,

eagerly. She could see his hand grip the arm of his chair.

She looked up at him, now, trying to read his face. "Indeed, I have," she said, but offered nothing more. He sat back; his eyes focused on his thoughts. Arthan did not venture for more information; he seemed reluctant to speak more of the matter himself.

She turned to the king. "Your Majesty, I believe I have little further to say."

"What you have given me already is considerable. I will let the marshal of the guard know your suspicions on the poison. It will no doubt help his investigations."

Controlling a violent fit of trembling, Cemirowl gathered up her bone basket and herbs. "If I may have your permission to leave?" she asked.

He nodded. "You are dismissed."

Cemirowl fled.

As she closed the door, she heard Prince Arthan say, "She seems like a fledgling hawk caught in a room full of cats. If someone did try to harm her, commoner or not, I'd set someone to guard her. It was a foolish move to bring her here."

"A more uncommon woman I have rarely met," was the king's wry response. But the king had more to say, and began speaking to his brother in a low, angry growl as Cemirowl firmly closed the door.

CHAPTER SIXTEEN

⟪◆⟫

C emirowl left the king's office, emerging into the hallway. She wished the hall was empty so that she could sag against the door. Instead, she nodded to the knights and gave a tremulous smile to Lady Soflia and Lady Harlyn, who were walking to the solar and their room. The two ladies moved toward her, as if concerned for the obvious emotion on her face, but Cemirowl could not face them. Clutching her basket and her pouch, she turned and fled.

Cemirowl finally found her room; she had to ask for directions, having taken a wrong turn at least once. Once there, she asked Les for some Clary wine. When the girl gave her the brimming goblet, Cemirowl thanked her and asked her to call Ewan.

"I'll have to go find him. He and Tellen were working the feast; he came, but left again when he realized you were with the king," Les said.

"I'll wait for him here," Cemirowl said, as Les closed the door.

Her mind was racing. As quickly and carefully as she could, she took off her ornate gown and pulled on a working dress she'd brought with her. She did not bother with the new working dresses Les had left out. She guessed a place with hundreds of spiders would be messy. She stuffed different things in her pockets that she thought she might need.

The midwife Abenne wasn't missing. She was dead. She had died somewhere in the vicinity of Prince Arthan's room, covered with white spiders. He had not told his brother this fact and no one, she believed, was looking for Abenne except, perhaps, herself. *Does he actually know that Abenne is dead?* she wondered. The spider and the midwife's ghost seemed to damn him.

Lady Terria had said this evening that he'd recently used the services of the midwife, secretly. She had no doubts as to why Arthan might need a midwife, but was angry that he'd go that far.

She laughed bitterly at herself. *He went farther than that, if I'm right. Murder. Two, no... three? Gracious Guardian, I hope I'm wrong!* With an odd, bitter comfort, she reminded herself that there was a great deal that she did not know. There were gaps in her knowledge in both court life and the myriad of people involved in merely tending the queen, only a few of whom she'd met. She consoled herself thinking, *You could very, very easily be far off the mark.*

It could also be completely unrelated. There was no reason to suppose that Abenne's death had anything to do with Queen Tidyri's death. Sir Amec had not been cleared as a suspect, and was under suspicion from those closest to him.

There was a knock at the door and Les came in with Ewan.

"You called for me, ma'am?" he asked, as Les closed the door.

"I know that it is late. I believe I need your help, if both of you can keep a secret for a while."

"Of course," they said in chorus.

"Do either of you know of an entrance to Prince Arthan's apartments or that part of the building? Something that isn't part of his living quarters, but part of the old building underneath?"

Les shook her head. "No ma'am."

"I might," said Ewan. "There are passages for servants and guards under all the buildings. But one part was blocked off years ago, while the king was building the Lantern Court for his mother. I know there are storerooms near there, even some used by that court. Mayhap there's an entrance there. I'll wager it's locked. Tellen told me about a door, I think, because he was moving some boxes and some kegs of wine or ale down there in those cellars for the cook's clerk and asked where that door went. It might not be the same door though." He looked at Les with a grin. "Knowing Tellen he could be talking about a different building entirely. There are stories he tells about ghosts and tunnels and the mystery of the ax man, who wanders the passages below the southern wall, because of the clanging you can sometimes hear— on a night with high wind."

Les nodded. "I've heard that story too. But that does not help Priest Cemirowl, Ewan. It does sound as if you can find what you're looking for."

"Well, if he's right, can we get there fairly safely?" Cemirowl asked him.

"It will be dark in the cellars this late," said Les, nervously. "Can it wait?"

Cemirowl thought for a moment. "I don't think I could sleep tonight without knowing and I may not have a better chance to search in relative secrecy. I've got to find out something. Are there any lanterns or torches we could use?"

"Sure, I can get some," Ewan said and, before Cemirowl could stop him, he scampered out the door.

"Do you want me to come too?" Les asked.

"No, I'll just have Ewan lead me."

"What if someone comes looking for you?"

Cemirowl laid a hand gently on the girl's shoulder. "Try not to give any information away." She paused. "If you have to tell them anything, tell them I've gone to the midwife." This was true, at least.

Ewan came back with a lantern and an unlit torch wrapped in a blanket. He seemed eager for an adventure.

"Let's go, Ewan," Cemirowl said.

Eagerly, Ewan led the way down to the cellars. Quietly, they made their descent down the service stairs, down a dark passageway, and to a part of the cellars that was clearly reserved for storage. Furniture and parts of tables stood next to barrels of wine in rows waiting for consumption.

Ewan said, "Someone's been here."

"How do you know?"

"Boxes have been moved," he said.

"Surely the cook or steward no doubt come and get wine."

"Aye, but the prince's steward likes things neat, and Sir Nevis, the steward's man hates boxes being laid on top of his barrels. It means extra work when it comes time to move them."

"So, you think that someone else has been here before?"

"Aye, and someone who knows nothing of Sir Nevis' temper! Or perhaps just the way he organizes his cellars," Ewan said with a grin. "But this is the place you'd find what you're looking for."

There was no obvious doorway, blocked or otherwise. Cemirowl wondered if this was already the end to the venture. Carefully they moved the lantern toward the wall, and looked past boxes and other stored items.

"This is hopeful, my lady," said Ewan, moving a box. Cemirowl reached for another one, and was surprised it was so light. She looked inside.

"Empty."

Ewan nodded and went to work with a will, stacking the boxes opposite the barrels. Soon they had the way clear and found the door. It was locked.

Ewan put his torch near the door.

"I know these locks, or ones like it. They're for the royal sets. Only Their Majesties might have those keys, or perhaps the lord steward or lord marshal might have it, otherwise. I'd guess. Oh, and the prince."

"Oh, surely not the prince, in this case," Cemirowl murmured. "He has his own means of accessing the cellar we wish to explore, no doubt." She looked at Ewan. "How do you know this... lock?"

"Oh, sometimes we have to know who can open up a cupboard or chest or door if we're to clean or move things." He bent to it again, examining it. "For a lock like this, a knight would have to ask permission, never someone like me. If ever I had cause, I'd have to ask a squire, who would send the request up ranks to get it unlocked. Never has happened in my lifetime, nor my pa's, that a servant could do anything but look at the thing." He turned to her again. "What are you looking for, my lady... er... Priest."

She gave him a wry look. "A body, I'm afraid."

"A body?"

She nodded. "Yes. I think someone murdered the queen's midwife."

"She's a commoner, or little better," he said with a shrug.

Cemirowl turned to him, and asked angrily, "Does that make her less worthy of notice?"

Ewan shook his head. "No. It's just that most nobles and the lord marshal would think that she was. At least compared to the queen, they might not care at all."

"That is, no doubt, why no one has missed her." She tried the door, but it would not budge.

"I take it there's no way to get in?" she asked Ewan. Adventure too soon over.

"Not unless you can divine a way," Ewan said, with a nervous laugh.

She laughed, surprised she hadn't thought of it herself. Cemirowl altered her focus a little and waited. "Is there a way in?" she whispered.

She nearly didn't catch the movement, the darkness obscuring her eyesight. She felt it more than saw it first: a tiny glimmer of a scurrying move. She held out her hand, willing Ewan to remain still, and saw it again. It was a little ghost mouse. The tiniest of her bones in her basket upstairs. It moved to a spot in the door and then disappeared.

Cemirowl touched the door. It was still solid to her, but she pushed a little harder and felt the wood giving way, but not by much. She handed the lantern to Ewan. "Here, hold the lantern and shine it so that I can see what I'm doing."

With both hands she was able to push the spot in a bit further. Ewan saw what she was doing.

"No, ma'am, let me," he said, and handed the lights back to her.

He grabbed a piece of wood and slammed it into the spot with a dull thud and opened up a hole. He put his hand through and felt around. She could hear him fiddle with the door. She heard the latch shift. He grinned as he opened the door, pointing at the key on the other side of the lock.

"Looks royal, but wouldn't it be strange for them to forget it?" he asked.

"Probably, but how would I know?" she asked him. "And why put a key in a door with boxes piled up on the other side?"

Cemirowl realized Ewan was caught up in the adventure, not realizing they had just broken past a royal lock for which there must be consequences. "Good work, but if anyone ever asks, I did this myself," Cemirowl said. "Now, let's go in. Quietly now, we don't want to disturb anyone upstairs."

Ewan nodded and paled.

They went forward and avoiding the stairs to their left which led up to the prince's apartments, Cemirowl and Ewan moved into the room that was obviously no longer in use.

"Do you want me to go in there?" asked Ewan, horrified.

He was staring into what was more than a dropped floor. In the torch and lantern light, it looked like a deep pit. Cemirowl looked up to the ceiling. They were underneath what looked like ancient framing, with newer stonework having been added to it. She was no builder, but massive rough stone stood against smoother stonework. She looked back down at the sinkhole; her heart began to pound. Its edges mostly did not quite reach the walls of the room. It was still large. *The Story of Soft Water!* Thade had once tried to build a stone castle on what was now a village green. The ground around the river was too soft and the foundations collapsed. He'd been forced to move upriver to a foundation of rock. Cemirowl was amazed that the whole building had not collapsed. Cemirowl swallowed the lump in her throat. *Well, it hasn't fallen yet.* Clearly neither old nor younger building had fallen.

"Hold on. I need to make sure that this is where I need to go."

If she could avoid it, she did not want to go down there. Cemirowl didn't know for sure that Abenne was there. However, if her body wasn't reeking up the prince's apartments above, this would be the likeliest place. Except for her animals and her grandmother's vague, but anxious presence, Cemirowl felt nothing. She closed her eyes and focused. Searching for that odd sense of 'tie'—as she called it—of a spirit's connection to its body, Cemirowl drifted deeper into focus. It was faint or, rather, far. She opened her eyes and focused on the light of the lantern, then turned to Ewan. He still looked pale.

She took the torch from him, and lit it with the lantern.

"How long will this torch stay lit?" she asked Ewan.

"An hour, I think, ma'am."

"If I don't come back in half an hour, then go get someone to find me. Don't come to find me alone."

"You're going in there?" he asked, appalled.

"Yes. I have to. Besides, it may not be that deep," she said to cheer him, even though she already knew it would be.

She went toward the sinkhole. Rough steps had been made with fallen stone and this gave her some confidence that others had gone down this way. Then she remembered what she was looking for. Of course she'd seen dead bodies before. Plenty of them, young and old. However, she'd never journeyed through a cavern to find a body more than three days old and further one which she suspected was covered in live and dead spiders. Even without the spiders, it would not be a pleasant find. She could go tell the king, but she could not abandon the pull of the ghost and her duty to the dead.

Carefully making her way down the stone steps, she came to the bottom and found herself in a small space. When she looked up, light from Ewan's lantern showed that only a small part of the sinkhole's rim was visible. She moved her torch around and saw a dark space. Carefully moving her torch as to not burn herself, she tried to see the shadow better. Crouching down, she saw that she could move into the opening. It would mean walking stooped over, with the torch in front of her. There wouldn't be room to move her torch about either, unless she squatted or sat, turned on her bottom at the risk of scorching her hair.

Clenching her teeth and breathing out a small moan of reluctance, Cemirowl went in. Even making her way stooping low, Cemirowl could tell that she was moving steadily downward. The walls she touched grew damp. Nothing else changed for a long while, but the size and shape of the tunnel. At one point she had to slide through stone walls, as the wall rounded into the passage. In the wavering light, it almost looked as if huge stones lay upon each other. The path, however, was choice-less. She could only go forward or back. Only at one point could she almost go up, when the tunnel opened, vaulting upward in a narrow, long chimney. Beyond the depth of her light, there was no way of knowing how far up it went. The echo of her voice came weirdly back to her.

Cemirowl began repeating to herself the litany of the four provinces and humors from choleric to melancholy. When she finished, she repeated the three choruses she knew best about sanguinity. Wondering when the passage was going to end, she began reciting some poems in praise of the gatekeeper. During her murmured renditions on the centered province, she'd begun to hear the sound of rushing water. It had been faint at first, but as she kept moving it began to grow louder. This journey was taking longer than she expected.

She was beginning to tire of the smell of torch smoke and dirt. Her eyes were burning from the oily soot. Her face was no doubt black. If she didn't come upon anything soon, she would turn back.

The tunnel suddenly opened up into a cavern. Heart pounding, Cemirowl was grateful that she'd been moving carefully. She leaned out and shined her torch into space. The fall would probably not have hurt her much, but no doubt it would have put out the torch. She looked up. Odd, tall, clearly natural columns stood in the cavern. They were not straight nor uniform, but slightly narrow toward the center and rather textured. Some of the columns had skirts that fanned horizontally around them. There were shelves running along the walls that corresponded to the skirts, broken in places. The fragile ledges reminded her of fungi fanning out from fallen logs. They were on the same level as her tunnel. Cemirowl noticed that the smell of water was stronger here.

She looked down again. The drop to the floor was not so far that she wouldn't be able to get back. A small pile of rocks stood along the cavern wall, not quite below her. When she dropped she would not disturb them, nor would the pile of stones make her landing awkward.

She sat down on the rim of the tunnel, holding her torch

carefully and then slid into the tunnel. For a brief moment the torch sputtered, nearly giving Cemirowl heart failure. She did not relish making the return trip in total darkness.

As the sound of her beating heart subsided, she realized that the sound of the rushing water was loud in this cavern. She moved forward to look for the source of the sound while her heart calmed. A glimmer of reflected light pointed the way, so she made her way toward the shifting gleam. Expecting a torrential river, Cemirowl was surprised that she found something only the size of a small creek. It had cut deep into the ground. Though the creek was not as large as she expected, she knew that she'd not wish to jump across it.

Looking around for a direction to go, and looking back the direction she had come, she realized that she could only follow one direction. There were no obvious outlets. The ground was a gentle slope and dusty. She bent down to touch the ground and realized that it felt like dried mud rather than loose dirt, silted rather than crumbly. There was a cool breeze, that smelled very lightly of salt, but it was a near metallic scent of minerals that was laden in the air. Nothing rich, she guessed, for mining, but rather like the soil from the best tended croft. But deeper, less organic. Less cow or goat manure.

She noticed that there were some odd looking white crickets that moved away from her light. A shudder came over her. She stood, trembling and explored deeper into the cavern. Cemirowl wanted the trip to be over, so she focused on the otherworld for a moment. She felt nearer the 'tie' of the midwife's soul than she had been, but that it was still far and faint.

As she walked slowly and carefully down the gentle incline of the floor, Cemirowl saw another stone cairn. Turning, she could still see the first one, though faintly, almost out of the limits of her light. She looked around, and noticed one near her, and realized it must have been a marker for her path, and not some natural rock formation. She went toward the new one which had been placed near the underground creek. From there, she saw another cairn on the other side and yet another one by an opening just beyond it. The opening was a large, pointed, uneven oval but it was clearly her path.

She took a breath and jumped across the only narrow place the creek afforded, as well as the lowest, and went into the hole. It was a short tunnel; her light was already reaching the other end. She felt as if she must be near the cliff wall, if her sense of direction was accurate. She was very willing to believe, however, that this sense might be completely wrong underground.

Cemirowl was grateful for the cairns, well aware of how foolish this solitary exploration was. With a faint breath of hope, she thought that, either way, the end of her journey might be close. She did not want to leave Abenne's spirit tied to this world, alone in these caverns. It was the funerary priest in her, the one who cared for the dead as well as the living, which made her continue moving. She could almost feel Abenne's anguish.

Still jittery and nervous she came upon a fairly open cavern. The first thing she noticed about this new cavern was the smell of ammonia, which had become rather overpowering. The cave wasn't as tall as the one she'd left and though the echo of the creek was clearly audible, here there was also a sound of dripping and, periodically, an odd humming whine that came with a light movement of air. The floor was dark and glittering. The ceiling looked jagged with deep shadows and odd, pale, jutting teeth. She couldn't be sure, but it looked as if there were other openings to other tunnels or caverns near the ceiling, but beyond her reach. When she looked for markers, she saw that a few of the stalactites were clearly marked with red cord.

Briefly, Cemirowl wondered why cairns had not been used, but was grateful for the sign that other people had been here before. She ventured into the cavern farther. Her feet squelched into deep mud. With a wave of distaste that roiled up through her loins and into her throat, she bravely moved toward the first marked pillar, lifting her skirts in one hand. With a shout she realized that the glittering on the dark, stinking mud were actually crawling, swarming insects.

Suddenly dark things fluttered around her head, having dropped from the ceiling.

She yelped loudly.

Holding her torch with an arm guarding her face, Cemirowl pulled her skirts up higher with her other hand and slogged her way at a sliding, disgusting run under stalactites and bats, from column to column. She came to a wall with an opening above the floor at the height of her knees. She'd have to stoop again, but she fairly leapt to the shelter. She sat for a few moments calming her heart thudding in her chest.

The first thing that came to mind was an answer to a mystery. She'd seen bats feeding on insects in the dark twilight of her forest home. Now she knew where they lived. She realized, because of the smell, what she'd been running through. The knowledge made her shudder and she fought to keep down the remains of her supper.

"Bat droppings," she said disgustedly, not even wanting to consider why the insects obviously adored it.

It had not been a pleasant adventure. As high as she'd held

her skirts, they were still touched with filth. Then she laughed.

"You silly wench! You should have run the *other* way!"

She should have gone back for help, told either Mercor or the king her belief that Abenne was dead in these caves. She was bitterly glad she had not. An embroidered handkerchief burned in her pouch, the bundle of it against her thigh under her surcoat. Cemirowl realized that if he'd been party to these deaths, she did not wish to betray Prince Arthan without proof.

You're hopeless, she told herself and felt tears come. She did not wish to regret the small kindness he'd afforded her.

Saddened, she stood, hit her head and the torch on the ceiling of the tunnel.

"Ow!" she cried and rubbed her head. She took a deep breath to not give way to more emotions. Taking a deep breath, coughing and gagging on the stench of guano, she stooped and moved on.

Even if it was stupid, Cemirowl did not want to go back through the bat droppings and insects yet. It would feel like defeat and silly after the worst was—hopefully—over.

Though the tunnel was shorter than the first, but longer than the second one, the ceiling loomed lower and she was forced to stoop even more. She scraped against the wall to her left once, making her arms and spine shiver.

The cavern into which she emerged stunned her. It wasn't wildly different from the first cavern, but it was more varied and something about it was awe inspiring and lovely.

The cavern was beautiful. There was only the hint of a stream, the sound of it only a trickle. In this cavern, the sound of dripping was louder. The echoes were melodic. Near her, in a straight fall from the ceiling were a number of long, thin pillars all grouped together that did not reach the ground. She reached out to touch the bottom of one, but it crumbled in her hand even as she felt water along its rim. It was hollow. She was amazed. "Like a flute," she said.

Along the wall nearby, the same straw-like formations seemed to fan out, creating stone pillars of grouped fans. Farther into the cavern she saw that the rough, natural columns had not all reached the ground. In the cavern she'd just left, the cones covering the ground had been covered in bat droppings. Moving through the forest of stalagmites and hanging icicles of stalactites, Cemirowl realized that they would probably one day meet and make the natural columns she'd seen in the first cavern. Some were near completion, but the ones that merely reached for each other enchanted her.

She looked to see the cairn marking her way back and looked for the next one.

She slid in a thin layer of mud. The torch fluttered. Through a break between some of the stone icicles, she saw a flowing curtain-like formation. Waves of what was probably fragile stone, if the straw-like flutes were any indication, was made beautiful by the layers of different shades and colors running through them. Trying to see it better, she saw another cairn, nearly in shadows at the other end of the cavern. It was lucky that she'd seen it, for the conical hedge of stalagmites she wandered through could easily have hidden it from view. She made her way through the blunt spikes emerging from the ground, and under the drooping teeth.

In the melodic dripping quiet of the place Cemirowl felt more at peace than she had in a year. She felt as if here, with enough light, she could find truths that eluded her. Standing still, breathing in the quiet, she touched the fear she'd felt inside herself the other night.

As she closed her eyes, she remembered the smell of the woods, of turned earth in spring and the moldering leaves of autumn. Slowly, as the scent of the cavern grew, an idea emerged. In all her walks in the woods Cemirowl had been building a wall between herself and the village; she hid from them as much as they had not wanted to make any peace with her. What she thought of as peace, at home, had been a hiding from the village and from herself.

This place was peace; not hiding, but centering. A place where she could examine herself. It was with sorrow of the thought she knew she wouldn't have been able to see it without having grieved for her mother. In the arms of a prince, Cemirowl had stopped hiding from herself.

The cavern felt like a home that she'd never known she'd been missing. There was no way that she could live in this place, nor should she. It was a retreat. Home and cathedral in one, but living happened above ground, even with the many complications in the upper world. In the brief hiatus, she calmly breathed in the clear and rich scents of water and earth and even the lingering acrid smell of ammonia rising from her skirts. In the short time she allowed the cavern's peace to touch her, she realized that she could now face the secrets of her abilities that she'd refused to think on or even explore.

Gently pushing away her regret, Cemirowl opened her eyes and moved toward the next cairn. There was work to do and a body to find. Even with the time limit of the torch, she did not regret the time she'd spent in the cavern.

An opening in a wall of columns, with two cords tied on

either side, led her through to the next cavern, like a doorway. She entered into another cavern, or another part of the same one. Bats were in this one too, but most of the droppings were at the bottom of the cavern below a ledge that ran along one side. Unless she dropped or slid down the cliff-like wall, the ledge was the only place she could traverse. The bottom of the cave was too far off for her to get back easily. The ledge was narrow in places, but not so narrow that one could not walk along it.

Even to Cemirowl, it was clear that bats had not been in this cavern long. She could clearly smell their droppings, but there was some other unpleasant stench rising as well. Though there were some rather tall, narrow columns, there were a few places along the lumpy bottom of the cavern that looked like teeth erupting from the ground. Along the bottom of the walls was one large dark spot, which Cemirowl suspected was another opening. Looking up, the teeth-like stalactites were emerging from the ceiling. Some of the curtains were also beginning to form. A number of bats hung among them and the teeth. There was more evidence of bats in other places, covered in the white crickets and spiders she'd seen in the other cave.

The sound of this cavern was eerie. It seemed to echo with an undulating moan, more pronounced than in the other cavern. It was almost as if the cave was breathing. Beginning to tremble, wondering what creature was making the eerie noise, Cemirowl forced herself to calm and allowed her mind to think of what the noise reminded her. She then remembered the surf. *I must be near the cliff, near the ocean.*

Her heart was thudding inside her, but Cemirowl focused on the otherworld again. Almost immediately, Cemirowl sensed Abenne.

She opened up her eyes and walking along the ledge, slowly waved her torch around, gagging on the rising stench of putrefaction. Roughly two-thirds of the way into the room, she saw a disconcerting heap below the ledge. Broken among the teeth, covered in spiders and beginning to be covered in bat droppings.

She made her way gingerly along the ledge and then lay down in the few droppings and spiders on the path. Lowering her torch, Cemirowl knew that she'd never be able to make the drop and get back without help. With the light shining on the woman's guano spotted face, there was no doubt that it was Abenne and not some odd cave formation.

For a moment Cemirowl wondered if it was possible that Abenne had not been murdered, but had fallen. The ledge that Cemirowl lay on, however, was one of the widest sections. Examining the area, she saw that gold coins also glittered near the body. For some reason, with the wide ledge, and the gold coins, accidental death seemed doubtful. Thinking of the offices for the dead and Abenne's unhappy spirit, Cemirowl wondered how she could solve the funerary problem. With ropes and help she could get the body and take it to its rest and bury it properly, even if Abenne was already, technically, in the ground. Here, however, there would be no way for her loved ones to honor or remember her. There could be no clean grieving if she left the body here.

Looking down at the midwife's body, something she remembered came to mind. Cursing herself for a fool, she realized that Arthan wasn't the only one to know about the cave. She was sure of it. If he'd secretly needed a midwife, and stupidly brought her through these caverns, the person he'd brought the midwife to would have known about the cave as well. Someone with more reason to talk privately with a midwife than a man.

Amec had given her another clue, suspect though he had been. If it was poison or yellow creeper that had killed the queen, she could not have been crying. The ladies Terria and Soflia had seen him leaving. The weeping he'd heard would have been by her killer. Had she planned to kill the queen?

Cemirowl knew who had killed the queen. But she had enough doubt to not want to make the accusation out loud. It was not merely doubt. Cemirowl simply didn't know enough about the court to be sure, she had no physical proof, and if portents and second-sight were not proof, neither were feelings.

Feeling tired and discontented, she knew that there were many more questions that she needed to ask. Though the questions would be difficult for their delicacy, their answer would probably set the thing in stone. Despite her doubts, the only thing that remained incomprehensible was the motive.

Cemirowl spoke the words to ease Abenne's spirit and cut her soul free. She then raised herself up and walked back up to the other cavern with the fragile flute-like hangings, the colored stone curtains and the pillars reaching toward completion. Cemirowl reached for the same sense of peace, but was too heartsore to recapture the feeling. Besides Ewan was probably fairly desperate for her return, if he had not already gone for help. She knew that she had been down here for at least the better part of an hour, if not, she suspected, a little longer. She hoped her torch would last for the trip back.

A light came from the other side of the cavern, and Cemirowl went forward. "Who is there?" she asked, guessing it was Ewan's search party.

Only one person walked through the hedge of stalagmites,

instead of a number of rescuers. Cemirowl's heart began to pound. Another stupid move: Cemirowl had told Les to tell anyone she'd gone looking for the midwife. Only one person knew where Abenne lay dead—and not someone Cemirowl wanted to meet alone in the caverns after leaving that body.

The person came forward, torch held high. Cemirowl was surprised to see that the person's face was hidden in shadow of a hood. The cloak did not seem to hide a dress. As her heart beat faster and louder, Cemirowl wondered how inaccurate her last guess had been.

"Who are you?" Cemirowl asked, unable to keep the fear from her voice.

"So, you think you're clever?" asked the figure angrily. The voice seethed so low that Cemirowl could still not confirm her guess. "Above yourself, perhaps? Think you could have him?"

Bewildered by this nonsense, but feeling as if someone else was swirling in a morass of misinformation as well, Cemirowl almost laughed. "What? Have whom?" she asked.

The cloaked figure said nothing, but continued moving forward. Knowing she was in danger, Cemirowl tried to circle around the cloaked person.

The only warning she had was the fluttering of cloak and wild sputtering of torchlight. Cemirowl was smashed into the stalagmites. They were harder than she'd expected. Sliding in the thin layer of mud, Cemirowl pushed back, attacking with her own torch. It was quickly knocked from her hand.

As they struggled, clawing and hitting each other, the figure's movement revealed a hint of long hair and Cemirowl knew her to be a woman. It was too dark in the wavering light to tell the color, but the realization gave her a wave of courage, even if she still couldn't see the face. It meant she was not fighting a well-trained man.

Unfortunately, the discovery did not help her as she struggled against this person's silent fury. Kicking, hitting and pushing, her attacker suddenly broke away, stepped back and then thrust her own torch in Cemirowl's face with a wordless yell of anger.

Arms waving, Cemirowl staggered back, tripped and slipped between a hedge of spires.

The world shifted. Pain thundered inside her head. Her eyes rocked back into her skull while fire seared her shoulders. Cemirowl's head squelched in mud, the right side of her forehead and face was splattered with filth. The woman leapt forward and pinioned Cemirowl within rising stone cones.

Even through cloth, Cemirowl's shoulders scraped against stalagmites. Her arm began to throb. She'd fallen with one arm pinned under the small of her back. As the woman crawled over Cemirowl's legs, she wedged them firmly between two lumpy stalagmites. Cemirowl was well and truly trapped, unable to move either of her arms, or her legs.

Cemirowl struggled, but her attacker set one knee upon her chest and calmly set her torch where it would not go out. The figure moved as if she had all the time in the world.

Cemirowl felt fear roil up from her toes, all the way to her scalp in a wave of helplessness. And another wave roiled up through her, as she remembered Ewan. If this woman, whose face she still couldn't see, whose identity she still couldn't confirm, felt such a wealth of patience, then Ewan may have been hurt. Cemirowl began to struggle in her need to find him, but her attacker leaned forward and wrapped her hands around

Cemirowl's throat and slowly began to throttle her.

In the intimacy of their positions there was even less doubt that the attacker was a woman. Cemirowl struggled to free either shoulder or arm, but could not.

Cemirowl had always believed that she'd face death with equanimity. She was sure that there were still some surprises for her, but she knew life did not end once her body had died.

Feeling the growing pressure around her throat, it was her whole body that rebelled against dying. Her body did not want the pain her attacker was forcing upon her. It wanted to breathe and it struggled, almost without Cemirowl being aware of it. The world around her seemed lit in sharp relief. Death was taking forever, the killer being hampered by the odd angle of Cemirowl's wedged body and the obstacles of the stalagmites in her way. The woman had to hold herself from sliding, even while she slowly throttled Cemirowl.

Peace came slowly to Cemirowl and she stopped fighting. Her eyes already felt dull and she could almost hear words from the dead shouting at her.

"Focus!" she finally heard her father say clearly.

"Focus," said her grandmother, and Cemirowl almost felt the touch of her fingers on her face.

Cemirowl looked up through the corners of her eyes at the dark face above her, the light glinting only on the nose and brow. It looked like a skull. It was like a glimmer of light in pitch darkness, or the feather touch of one hair on the arm.

Sensing the soul inside the figure, as if it was the skull of a dead animal, Cemirowl whispered to her, "Stay with me."

The change was not immediate. Cemirowl's world was growing dark. The sound of the realm of the dead seemed nearer, as if that world had its own noise, like that of crickets calling, or the burble of streams. The realm started to grow more distinct.

Cemirowl, looking up toward the top of the far wall, saw her grandmother standing over her. In a peaceful wave of recognition, Cemirowl thought, *You look like me.*

Like humming, there came an echo of voices from what seemed like vast numbers of spirits coming to Cemirowl. Abenne was there, her grandmother, her father, Meelac and countless others she did not bother to identify. They reached for her and for her attacker. The woman's hands loosened with a gasp.

"What? Who are you?" the woman cried out, stepping back.

Painfully air came back into her lungs. Cemirowl gasped for breath. In a sudden swirl of vertigo, the living world slowly and painfully came back into focus. The images and sense of the spirits faded. With a deep breath and another swirl of vertigo, Cemirowl was able to release an arm, but little else. Her attacker's body weight had wedged her in between the stalagmites quite firmly.

From her trapped position Cemirowl craned her neck and watched as the woman looked wildly about the cavern.

The woman's hood had fallen back but she stood in shadows cast by the sputtering torch. Cemirowl barked in frustration. The figure had her back to Cemirowl. The woman was waving her arms about, brushing off the touch of the dead, flinching and stumbling.

Above the sound of her own labored breathing, Cemirowl could hear the woman's breath come in hyperventilating gasps. "No! This isn't happening! You can't!" she wailed.

In an aching effort, Cemirowl craned her neck further to look. The world spun, shifted to firmness and spun again. One figure, hair glowing and long, came through the assembled spirits. The spirit walked stately and beautiful. Walking her way slowly toward her killer, Tidyri raised her arm to slap her.

Cemirowl's attacker gasped and cried. "Help me! Oh help me!"

The sounds echoed weirdly throughout the cavern. She turned and fled, weaving and stumbling as if she were dizzy. *Vertigo,* Cemirowl thought.

Cemirowl struggled as another voice came echoing through the cavern, calling out, "Help is coming!"

Cemirowl could not even croak out a response. She tried to wriggle free. With her one arm free, she pulled against a stalagmite and freed her torso to some degree. She could not move much else. Light came near. Cemirowl could only hope that it was her own rescue party and not unguessed confederates of the wailing person in the cavern.

A growing light and shadow loomed over her, wavering. She looked up.

"Well, it seems as if you're well and truly stuck," growled Arthan. "I should leave you down here for stupidity. What in the world possessed you to come down here alone with only one poor, frightened boy as a guard? In the middle of the night, no less?"

"The spider," she croaked, reaching for his hand.

He grabbed her wrist and pulled, giving her enough leverage to free her other arm. She pushed herself up, while he pulled. The force nearly threw her into an embrace. She pushed back and stumbled back from him. She was free, and standing, hand to her throat, still gasping for breath.

"Thank you, Your Highness," she managed to croak out.

"I'm assuming that you're not alone as your groom was

found with a lump on his head and we find you stuck between stalagmites with something that is not a trick of shadows rising on your neck. Where is she?"

"How did you guess?" Her voice came out hoarse.

"Don't talk, just point. We'll get you some wine to soothe that throat later. We'll take care of the person who did this."

She gestured in the last direction she'd seen the terrified woman. The marshal of the guard and another knight went off in that direction. Arthan took out a handkerchief and began to wipe the mud off her face.

"I'm sorry it took me so long to get here," he said. His voice, though still gruff, was gentle. "After you left, there were things I needed to tell my brother. It wasn't till my brother finished shouting my ear off and I was able to get back to my rooms that I realized your seeing the midwife might mean more than seeing her in the flesh. If you had seen her spirit and had connected her with the spider, she could only have been in one place. That is how I knew."

He paused for a moment and clutched her shoulders and looked intently in her face. "I'm sorry that you couldn't tell me."

Cemirowl began to sob. "For a while, I was afraid it might be you," she admitted, hanging her head in shame.

"That doesn't surprise me," he said gently, and then more angrily added, "She did her best to implicate me, without being obvious about it. A good number of people were quite ready to believe I want the throne. The marshal of the guard told me about the rumors that had been circulating around the castle, which wasn't a pleasant interview, to be sure."

"But it was stupid," Cemirowl said.

"No doubt you are as faulty as any of us. There were a

number of better suspects. Even the Honorable Ferran was questioned. He had not great love for the queen." He paused, then said, "I did not truly know what she had done till I realized how you must have identified Abenne. It was my stupidity and foolishness that led to this pass and gave her the means to wreak the havoc." Cemirowl noted he could not say her name. He continued, "I wanted to find Abenne myself; when I thought you had seen her, I had hope that I could find my answers through her. It was staggering to realize that she must have been dead and for some time as well. I did not know what to think when I saw that poor boy above the caverns."

The two knights came back with a hobbling figure between them. "She broke her ankle, Your Highness."

"We don't have anything to bind it with, here. We'll have to take her back up before we can fix it."

The figured moaned, "Please, no! Make them go away!" she wailed.

The marshal and the other man took a stronger hold on her, as if she would begin to fight going with them. She clung to them instead. With a shrug, the two dragged her to the other cavern.

As they slowly made their way back through the tunnel, Cemirowl stopped the prince. "The midwife! I found her," she said, gesturing behind them.

"We'll have to come back and get her. You need rest."

Cemirowl nodded. Her whole body hurt. After the grueling ride to get to the castle, she'd thought her legs would hurt for weeks. Now, as she painfully stooped forward into the cave, she realized it was nothing compared to her new aches and bruises. *What a delightful trip this has been!* Cemirowl thought wryly.

She stopped at the entrance of the cave filled with bat droppings and insects. She'd known that she'd have to go through it again, but the prospect of comfort and a bed gave her courage, even as Arthan pushed her into the cavern. She thought wryly back to her reading with Harlyn. The passage hadn't been metaphorical. It wasn't what she walked through that made her queasy. She would always wonder if she might have been able to read that Harlyn was the murderer from that throw. It didn't matter. Even if she had, it wouldn't have been proof.

When they finally made their way up the stairs into Arthan's apartments, the king and his guard were waiting for the prisoner. Light shone much more brightly, painful for a moment. Cemirowl could finally see her attacker's face and confirm her identity. The confirmation fell flat in the face of all that this woman had done.

Lady Harlyn quaked, miserable and moaning in a heap as two knights bound her ankle in splints. She was not wearing a dress, merely her pantaloons and a shift cut high, prepared for spiders and bat guano.

King Larthor looked at Lady Harlyn's miserable face and then at his brother and at Cemirowl. "Are you sure?" he growled.

Arthan said, "Yes, Your Majesty."

Cemirowl only nodded.

With a nod, the king's guards moved toward Harlyn.

Cemirowl started forward. "Your Majesty..."

"It will wait," snapped the king as they took Harlyn to a cell. Larthor followed but turned at the door, saying, "It is late. Get bathed. You all stink. I want explanations in the morning when you smell better." He left the room and slammed the door.

Arthan turned to Cemirowl and pushed her in the nearest

seat, despite all the filth covering her.

He looked at a yawning valet and said, "Wine... Clary."

It was brought forward and Cemirowl drank the sweetened wine. The honey eased her throat.

"I think your neck will be black by morning as well as the rest of you," he said sadly.

Cemirowl began to weep, leaning forward, the goblet of wine hanging from her hands between her knees.

"What? What is wrong?" he asked, kneeling in front of her, taking the wine and setting it on a table nearby.

She shook her head and sat straighter, looking up at him. "I was frightened," she said. "She was trying to kill me."

"That is not an event someone would rush toward with glee."

She shook her head again. "I called her."

"I don't understand."

"When I find animal bones," she said hoarsely, "I call the spirit to stay with me. I couldn't move down there. She was choking me... and I called her. She can see the dead now. She doesn't understand. She can't, and she's terrified."

Arthan paused for a moment. He handed her the cup again. "Drink. Perhaps I'm angry and tired, but I'm not feeling at all sympathetic toward her. She's going to be executed in a few days. She killed two people and tried to kill you."

"But it drove my mother mad," Cemirowl wailed.

Arthan rocked back on his heels. The scent of clean straw and dried herbs rose up and mingled with their cavern stench as he shifted his weight. After a moment he asked, "Are you worried about her or something else?"

Cemirowl thought for a moment. "Her, a bit, but rather

what I've done. It was easy."

"Ah! That frightens you," Arthan said and stood, gesturing for wine himself. He sat beside her.

"There is so much I don't know."

"Then learn. Now I want to know when you realized that I might not have killed my royal sister and queen," his voice was wry. She looked at him. His brooding temper could not hide the hurt in his eyes.

Cemirowl took a sip of wine, and set aside her own fear. He was right, she would have to learn. For the moment she had to focus on Arthan, and the betrayal in his words. She was glad of the honey: it soothed her throat. She tried to speak, coughed and drank more wine. The cup in her hand trembled. "When I saw the midwife, different clues came together. I'd been told rumors that you'd called her in secret. That was stupid of me. I know whom midwives attend. I do not know why I was distracted." She drank more wine as she became more hoarse.

"You've had a complete shift of surroundings and society, on top of everything else! It is no wonder," he said.

Cemirowl shook her head. "My parents may have been peasants, but my father was a reading man, a thinking man. He raised a thinking daughter." She shook her head again as her voice cracked.

"Thinking or no, you have not lived much in the world I understand?"

She drank more wine. Arthan didn't seem to understand. She tried again. "Regardless, when I saw Abenne's face, I realized then that you weren't the only one who knew of the tunnel—I'm guessing it is a tunnel?"

Arthan nodded. "It goes down to the sea. You can reach the

entrance if you start out at the east end of the beach, when the tide is about three-quarters of the way out. Otherwise you get caught by the tide. You would have to be very lucky to not drown. Harlyn could have seen Abenne when the midwife was visiting the queen, but she said she did not want such a *delicate* conversation to be overheard. Too many would know our secret. I wondered, afterwards, because the exchange did not take long, but she'd pleaded for me to help protect her honor." Arthan shook his head. "I don't know. I rather felt more like a puppet than a prince at times."

"Did you care for her?" Cemirowl asked softly.

"No," he said more vehemently than Cemirowl expected.

"Then why..."

Arthan leaned back in his chair.

"Oh Good Keeper," he seethed through clenched teeth. He turned to Cemirowl. "I loved Boduscia. I spent the months after her death furious at everything. I hated that she was gone. Larthor had to talk to me quite often to control my temper. Harlyn came some weeks later to attend Tidyri.

"Even then she didn't appeal to me. Well, actually no one did, really. I had not invited her. Harlyn came to me in the middle of the night. Doubtless my servants knew about her, but they did not gossip, for which I'm grateful. I'm not sure how it started, why she... What made her believe I..." He could not finish. "We both kept it secret—or I did. Rumors I overheard, nothing was ever mentioned beyond her interest. My brother ordered me away, and I'd planned to send her to the country for her pregnancy, confirmed by Abenne. But by the time I'd made arrangements, she'd lost the child."

He paused. "Even before I left, I'd taken to barring my

doors against her at night. Harlyn was everything Boduscia wasn't. I'd let it happen more than once. I wanted to bury all my grief, though I didn't want to betray her memory. In the end, I did worse than that in bedding Harlyn."

"Why did you show her the tunnel?"

"I didn't show her the tunnel. I only brought the midwife through it. Harlyn knew about it, though. She waited in my rooms, and saw me bring the woman up through the cellar stairs. I betrayed the secret of it because I felt trapped, which if you think of it, is incredibly, tragically ironic. It would never have happened if I had been in my right mind."

He took a deep draught of wine and shook his head. "Larthor put my apartments over it, so that it would *remain* secure. Harlyn could make such a ruckus when she wanted. I was exhausted in grief, depressed by the relationship and disgusted at my own folly.

"It was that which killed any sentiments that I might have had for her. She could seem so kind and generous and willingly self-sacrificing. About that time her lord, Duke Ross, tried to get her to marry. She paid a great deal of money to stop the match. It was a gesture that I misunderstood, adding to my error. I thought she'd lost her heart to me. I tried to make up for my folly by asking my brother if I could wed her instead."

"But you hated her?" Cemirowl croaked. She drank the last of the Clary in her cup.

"And I hurt her. No matter how conniving she might have been, I played a part in her ruin."

Cemirowl looked at his face, shocked. In a small voice she asked, "And you would have married her for that?"

Arthan nodded, asked for a refill for Cemirowl and himself.

"Larthor refused, which I actually thank him for—even if I haven't admitted it to him yet. He sent me away to be out of her clutches for a while. He planned to send her away with reasons other than her interest in me. It was obvious that Harlyn was spending herself into debt."

"But why would she kill Tidyri? I know that she did it, but for the life of me, I cannot understand why! It seems such a petty revenge."

"I can guess, but it isn't pretty."

"What in these past few days has been pretty?" Cemirowl asked.

Arthan looked at her for a moment. He grew very still.

Cemirowl regretted the words, for there had been moments of beauty, ones that even they had shared. He did not say anything about that, though, and Cemirowl finally turned her head and took refuge in her wine as he seemed to taste his own realizations of the past few days.

After a moment he answered the real question. "I had already made it clear to my loyal household that even if I could not avoid her in the majority of the palace grounds, I did not want to see her alone in my rooms. With all those devoted servants barring her, she probably could not get to me in any way that would hurt me without implicating herself. She couldn't get to Larthor, whom I know she was furious with for refusing his consent. I do not know that she found out that he'd planned to send her away, but it's possible. The one person she could attack that would hurt both of us was Tidyri, who was as available to her as the ocean is to a fish. She just had to find a way to do it."

Cemirowl nodded. She thought about the reading she'd done, and wondered at the idea of revenge. What she had seen from the reading was more akin to desperation. Whatever anger had been there had not been enough for that level of retribution. She thought about what Harlyn had asked in the reading, and remembered jealousy—but Cemirowl knew Arthan had not been in love with the queen.

She asked the question, "Why kill Abenne?"

"I'm assuming no matter how she learned about the poisons, Harlyn saw the midwife whenever Abenne came to visit the queen. Even if she couldn't ask for advice about her pregnancy in public, she could at least ask to meet her in the tunnel for a more private interview. There, she somehow got the poisons she wanted and used it on Tidyri. She couldn't leave the midwife as a witness. My last question is how did she get in?"

"When we saw the door, Ewan suggested that it was a lock that opened by a royal key. The queen's keys, did she have use of them?" Cemirowl asked.

Arthan looked surprised, nodded, but said nothing. He shook his head, hand to his face with renewed grief. "So she used the queen's own keys."

After a quiet moment, Arthan added, voicing some train of thought of his own in a low mutter, "I thought Abenne must not have been in town. By then she was probably dead. If it was the same day or night before Tidyri's death, low tide had started turning back long before dawn."

Sipping her Clary, Cemirowl was deep in thought. *Keys, poisons, tide, agreements with the midwife...* Cemirowl had cause to know that Harlyn was free with her gold even when the recipient was doomed in that lady's eyes. A midwife may be swayed to traverse caverns alone for gold. "She planned it," she said finally.

"Yes," he said gently.

"And while the queen was dying, she cut her hair while Tidyri couldn't even struggle."

"Yes," he said again.

There was silence for a while and Cemirowl heard Arthan drink from his goblet. She stared at the floor. She was tired. She was exhausted. She stank. It had been a long, emotional day.

"I want to go home," she said.

Arthan laughed softly, but not untouched by sorrow. "I don't think you can leave tonight," he said gently.

Cemirowl looked at his smile and in his dark eyes, still touched with grief. As tired and sore as she was, she realized that it would be very hard to go home. Events had tied her to this place. She ached at having to deal with the wariness of the villagers and now the boredom, but she wanted to walk through woods again, be in solitude. She'd tasted of wealth and consequence. It was not the dress, but the sure knowledge that there must be more books than Tonn's *Treaties on the Offices for the Dead* in the palace chapel. Her eyes drifting to the floor again, she stood.

"You're tired, I'll have Talbert take you to your room."

She nodded, and quietly made her way back.

Les was bleary-eyed, but helped her out of her filthy clothing.

"I'm not sure I can get this clean," Les said.

Looking at the clothes with revulsion, Cemirowl said, "That's fine, I don't want to see them ever again, anyway. How's Ewan?"

"He's got a lump on his head but the guard marshal commended his bravery, so he went to bed happy."

"I'm glad," Cemirowl said. "Remind me to make a poultice of consound for him, to ease his bruise." With a sigh, she sank into the tub the king had been kind enough to order. The water had cooled somewhat, but it helped ease her head made fuzzy by wine.

Les scrubbed her hair and her back, helped her dry off, dress for bed, and then tucked her into bed. Cemirowl could not face the dark alone, not with what she'd done, and seen, and learned. Lips trembling, looking up at her servant, she asked softly, "Stay with me, Les. I don't want to be alone."

Les nodded and pulled a pallet out from under the bed. Cemirowl was surprised to see it, but in general needing privacy Cemirowl was grateful that Les had not assumed she could use the pallet. With a hand toward the edge of the bed Cemirowl was comforted by the girl's presence.

It was only a few hours after dawn, but despite the early hour, Rimmel brought Caballier Mercor word of the Bone Reader's and the prince's discovery.

"That is good news," he said, as a valet brought him some weak morning ale.

He nodded thanks and took a draught.

"Give me a moment of peace?" he asked calmly. Rimmel cleared the room, closing the door himself.

He almost fell to his knees in gratitude. "Not Amec!"

He had not spoken to the king about his knowledge of his beloved's brother. He trembled in the relief of what he might have done if he had! He called Rimmel back to help him dress. It was vital that he tell the ambassador, and his friend, the news.

In the morning Les helped Cemirowl into another new dress. Earlier that morning, with a knock that woke them, a page delivered a necklace Arthan had sent. Holding the bejeweled thing that implied there were more court appearances ahead, she realized that facing the terror of her abilities would have to wait. She had duties to others, Harlyn, Arthan, and the king, that needed attention first. Her ghost animals swirled around her, comforting her in her surge of panic. They were proof she could put grief and fear aside. Years of acting as a priest had also taught her the ability to set her own needs aside.

The collar fit loosely around Cemirowl's neck, hiding her bruises. Though the dress was nicer than her clothes from home, it did not do the necklace justice. Les put aside the gift reluctantly, and found a thick ribbon that served better.

While Les combed Cemirowl's hair, Ewan came in with bread, cheese and watered wine. Together the three feasted. He was clearly excited and had been awake even earlier getting news and being praised for his part. Cemirowl lauded him for his bravery and put a poultice on his sore head. Les had only seen the filth and the confusion the night before and had not heard the whole tale which Ewan told with great enthusiasm. Les was awed that Cemirowl had helped to find the queen's killer.

Cemirowl would have loved more rest; her body was still aching and her throat hurt. However Ewan and Les carried most of the conversation in their rumors and awe. Cemirowl gently corrected an assumption here and there, skirting the secret of the caverns. She did not wish to be the one who made the security of the castle any less fragile.

There was a knock as Ewan was telling a tale of another caballier lauding his bravery. A valet had come to fetch her to the prince.

Entering Prince Arthan's rooms, Cemirowl curtsied to him, "Your Highness," she said, feeling shy again. She wondered at her presumption of the night before, lulled by exhaustion, wine and the comfort of his rooms. She would make an effort not to be so rude or informal now. She stifled a yawn and decided that she would sleep for the first ten days after her return home, with her bruises packed in a poultice of consound.

Arthan gave her a wry smile and said, "I thought you might wish to see Lady Harlyn. I understand she's been wailing all night. You might be able to gain some understanding of what you were able to do last night and... possibly ease her mind."

It was a considerate gesture, if a hard one for both of them.

"Thank you. I do wish to see her, Your Highness."

They made their way down the corridors and gardens that took them east, past the ambassador's suites, more barracks, and a grim courtyard stained in blood. He led her down the stairs to the dungeons. A bored looking caballier, and a few watchmen sitting on pallets on the floor were playing dice in a space cleared of straw, but stood when the prince and his companion entered.

Arthan nodded to them and led Cemirowl to a narrow passageway with doors on either side. He knocked at the first door along the passage marked with four more doors. As Arthan waited, leaning on the doorjamb, his arms were crossed. He fiddled with the pendant brought out from his shirt, his fingertips turning white.

Whatever Arthan had said last night, his face betrayed some concern for Lady Harlyn. Pain was etched around his eyes. His mouth betrayed, not regret or loss perhaps, but, that though the predominant emotions he felt toward Harlyn might be antagonism, there had been enough shared kindness between them that he'd regret the last hours of her life.

A beleaguered looking guard opened the door. Harlyn sat crumpled in the far corner. Her hands were mitted and bound in front of her. Scratches on her face revealed why.

"She tried to tear her eyes out," her guard said by way of explanation.

"How else is she doing?" Arthan asked him.

"She's quieted down this past hour, Your Highness."

Not even Cemirowl's mother Ferioul had looked quite so wretched. The ankle had swollen in the night, as well, but it was clear that her incarceration was not the source of Harlyn's distress.

"Good God! Was your mother like this?" Arthan asked, but so softly that Cemirowl barely heard him.

"Similar. More listless and wasted... but she had long understood it was futile to fight. She had lived with it longer."

Torn between pity and guilt, Cemirowl decided not to do

this again to anyone.

She went forward and tried to see if Lady Harlyn would look her in the face, but Harlyn's eyes were unfocused. Focusing, centering, Cemirowl tried to see if there was any way that she could understand what she had done. If she could, then she might be able to change it.

She sat down on the floor and focused even deeper. Cemirowl could not see anything different, but the spirits around Harlyn became clearer to her. Their actions toward the lady showed that they had already judged her.

Rising from her concentration, she stood and turned to Prince Arthan. "I wish I had not done it," she said. "I can't help her."

"Even if she deserves it, death will be a blessing."

Cemirowl said nothing about the anger of the spirits surrounding Lady Harlyn.

"Let's go," Arthan said.

As the guard opened the door, Lady Harlyn began to murmur. They both turned. Harlyn looked up, eyes unfocused, at the three people. She was mumbling incoherently, then her eyes caught and focused on Arthan.

"Arthan!" she called out. "Please help me! They have it all wrong!"

Prince Arthan flinched as if he'd been slapped. "What do they have wrong, Lady Harlyn?" he asked, his voice strained.

"About me! Cemirowl was going to accuse you of the queen's murder! I just know it! I had to stop her! I went to talk to her! I followed her down the stairs," she wailed and flailed her bound hands at creatures only she and Cemirowl could see.

"Oh please, don't come closer!" she cried. "Cemirowl, help

me! They're all around me! You know I'm your friend!"

Arthan stepped one step forward, in front of Cemirowl. "There is a great deal of evidence that accuses you of the queen's death," he said.

"But she is here! It was all a dream! I didn't even cut her hair!" Harlyn gestured to the pallet next to her, wailing. Turning to the figure sitting stately on the pallet, she said, "Am I still in this dream? Tidyri? It never really happened, did it?"

Cemirowl stepped back in the wave of revulsion that came from the queen and Harlyn curled up and sobbed. "Are you dead? Aren't you dead? I just don't know, now!" Harlyn whimpered. "You were going to send me away," she wailed, "and keep him for yourself. I couldn't stand it, but you're here now. Do you forgive me, then?"

Cemirowl was the only one who caught the ghostly part of the exchange between Tidyri and Harlyn. "Keep who?" Tidyri seemed to say, just as confused as Cemirowl.

"Arthan," Harlyn said aloud, looking at Tidyri as if she were alive, gesturing toward the prince with her mitted hand. "And I could see *her* leading him away too!"

Cemirowl looked at Arthan in consternation. The real motive for murder. She hadn't killed her queen, and friend to revenge herself, but to try and keep him.

Arthan blinked, leaned forward. "Lady, surely you do not think Tidyri and I..." he began.

Harlyn lurched as she turned to face him. It was odd for Cemirowl to see the shift of Harlyn's reality, to recognize what she'd only experienced alone.

"But the king..." Harlyn breathed, "he could not have a child, and you... I knew you could. And the way you spoke to her that day!"

Arthan stepped back as if slapped. The guard gasped. He was pale. "No..." he was saying. "Never. Not my brother's wife!" He paused, and looked at Cemirowl. "I only offered to buy her a new book of poetry from a bookseller in the city!"

Cemirowl turned to Arthan and laid a hand on his arm.

Harlyn stumbled up from the pallet with a screech, "Don't touch him, you witch! If I killed her, I can kill you too!"

Arthan stepped forward to protect Cemirowl. He struggled awkwardly with Harlyn.

"No! Harlyn, never did I love the queen in that way. She was my sister, my brother's wife. You had no cause to kill her."

"Kill her? But she lives! Can you not see her?"

"She lies buried in the crypt beside my wife, mother, and sister. You were there."

Harlyn struggled out of his grip with a moan and stumbled back, tripping on the pallet and sliding into the corner.

"And what of your attempts to poison the priest?" Arthan asked.

Harlyn put her mitts to her head. "I didn't care if she lived or died. I would have been happy if someone else drank from the tea I left in her room, discrediting her. Anyone would have served," she spat. "I hated what she might see, and I hated you all!"

Arthan and Cemirowl looked at each other. There was nothing they could do. They turned to leave. Arthan spoke to the caballier, then the guard shut the door behind them.

Silently they made their way back to his apartments.

"Leave word with the king's men that we await his pleasure in my sitting room?" he asked a page, who nodded with a "Yes,

Your Highness," and scurried off. He ordered most of the other people gone.

They were silent for a long while, standing apart, but staring out different windows. Noise from below roused them from their reverie.

Arthan looked at Cemirowl, then went to investigate. She followed.

The smell should have warned them. Before they reached the stairs, the marshal of the guard and a few other knights brought the midwife's body up to the room, carried on a pallet.

"Pardon us, Your Highness, but we need to take her to the chapel and the way through the cellars is blocked at the moment," said the Lord Marshal.

"The cause of her death?"

"We examined her, Your Highness, when we put her on the pallet. She had broken ribs, not bad. Even in the poor light we could see." He paused. "She probably died of a bruised lung."

"So she fell?" asked Arthan.

The marshal shook his head and held up the guano stained weapon in his hand. "We found this cudgel at her feet."

Arthan nodded and the men took the body from the room. The marshal turned. "The tunnel is being filled and pitch being poured over different layers of rock and stone. King's orders, Your Highness," he said, and made his way out the room.

"What a shame that beautiful cavern will never be seen," Cemirowl said when he'd left.

Arthan turned to her.

"You found it beautiful?" he asked. There was a note of pleased surprise in his voice.

She smiled sadly at him. "It was one of the most peaceful

places I have ever been."

"I know what you mean. I explored the caverns for Larthor when it seemed prudent for someone to know them better. Clearly he sees it as a liability now." After a moment's pause he added, "With clear and adequate reason."

Arthan collapsed in his chair, with his face in his hands. "Damn her!" he said.

Cemirowl came close, but made no move to touch him. He would see her nearby if he wanted her.

He looked at her. "You and I both feel pity for her, now, but can you imagine the cruelty of a woman who would poison her friend then humiliate her while she could not fight back? But now we also know that she could also smash a woman's ribs and, probably hearing the woman call out for help for quite a ways, the way those chambers carry echoes, would not go back and help?"

"I don't understand, Abenne…?"

"Don't you know? A bruised lung doesn't kill right away. Depending on the severity of the injury it will drown a man—I've only seen it in battle—slowly in his own blood."

Cemirowl grew sick.

"I feel filthy," Arthan said after a moment.

Something in the way he said the words, so unguarded, Cemirowl was embarrassed. She turned from him, but laid a hand on his chair. She heard him sigh, and saw a movement of his arm, as if he would have reached up to her hand, but he dropped it with another ragged sigh.

They were summoned then. Not looking at each other, they both made their way to the king's office. Yet, despite the sudden emotional distance, she felt tied to this man in a way she'd never shared with any other. It was nothing more than shared events and emotions and an intimacy that was in no way physical. It was nothing she could explain to any other person. Distressing as their thoughts were at the moment, the bond was oddly comforting.

The king was standing by his desk, but had turned looking out the window. When the two entered, he turned and nodded to the knights who closed the door behind them. Larthor looked as if he had not slept.

"I called you two first, as I believe you both know the whole of these appalling events as much as any can. The tunnel and that connection will not become public knowledge," he ordered.

Larthor turned to his brother, "The intimacy of your relationship with Lady Harlyn will probably come to light, but I'll suppress what part you played in teaching her a way to, even unknowingly, help her kill my wife."

"Thank you, Your Majesty," Arthan said.

Larthor sat down and looked intently at his brother. "I know you well, Arthan. She used you for viler purposes than those for which you used her."

Arthan sunk into the chair, pale. It was a cruel statement, but it probably had more impact than any kindness anyone else might have offered.

After Larthor examined his brother a moment, he offered more gently, "It was *her own* choice to use the confidences you shared with her. Whatever else you shared with her, all relationships are based on some degree of trust. I might fault you in betraying the palace, but I fault her more for betraying *your* confidence to murder."

He paused again. "We were not at war with her, Arthan. She was a well thought of lady attending the queen. She was kind to the children, playing with them. She was helpful with any of the women creating their tapestries and sewing. She sang and laughed often, even if some of her jokes were barbed. However, even Tidyri, who did care for her, knew that Lady Harlyn was also a gossip, and that she was depleting her resources in an attempt to gain position. Tidyri was preparing to send her home. We all knew she had a temper."

"I wish we'd known of her cruelty," Arthan said, not looking his brother in the eye.

Larthor said roughly, pointedly, "We all try to hide our base humors."

Arthan was silent for a moment, but then looked up at his brother and said, "You are right, brother."

Cemirowl could see that the tension had left his face, even his body. She sighed softly in relief. She could still see worry, grief and sorrow, but the self-destructive tension was gone.

There was a knock on the door. Larthor cautioned them to keep certain things out of their tale, he would hear of them later if needed. He then called out for those waiting to come in.

The marshal of the guard, the ambassador, Caballier Mercor and a magistrate came into the room. Two clerks came in and were seated at a table behind Cemirowl and the noblemen. Caballiers brought the clerks parchment, quills and spare inkpots.

"You are all here," said King Larthor. "We can begin."

Caballiers helped the noblemen to the chairs, seating them in front of King Larthor's desk in a half circle. Cemirowl was seated between Arthan and Caballier Mercor, who took her hand briefly before sitting down. Squires brought wine, setting small tables between every other chair. A squire leaned forward and gave Cemirowl wine from a different pitcher, saying softly, "Clary."

As the room settled into silence, King Larthor began.

"We are assembled here today to judge the accusations made by my brother of Lady Harlyn causing the death of Her Majesty, Queen Tidyri and the midwife Abenne, as well as the attempt on Priest Cemirowl's life. Does any of the present company have anything to add?"

"Who stands for Lady Harlyn?" asked Mercor.

The king nodded to the magistrate as that man spoke. "I do, but she is not fit to be questioned, Caballier, Your Majesty. She seems quite mad."

A brief look from King Larthor, Cemirowl realized he knew the cause of Lady Harlyn's madness. He said nothing.

The marshal leaned forward. "So there is no one to speak in her defense?" he asked, concerned.

Cemirowl hesitated a moment. "Your Majesty?" she said. "Perhaps the Ladies Soflia and Terria might know some of her movements that day and on days prior?"

"It is a good thought, Priest," Larthor said, and gestured to a caballier to fetch them. Chairs were moved and the ladies brought in.

Arthan related the weight of his accusations. That she'd attempted to physically throttle and kill Cemirowl was easily proved, by her showing the bruises on her neck. The poison she'd used on the queen affirmed by the description from Cemirowl and a reference in a book brought in by Lord Marshal Buce. His attendant caballier handed an herbal to the king, with the pages marked. The probable means of Harlyn having acquired the poison creeper was accepted. She could have easily identified the plant in the gardens, but not necessarily know about the root. The ladies doubted that she'd dig up a garden plant.

The ladies could not offer any testimony on Lady Harlyn's movements that would either hinder or help her. They had not seen her, but could not confirm that she was where she had said she would be either. Both ladies, however, confirmed a sudden interest in reading obscure herbals in the weeks past, and they knew she had been making infusions for herself for headache. She was also willing to dose them as well in her generosity.

Cemirowl kept her gaze fixed to the floor, hoping that neither lady would guess how close to danger they might have been. Even had Harlyn's concoctions not been made of true poison, the woman did not have a cautious hand or adequate understanding of possible overdose and danger.

The marshal then spoke. He had been tense, and finally leaned forward.

"I have more evidence, Your Majesty," he said. Cemirowl looked at him. He did not look happy. He kept an eye on his king while nodding to the knight attending him. The caballier, clearly also unhappy, placed a package wrapped in cloth on the king's desk.

"We searched Lady Harlyn's personal trunks and wardrobe, and found this in a locked chest," Buce explained. "We did not have time to prepare you for this, but I feel it bears the weight of the prince's arguments."

The king pulled apart the windings of the package and found a satchel similar to Cemirowl's herb bag inside. He pulled out labeled vials and bags of herbs. At the bottom of the bag was a bundle wrapped in cloth. The cloth was ornate and one of the ladies gasped softly in recognition. Carefully he rolled it open. It was Tidyri's hair.

They were all silent as the king took careful control of

himself.

"Is there any doubt?" he asked, gruffly.

"I gave Lady Harlyn that veil to match one of her dresses, Your Majesty," said Lady Soflia softly.

Clutching the coil of hair, the king handed the satchel to Cemirowl. "See if you can find any yellow creeper," he ordered.

She went through the bag, found remnants of button bloom lining a vial. After a moment, she found a small, red marked vial. Cemirowl opened the vial, took the root out, sniffed and tasted, confirming that the label matched the contents.

She looked up at King Larthor and nodded. "Yes, it is here," she said softly. She did not doubt it was the same used to kill the queen. She pointed to where the root had recently been cut. Cemirowl laid it down and turned her face away, unable to prevent a tear from falling. Briefly Arthan caught her eye. She would not tell him, nor the assembled that, by the size of the root's scar, the dose had been massive. An ache pounded in her chest. It hurt that Harlyn had been so... uncaring of the pain she caused, and that Arthan had been, for a time, her object. She had not been a woman to ease the heart of a grieving man. Cemirowl bit her lip and turned away.

Soon after, the company was dismissed for luncheon, but Larthor kept his brother with him for more discussion.

Once in the king's sitting room, Mercor and Terria sat Cemirowl down at a low table and sat beside her. Cemirowl felt dull. She felt as if she could not look up to see anyone, and was relieved she was not in vestments. Harlyn had spread more pain than joy. The two sitting next to her were also in pain of disbelief and loss. They picked at their food. Sir Quormen came and sat next to Terria, and was given an account, in low tones. Not much else was said.

Cemirowl went to her rooms and went back to bed till dinner. Again she joined the king's household. This meal was somewhat less morose. Lady Terria talked quietly about her family and her plans to soon return to their house in the city. Though Sir Quormen looked desolate upon hearing the news, Cemirowl guessed that he would soon learn directions to that house.

It was also gratifying to talk about books, for though she'd not read many, not having been available, she'd been told about the contents of some of them mainly by her father, who had clearly missed reading in his life in their village. When he could, he'd spend much of his meager income on books. Having memorized the few books she did possess, she'd wondered about those others. Lady Terria was well read, as was Mercor. The conversation became animated as they all took comfort in avoiding topics touching on death or the coming execution. Cemirowl was offered the use of two books from Terria and one from Mercor.

"I'm so sorry that I had not realized your passion for reading till now!" he said.

Cemirowl smiled wryly, "We have been a trifle occupied with other matters, Caballier."

But the business of the evening was not over. After they

finished supper, a small group of people, standing in the outer bailey, witnessed the execution of Lady Harlyn. When it was over, Larthor and Arthan had the look of two men who would, together, get very, very drunk.

Cemirowl and Ferran performed the rites for the dead, but both priests let paid wrappers perform that duty. One of them, Fenna, asked if they could discuss wrapping at a later time, to which Cemirowl agreed. Ferran had voiced no complaint with Cemirowl performing the soul cut, nor the deeper mystery of gating before the ladies came to prepare the body. He stood next to her as she performed the rite, grim and unsmiling, echoing her words firmly.

Besides the caballier who had been Harlyn's only vassal at court, they were the only ones who felt any reason to sit vigil over her. Cemirowl was disgusted that Ferran and she were, in varying degrees, obligated to sit due to their ordination. The vassal, without saying a word, clearly indicated that he was also only there for duty's sake. He'd given his feudal bond to her father and affirmed those vows to Harlyn herself.

Through the night Cemirowl hunted for any sign that Harlyn had returned. Ferran finally noted her distraction.

"You are not at peace, Priest."

She shook her head. "Having performed this office for a number of people, I realized recently that a person will grieve for years if there is any reason to think that the dead did not find peace. I'm having trouble because I do not *want* Harlyn's spirit to have peace. That is haunting my thoughts now—waiting to see her come back, vengeful."

Ferran nodded. "You played an important part in this whole tragedy," he said gently. "It touched you deeply, both in what you gave to the principles, and what you yourself discovered, but further with her two attempts on your own life. It will take time for those emotions to fade. The first step will be to forgive yourself."

"*Myself?*"

"I believe that you reproach yourself on two scores: one for having, I understand, briefly given her a taste of your own gift and the other for reproaching yourself for your rather understandable anger."

"What?" she asked, surprised.

"Once you forgive yourself for the anger and your self reproach, you'll be able to accept that the emotions you feel are honest and just. Lady Harlyn hurt a number of people very deeply, including you. With the tensions and high emotions of the past few days, you've probably connected your heart to a number of those people also hurt by her."

Cemirowl was silent.

"Center yourself first, then look at your hurts."

With a wry laugh Cemirowl said, "Does not our philosophy say that we must attend to our hurts so that we can come to center?" She said it teasingly

He smiled at her. "To put it a different way, be sanguine with those humors that feel so out of place. You must accept that your feelings are natural and just. In accepting your anger, you will be sanguine."

Cemirowl slowly smiled and understood. "I will."

"Then comes the hard part," he said.

"And that is?"

"Forgive Harlyn as well."

"That *is* hard," she said, clenching her teeth. Her mind was full of Tidyri, the king and the child that would never be born, and the gasping echo of bubbling breath from Abenne as well.

"It can be done, though. Many years ago, while I was still living at home, my father beat my mother to death in a fit of anger. It took a long time to realize that there were many reasons he was so... out of humor. I had teachers and mentors aplenty in my time and training. Even with all their help, it took a great deal of time before I realized, with what I could remember, that my father was grief stricken and had been grief stricken long before he'd hurt my mother.

"He was so trapped in being unable to conquer his own internal hurts. My father died unable to escape his choleric attitudes, or the melancholy that was so debilitating, nor his languid phlegm. It was a vicious cycle with which he could not find peace. When I saw the trap my father had lived in, I began to forgive him. Before I could truly do that, I also had to see that I had been using his actions and my own anger toward him to justify the trap I was creating for myself. It was, perhaps, a trap less violent, but for me and my own happiness, just as dangerous."

Ferran was silent for a while. "I don't think that forgiving him took away his own responsibility for his actions, but it helped *me* a great deal to acknowledge the hurt that he died with. Whatever those hurts were, I was able to let go of mine.

"I find great truths in our religion. Had my father been able to come to some sort of peace before he'd hurt my mother, he would have been able to find the place to examine those things that trapped him."

It was a startling idea. "I think that I will have to ponder this further, but... I can already see that your view is profound, Honorable Ferran. Thank you; it has been some time since I could debate with my mentor, or fellow student like this. My father also enjoyed a good philosophical battle as he taught me."

He smiled. "You are most welcome, Priest. To my deepest sorrow, it was only during the vigil for the queen that I was able to truly come to peace with this idea even though I had begun upon this path and these thoughts years ago. If I take the time, and no longer press them to be firm and whole, one day I hope that I can write the philosophy of the four provinces. It would, I hope, honor the queen."

She nodded and was thoughtful the rest of the night.

CHAPTER SEVENTEEN

———————— «‹•›» ————————

H arlyn was buried in a graveyard outside the city without any fanfare or anyone but her vassal and the diggers attending. Cemirowl rested, reading one of the books Terria had left for her in her room. She fell asleep before she was five pages into the book.

Les brought her another dress, as lovely as the vestments of the other day to wear at dinner. It had been in the making for nearly three days and was a gift of thanks from the king. Though her new vestment was studded with gems and this one was not, Cemirowl suspected that the cloth and embroidery alone rivaled its cost.

Feeling like a scruffy peasant, she knew that she could not either be so rude or courageous as to refuse to accept a king's gift, or refuse to wear it. Despite feeling inadequate, she wanted to put it on. The gown was gold velvet, figured in a simple, discreet pattern that terminated at the neck and sleeves with flowered embroidery of a deeper gold, the leaves embroidered in dark green. The overdress clung close to the bodice, but without restricting movement. Its dark green was woven with a leaf pattern embroidered at random in gold thread to emphasize the design. Arthan's necklace was not out of place with this dress, so she wore it. Bruises did not suit this dress.

Les did her best to match the colors with ribbon that she found. Using two different ribbons, she wound Cemirowl's curls around her face, but loose, bringing it into a long braid that fell down her back. For once she was glad she'd not cut her hair fully, indicating a marriage to her office. She felt more at peace with herself, and knew Meelac had been right to forbid those vows.

After the dinner, the king had his guests adjourn to the queen's solar. A number of noblemen were already in the room, listening to the music and talking. The queen's family would leave in the morning, knowing her killer had been caught and executed. She took her turn in the line to curtsey to the king, and thanked him for the dress.

Arthan approached her as she moved away. She thanked him for the use of the necklace.

"You are quite welcome; it is yours. It is far less disturbing than blackening bruises," he said with a smile.

Ferran approached and stood nearby, bowing to the king and prince. The king acknowledged his arrival with a short nod, and waved for them to approach.

"Priest Cemirowl, I wish to appoint you the King's Priest and as an advisor and colleague of your brother, the Honored Ferran, with his approval."

"Your Majesty!" she said, stunned.

"I wish for you to perform the offices of my funeral if you outlive me."

"I hope that day is long in coming, my king, but I would be honored," Cemirowl whispered hoarsely.

Larthor was about to add more, but a caballier approached

and conferred with the king in low tones. Larthor sighed, and excused himself with a nod to his brother, to speak to a group of foreign dignitaries.

She looked up at Ferran. "What does that mean?" she asked him. "Does it mean that I will have to stay here?"

She did not know if she would be able to stay at center in the palace. Even as she longed for the caverns, which were not reachable anyway, she also longed for walks in the woods. She'd lived too long in solitude to wish for an extended stay. *How ironic, this is too much life, when I just asked to live,* she thought. She knew she was trembling.

Ferran shook his head. "You may stay anywhere you wish, only be available to the king if he wishes your council. I will help you make arrangements, later, if you wish. The full honors of the appointment will be conferred in a ceremony at a later date." He smiled at her. "Sir Kamin has requested a game of chess. I must show him that even a priest can prove his excellence in strategy."

She grinned as he left.

"Do you know where you will go?" Arthan asked.

Cemirowl shrugged. "I only have one home, Your Highness, a small cottage, on Sir Thade's hunting grounds."

"However did you manage that? I know Thade well enough to know that even if he can't swing a sword to save his life, he is jealous of his hunting ground!"

"My father had it built, but I never knew how he managed it. It has been a mystery that only Sir Thade might be able to answer. I've never had the opportunity to ask him. I was too low to enter his door without my father."

Arthan chuckled. "It is possible that you may very well outrank him now."

The thought stunned Cemirowl and she stared at him. Before he could explain, he was called away.

With the tensions of the past few days, the king had asked musicians to play for them and games to be set out on tables throughout the solar, giving the assembled a small holiday from normal duties.

Two musicians playing vihuelas entertained the company. The music, strummed lightly from the strings, brought a sense of content to the room.

The ambassador, Lady Soflia, Sir Quormen and Mercor were in the room, among a good many others she could not name. Lady Terria was organizing her removal to her home, and left after congratulating Cemirowl.

Lady Soflia explained that she would be moving to her future husband's estate soon. Mercor, Sir Quormen and the ambassador were deep in conference at one set of chairs. Soflia was drawn into a discussion that did not include her.

Feeling abandoned, Cemirowl went to the expanse of windows and looked out to the ocean.

At dinner, Terria had asked Cemirowl to affirm or correct some of the rumors that she'd heard so that, when in the city, she would not carry false tales. Through Terria's cautious questioning Cemirowl had realized that no matter how much her own knowledge, herb lore and even stupidity had helped her discover Harlyn's guilt, it was her 'magic' that carried all the stories. Even Arthan's part in the whole tragedy had been lost, from his affair with Harlyn to his near belated heroics. It was a dubious blessing.

She'd been a village priest before she left. In the space of three long days her reputation had gained gigantic proportions, a reputation which had been inaccurate from the start. If the tales of her ability were already so mythic, in one day within this palace, what would they become around the countryside?

Watching the waves crashing below her, Cemirowl realized that even if it added to this mystique by appointing her to a higher rank, the king was showing his support.

She could not go back home. Not to live. The bones had predicted change and it had come. *At the very least I have three new dresses, now. I can sell them to create the peace I need.* She'd lived alone in the woods. She would survive.

She felt movement beside her and turned. Larthor stood by her shoulder.

"If you would do the honor of accompanying me, I would like a word with you in private," the king said.

She curtsied awkwardly and followed him to his office. With the doors guarded on the outside, the king set her in one chair and sat down next to her. There was no desk between them this time. He said nothing for a long time, staring at the floor.

Finally he turned to her. Even sitting down, he looked down at her, being so much taller. She could not help wondering what he would still need of her that would cost him so much effort. He finally spoke and his voice proved how difficult his request was for him.

"Priest, would you let me see Tidyri?" he asked, looking down into her eyes.

"Your Majesty..." she began. Growing pale, she took a deep breath. "Are you asking me to give you sight?"

"Yes! I just want to see her!" he begged.

She clenched her hands in her lap and stared at them. It did not take her long to think of her answer. "I'm sorry, Your Majesty, I cannot do that. I do not know if I could take it away again and you are the king."

He bowed his head. "I know. I just thought I should ask. I miss her so very much."

She realized that Larthor had asked something that he feared, but had also wanted a part of. It was a mark of courage even if it would not help his grief.

She could not be surprised he'd asked. As often as the villagers had hated her for being able to see their dead, some had begged for some tale of their doings, or proof that they'd found peace. Because they could not let go, they could not heal or move on. It had taken some painful lessons, but Cemirowl knew that discretion was far better than any description of their loved ones' afterlife.

She turned her face away from Tidyri, who was touching her beloved's hair.

Cemirowl gave him a moment, knowing he was grieving. He soon looked up and studied her face. "You are also not deceived by my awarding you the role of my funerary priest, are you?"

"No, Your Majesty." She had already guessed that he'd used her notoriety to detract from any rumors his brother had been associated with a killer.

He smiled wryly, his beard quivering as he attempted to hold the smile on his face. "Neither of us can get what we wish for, can we? No matter what accolades I give you, what you have done here will only add to your reputation. Your connection with nobility here, because of your actions and aid to myself, will also further remove you from your village community. It was the best I could do: give you a living to help you survive it. Do you mind much?"

"Your Majesty, I cannot change that. I knew that I was not part of their lives long before I came here. My mentor was the only one who bridged my world and theirs. After he died, though some of the old ones called upon me, even I could see that they no longer wanted me. I suspect that our roles and abilities trap us both. You are a king, and I... priest that I am... am also a Bone Reader. You do know that it is in respecting yours that I must refuse you?"

He nodded. "Go now. I have much work to do..." he said standing, and then smiled wanly at her again as he laid a gentle hand on her arm, "...and much time to take to mourn."

She left him, feeling as if a door had closed between them, not just the door she shut. King Larthor would honor the office he'd given her, but it would be a long time before he would be able to see her and not wonder if Cemirowl could see his beloved when he could not.

Arthan was sitting as if in vigil in a chair outside the office. He stood abruptly when she came out the door.

In two strides he stood close and asked her softly, so the knights guarding the door would not hear, "You refused his request?"

She looked up at Arthan. "Did he tell of his intentions, Your Highness?" she asked, softly.

"No, Priest, I merely surmised them. I know my brother well and have felt the temptation to ask you if you had seen my wife. I assumed that he wanted more than that. Did you refuse?"

"Your Highness, I have far too much respect for him as well as his office to overcome even my own reservations," she said firmly.

He looked blankly at her for a moment.

"I refused him," she said.

He let out a relieved sigh. "I had hoped you would. I did not know if his position... his authority would have swayed you. Come, let us take a turn in the garden. I believe you need a breath of fresh air," he said, offering his arm.

She felt her shoulders ease and smiled up at the prince and then placed her hand in the crook of his elbow.

E • N • D

ABOUT THE AUTHOR

Mab Morris lives in Dahlonega, Georgia, with a number of cats and a Celtic labyrinth of her own design. Her storytelling and her love of fantasy began at a very young age, where she was drawn to Ursula K. Le Guin and J.R.R. Tolkien. Mythology, history, and folklore are her passion.

She writes mystical fantasy books set in the past, present and future of the world of Ihyel, where demi-gods and mortals alike struggle with their fate. She also writes the murder-mysteries of The Bone Reader, about Cemirowl who speaks with the dead, and the Regency adventures of gender-fluid spy Alex Goodward.

Check out www.mabmorris.com for more info.

OTHER BOOKS BY MAB MORRIS

APPRENTICE

Book One of Sen of the Woods

The world is changing, perhaps not for the better.

The Doctor-Diviners, keepers of old lore and healing, are fading away as their craft is usurped by Science. Soon the workings of Medicine will be guided only by rationality, and the mystic arts of divination and calling out to the ancestors will be lost. The lowly apprentice and foundling Sen is one of the few who sees the value of the old ways, and seeks to preserve them. Raised by Grandmother Turani in the woods and speaking the old Ndeb tongue, she is skilled in her craft and diligent in her study.

But her path to becoming a Master Doctor-Diviner is interrupted when a chance meeting reveals her parents may not be unknown. The Lady Ravantha - brooding, damaged, and dangerous - believes Sen is her lost daughter. Sen believes otherwise, but visions of the past torment her dreams and unsettle her waking. And always, always, Jackal and Crow mock her with their laughter at how much she does not yet know.

Sen of the Woods wants nothing of the life being chosen for her, but she will have to step carefully around Ravantha. For she is a healer above all, and she will not ignore someone in pain.

APPRENTICE is the first in the trilogy of Sen of the Woods, about one life's fight with fate and destiny.

Fate of the Red Queen

A Standalone Novel in the World of Ihyel

"I am not defeated! If my body falls, it is only that alone which dies!"

Faced with a war she could not win, the Red Queen sealed her country's fate with her final sacrificial pledge. Yezgyin was locked into undeath, the people and their enemies alike cursed to neither live nor die unless the spell could one day be broken.

Centuries passed, and history faded into legend. Kuen, a newly anointed Red Nun, escapes a vicious attack on her convent, and flees into the Jungle of the Dead. Amid the ruins of lost Yezgyin, she mourns the death of her mentor and all she has known, utterly lost to her grief. But the jungle whispers of her, and its otherworldly inhabitants welcome her as their new Red Queen, the one who will break their curse.

Kuen must find her way through the demands of the past and the hopes of the future, as the Red Queen's ancient adversary returns to win the war that never ended. With the life and death of Yezgyin at stake, she must fight for her own fate, or she and the people of the Jungle will never truly live again.

FATE OF THE RED QUEEN is a standalone novel set in the mysterious world of Ihyel.

www.ingramcontent.com/pod-product-compliance
Lightning Source LLC
Chambersburg PA
CBHW020432030726
47495CB00006B/1761